LOLLY

LOLLY

An Entertainment by

Judy Romberger

DOUBLEDAY & COMPANY, INC.
Garden City, New York
1981

TO:
JIM
ANDREA, SUSIE, ALISON, JOHN

All the characters in this novel are fictitious, and any resemblance to actual persons, living or dead, is therefore coincidental.

ISBN: 0-385-15860-2
Library of Congress Catalog Card Number: 80-2062
PRINTED IN THE UNITED STATES OF AMERICA
FIRST EDITION

CONTENTS

SPRING

PROLOGUE

"Mother would call it love"

For weeks, Paul slinks off to work before I officially awaken, probably so he can avoid facing *me* with the memory of *her* still fresh, hours later, like a dependable deodorant. Then famed husband of many years moves out.

The following day, Reginald Wendell Bennett III drops by. We collide on the stair landing. I have just shampooed, braided my golden locks into two sloppy pigtails, and wear a slightly damp football-jersey/nightgown. Reg and I stand there not knowing what to say. At least I don't. What comes to mind is revised screen dialogue: "Of all the gin joints in the world, did you have to show up here, at this hour?" Does he realize I've been crying?

Old friend and I descend slowly to the kitchen, where Mother's maid lingers over the dishes. (When the ancient

black woman first heard about "Lolly's troubles," she com-
mandeered our vacant servants' quarters. I think Pearl
believed that if she waxed behind the refrigerator, Paul
Whitman wouldn't leave.)

I ask, "Reg, what happens to people?"

"I don't know."

"Please tell me."

"They make mistakes."

"Divorce scares me. Do you believe in divorce?"

"Let's say I'd rather believe in marriage."

"I believe in *façades*."

"I can't be angry at Paul for you, Lolly. He and I've been
friends for over twenty years."

"The way we look on our Chistmas card. Terrific! Don't
you agree? Paul's pipe. The Saint Bernard wearing his
brandy keg. The girls' Florence Eiseman dresses and hair
ribbons. My plastered-on smile. Did I ever tell you I was
elected 'Most Congenial,' senior year in college?"

"Just don't expect me to hate him."

"Reg, what do you want? You used to be so nice to me.
Once, at the Mona Kai dance, you stuck your hand up my
sarong."

He shakes his head. "Want?"

"I was very jealous when you married Bev. She was
pretty, but I didn't find her equal to you. My hero! With all
those medals from Vietnam."

Paul's ex-fraternity brother examines his fingernails.

His wife must still be too painful a subject to discuss.
Why did she give him custody of their children and—

Reg grins at me. Who in their right mind would leave
dear Lynda and little Richie and this man? For years he has
ridden off into my sunsets like a film cowboy.

"You used to be so nice to me."

"I was nice to everyone."

"Remember how friendly I acted? That beer bust at Sor-
rento?"

"Lolly, *you* were friendly to everyone."

"More coffee?"

"I'm already late." RB III stands.

"Fucking bastards. You're all a bunch of fucking bastards." I swear only when in a complete rage.

"Yessir!" Pearl agrees. "The one man you can count on is the Lord Jesus, and I ain't totally sure about that."

RB III grabs me firmly by the wrists; my fingers droop like week-old carnations. From this semi-wrestling stance, we move into an embrace, our steps choreographed by frustration and sadness, with a *demi-plié* of desire. Mother would call it love.

My cowboy shelters me in his arms. Tentatively I explore this warm cave. He smells like Old Spice. *Nobody* wears that after-shave any more. It seems corny and safe. Dare I put faith in a smell? He says, "You're going to be O.K., Lolly."

Immediately after the interlocutory judgment is entered, Reg and I agree to spend an evening together. For old times' sake. When he tromps into the Milan Avenue entry hall wearing a three-piece suit, boots, and Stetson hat, I confess, "I'm nervous." I cling to the banister. I had thrown on a pair of Calvin Klein jeans and an understated French silk blouse so this cowboy wouldn't think I expected him to take me any place fancy.

"Uncle Reg!" Jenna acts leery of the See's candy he offers.

"Thank you." Mouse hides behind my back.

RB III hands me a single red rose. I stick the stem between my teeth. He laughs—uneasily.

Pearl, who answered the door, barricades it. "I'll be expecting Lolly home by the time Johnny Carson's off. You hear?"

(I've always had to hurry back. First because of my parents' rules, next the sorority lockout, then baby-sitters' curfew, now the maid's dirty mind.)

6 LOLLY

We drive to the beach and eat cold chicken and potato salad from Colonel Sanders containers, drink two bottles of Chenin Blanc. I write REG in the damp sand with my big toe near a clump of putrid kelp and a dead seagull petrified into a position of descent. He adds: LOVES LOLLY. That makes everything alright, doesn't it?

I have adulterous thoughts about RB III and feel guilty. Except, legally I am no longer Paul Whitman's wife. The wedding ring's in a drawer. The title "Mrs." lingers like bathroom smells. At least in my head.

About nine-thirty, we boldly shed clothes, agreeing to skinny-dip in the moonlight. I act coy, which completely unnerves me. I'm brave in a hot tub. I guess there is safety in bubbles.

Why am I so scared? Shaking, even?

Because I don't want my lack of experience to show. I am too shy to look directly at him. "I'll race you to beyond the breakers!"

There, treading water, I sneak glances. Freckles dot his shoulders like nutmeg sprinkled on eggnog.

"Come here."

I refuse to budge.

"You look like a sea goddess. I'll crown you with seaweed."

He swims over. "You're shivering!"

"No!" spoken through chattering teeth.

We hug and a school of small fish dart between my legs.

He holds me close for warmth. I can feel him below. Does RB III realize this? I finger the cowboy's blond chest hair, try to seal the moment in my memory like the violet Mouse trapped in plastic: a Mother's Day present.

We cover up with towels, sit on the shore to watch the 727s take off from LAX in the distance. I remember that this handsome man is nuts about flying. He rubs my back, turning me toward him.

"Have you had others, Lolly?"

What a rotten question! "Of course!" One and a half, to be exact. Paul Whitman, husband of long standing, and Scooter Barnes, the guy I went steady with during high school. Scooter didn't go in all the way.

The air smells of salt water and oil. If you dig down deeply enough with your fingers, the sand still feels warm.

"There goes a flight to Hawaii!"

"Hawaii's that way."

"Fly me somewhere in your plane!"

"Over the rainbow?"

Our lips meet. I've kissed like this before, in dreams.

We reach for each other at the same time. I am high with anticipation, remember that dumb college joke: if you drink beer and screw on the beach, you'll get sand in your Schlitz.

Melting together, I don't expect to feel anything and—quickly gasp with surprise.

Afterward. After which time and which way? I confide, "Reg, I didn't realize it could be this wonderful."

"Neither did I, Lolly Bare."

I believe his words frighten both of us.

Why is this sex so great? Because I have nothing to lose. With Paul, my marriage was at stake.

After five nonstop hours, I ask Reg if we're engaged or what?

The next afternoon, my almost-ex-husband's young girl friend calls. "I'm so glad you went out with Reg, Lolly. It's good for you."

I want to discuss what happened on that beach with somebody, but not Sheri. Or Mother, either. She'd be shocked we didn't go to The Beverly Hills Hotel. Or Pearl. Or Jenna and Mouse. Or married friends. They'd think I bragged. Maybe Paul.

When Paul gets on the phone, he tells me he is delighted I've *seen* his buddy. "I hope you wore decent underwear. Not those horrible things with the drooping elastic."

"I borrowed Jenna's." Savoring the memory, I recall that when Reg undressed me he discovered mint-colored Growing Girl, size four.

Half of me feels numb, the half that receives final divorce papers in the mail; yet another secret part is Cinderella at the ball. The result? I either cry or act ecstatic, confusing the children. As Reg and I continue to date—if that's the word—I become more adept at spreading peanut butter on three different kinds of bread for my daughters' and his daughter's and son's sandwiches at six-thirty in the morning while residue from recent lovemaking trickles down the inside of my thigh. The cat, Governor Brown, sniffs suspiciously.

Pearl promises, like a fairy godmother, "The man's shopping for a wife. He needs a mother for those sweet children. Take my word and start packing your trousseau. Mr. Bennett's going to pop the question."

He does.

In a matter of days, I wed Reginald Wendell Bennett III and move with him and Lynda and Richie and Jenna and Mouse to his ranch, somewhere north of LA, blinded—according to my shrink—by fantastic sex. Also, the Milan Avenue house sells, leaving my girls and me with no place to live.

Would I have gone through the ceremony had I any inkling of what lay ahead?

SUMMER

1

"Mom's new boyfriend's father is . . ."

Dining in the ranch kitchen, my new husband and I listen for the telephone. Reg expects his attorney to call back. Mr. Scheffer is a custody specialist with a degree in psychology. I've come to dread his legal opinions. They seesaw for and against us daily, swinging me dizzily up and down. How much longer can our *blended* family hang on? Another month? May. June. July. Gone like popsicles dropped on hot cement. A sticky legacy remains.

Last Tuesday (or was it the Tuesday before?) I found an orthodontist. This tooth fairy arrives from Ventura once a week to grant rural children Pepsodent smiles. One mother transports her son with malocclusion forty miles over mostly dirt roads. However, Mr. Scheffer advised me to postpone

Lynda's treatment until after the trial. That way, the child wouldn't have to change offices if she ends up living in town with her mother.

Tomorrow I'll search for a library. Do we need a lawyer's permission to join the summer reading club? The phone book promises a county branch in Fillmore. Unless we drive to the water slides again. The four children beg to ride those slippery canals. Yet I dread leaving the ranch. Bev, Reg's ex, still may be having us followed.

It's five minutes after seven, according to a plastic chicken with Roman numerals on her stomach. Back in town, I wouldn't have allowed a corny kitchen clock. How late would Mr. Scheffer call? We sat down to dinner one bottle of wine ago.

"More zucchini, darling?" Lately, I act uneasy around Reg. He suddenly has *expectations*. Box boys at the local market don't. There's very little competition here. These deprived teenagers think it's enough for one to have good legs and wear tennis shorts.

"Don't stick your ear of corn into the butter dish!" The cowboy speaks crossly to his young son instead of answering me. In my husband's college graduation picture, snapped in 1959, he resembles Tab Hunter—an idol of my teens. Currently, squint lines web around his eyes.

Mouse listens. She doesn't know what to make of her stepfather. At first my younger daughter turned away from his good-night kisses. Now the ten-year-old trades one peck for Reg's recitation of Maurice Sendak.

"Pass Richie a butter knife." Before, I would have remained silent. Marriage does alter relationships. We legalized our arrangement and departed for the country in order to provide a wholesome environment for the children. But the ploy backfired. Either the ceremony, or the move, or both, infuriated Bev. She has surfaced like an enemy submarine.

"Are you guys fighting?" Mouse fiddles with her wire-framed glasses—a pigtailed John Denver.

Richie interrupts, "My Mommy hates Lolly."

"Your corn, son!" Reg acts exasperated. The Stetson he wore earlier indented his hair in a strip above the ears. He seems to sport an invisible headband.

I stare at the clock.

"There are six basic positions for intercourse," Lynda quotes *The Book of Lists*. My stepdaughter, age twelve, is our resident authority on sex. She pooh-poohed an old copy of *Seventeenth Summer*. It's boring compared to Judy Blume's *Forever*, where the hero calls his penis Ralph.

"Mommy was a virgin on her wedding night," Mouse defends, smearing a buttery finger on her right lens.

"She couldn't have been when she did it with *my* dad. It was her *second* time," Lynda argues.

"Everyone was a virgin in the fifties," Jenna says, which surprises me. My teenager rarely speaks. Unless the subject is horses.

"Things were different then," Reg adds. How nice to have someone on *my* side.

"Mouse, let me wipe your glasses off." This daughter underwent heart surgery five years ago. She has fully recovered from the operation, but I haven't.

"Not everyone," Lynda contradicts. "Didn't you see *Grease?*"

"What's a virgin? Like a forest?" Richie asks.

"Tell us the six positions." Mouse obviously has no idea.

Only five come to mind. I defer to Reg, handing over my youngster's glasses.

"I don't think this is appropriate dinner conversation," he admonishes.

"Lynda said it first."

"You found sex an OK table topic with Pearl," I accuse. When we were dating, RB III had told the maid that he shaved off his beard to prevent thigh abrasion.

Lynda continues, "An overnight lover isn't supposed to eat breakfast at the table with the children."

"Where did you see that, Lynda? Amy Vanderbilt?" You can't buy reading material out here that supermarkets or feedstores don't sell. I took B. Dalton's for granted.

"What should he do? Have breakfast in bed?" Reg teases. This seems to confuse Mouse. Her own father used to act very serious.

Jenna picks kernels from an eyetooth wire. (Her ex-orthodontist forbade corn.) She's extra talkative tonight. "Mouse and I tried to bring *our* dad breakfast in bed on Father's Day. The bedroom door was locked."

"Sheri locked it," Mouse reveals.

"Oh, really?" I'm always eager for information concerning Paul's twenty-one-year-old girl friend.

"Daddy and you never locked your door, did you, Mommy?" This little sweetheart finger-paints her lenses again, adjusting the frames.

"Not very often." I don't intend for my words to sound derogatory. Reg's custody battle has contaminated me. I no longer feel secure regarding Jenna and Mouse. Paul could request that the girls live at the beach with him.

"What are the positions for?" Richie's a blond-haired, blue-eyed echo of Reg.

Lynda and her father speak simultaneously. She says, "Sex." He, "Lovemaking."

I reflect, this man and I make love from sex.

"Mom's new boyfriend's father is rich. His factory makes Singer sewing-machine parts," Lynda advises.

"Hiroshima's from Tokyo." Richie stretches his eyelids until they slant. "He's Japanese."

Reg seems to concentrate on cutting the lad's remaining meat into bite-sized pieces. I figure my husband tests this information to see if he's become immune to his ex-spouse, like desensitizing for bee stings.

Mouse shoves her chair back. "I set the table, so I don't have to clean up."

"I did the breakfast dishes," Jenna declares. "Including that disgusting saucepan with oatmeal burned on."

Lynda bargains, "I'll take my turn tomorrow."

"Why should I do anything?" Nine-year-old Richie avoids his father's eyes. "This isn't my *real* family."

"Lynda is," Mouse retorts.

"We all need to help," I mimic some child psychologist, envying women who booze all afternoon so that dinner becomes merely a blur in their consciousness.

"Drink your coffee on the patio, Lolly," Reg suggests. "I'll take charge in here."

I ease through the screen door, escaping into the summer dusk. Soon laughter drifts outside. I listen without becoming involved, like hearing a news broadcast about the Middle East.

I recall when Reg announced our wedding plans to the four children. The six of us, sporting Mickey Mouse hats, were riding the Matterhorn at Disneyland. We occupied three cars. I held on to Mouse. Lynda crouched behind me, in front of her father. Jenna rode with Richie; she kept his ticket, popcorn, and jacket.

As the roller coaster plummeted from the darkness of a tunnel into the glaring Southern California sunlight, Reginald Wendell Bennett III yelled, "Lolly and I are getting married!"

Lynda screamed back, "Why don't you just live together?"

"We'll move to the ranch," her father continued as the bob-sled-on-a-track braked to a stop.

"Can I bring my horse?" Jenna didn't act concerned about any other details.

Richie wanted to know, "Should I call Lolly Mommy?"

Mouse whispered into my ear, her fingers entwined with

mine, "If the Blue Monster Man comes in the night, can I
still climb in bed with you?"

Reg bought six ice-cream cones. We ate them, clustered
together on a Main Street park bench. Richie let me wipe
strawberry smudges from his face. People walked by and
smiled. The lights turned on all at once throughout the
amusement park, delineating the unreality with tiny white
bulbs. I thought our life would be a series of Kodak Golden
Moments.

Eventually, my husband joins me outside. Embracing, we
watch the sun set on the mountains. The sky looks too beautiful to be real.

"I love this old place," Reg admits.

"I know."

"Especially now. With you and the four children here."

Sometimes I feel that I'm removed from myself as if I
watch my actions at a safe distance. It's similar to seeing
oneself in a home movie. I am that way presently.

"Did Mr. Scheffer suggest you deny the two-week visitation?"

"No. It's my idea."

"Richie said that Bev dislikes me."

"What do you expect?"

"I like Sheri," I lie.

"I'm sorry I snapped at him."

"We can't live with the tension much longer. Bev asked if
I ever worry that you married me instead of hiring a housekeeper. Pearl thought you needed a mother for your kids. I
don't mind *that*."

"Who does Bev think she is, demanding to have Lynda
and Richie for two weeks?"

"Their mother."

"After ignoring them all summer—since January, really.
No, she can't see them for two weeks *now*. Not this close to
the latest trial date. That's too much to ask. Hawaii, my ass!

It's a ploy. She has no airline reservations. I don't trust that woman. I know her, Lolly."

I listen to myself say, "Are you sure it's not legit?"

Reg pulls away abruptly. He seems to ignore my statement. "She can't! I don't care what her dip-shit attorney tells her!"

The custody issue worms its way through our relationship like an intestinal parasite. I change the subject. "We visited the Museum of Natural History in Santa Barbara today. I liked the fire that glows in the teepee with the Chumash Indians frozen into position around it."

"All Bev wanted when she left was her freedom."

"Richie liked the nose on the timber wolf blackened with shoe polish."

"Freedom from *me* and Lynda and Richie. My ex was dying to relinquish custody and do her thing. You know why she's changed her mind? Because now the children and I are settled. *Happy.*"

"Oh, darling!" I stand on tiptoe to kiss him.

"Reg!" Jenna calls across the patio. "I forgot to tell you: there's wire down in the north pasture where the road curves."

Mr. Tall and Blond swings around toward my daughter.

"Would you let me fix it?" In town Jenna refused to make her bed. "*Why should I?*" She used to argue, "*If I don't Pearl will.*" I felt the same way about cooking dinner. Obviously, my mind still suffers jet lag from that other life.

"Why don't we take a look together, Jenna. Come along, Lolly." Reg invites me to mend fence. The hardest thing about our situation is carrying on normally. The children are waiting to see if I will unpack my crystal.

"Me too!" from Mouse and Richie.

Lynda remains behind to play the upright. Dare we leave her here alone? "Minuet in G" assails us from the porch. Through the window, I see the wavy-haired silhouette: a cameo of her mother. Bev played piano in the talent portion

of the Miss Marine Corps contest, where Reg met her. He
claims to have fallen in love with the beauty queen's inten-
sity at the keyboard.

My husband and I hold hands, and each grasps one child.
Jenna ambles in front wearing baggy overalls that disguise
her figure. This teenager camouflages a goddesslike beauty
with tangled hair and sloppy clothes. She totes baling wire
and clippers. The children's horses canter up on the far side
of the fence. The donkey falls in line behind the pony. The
dogs tail the donkey, like private detectives. The cats chase
the dogs.

"I love you, Lolly Bare." Lover Boy nuzzles my neck.

I feel like an immigrant in a new and promised land
called remarriage.

*When I'm high, I think I'm a kite in the wind that'll drift
off. My husband kneels on the floor then and grips me by
the knees. I can't believe in permanence any more. 'Happily
ever after' is just for the movies. Sometimes I speculate that
there's nobody inside me, just eight-track tapes of screen dialogue. The only time I act real is when I'm in bed with
Reg. At first, I believed even that was a script. When I realized it wasn't, I truly fell in love with him.*

*Right this second, behind my eyeballs, a carefully edited,
large-screen adaptation of my life is playing. This comic version of* The Laurel Andrews Whitman Bennett Story *por-
trays a fun and adventuresome journey to a ranch in the
country with RB III and assorted children. The scary ex-
wife with evil schemes melts when you throw water on her,
like the Wicked Witch of the West.*

*The heroine inside my head isn't wary of sparkling
Mexican-blue-glass skies. She doesn't agonize over spring
wildflowers; spring wildflowers which momentarily dye the
pasture pink and white and orange and purple and yellow
before being plowed under. That Lolly wasn't weaned
rather late from flashing neon, police sirens, street lights,
and a liquor store that delivers.*

"Daddy," Richie whimpers. "Are we going to Hawaii with Mommy on Monday?"

Reg shakes his head, meaning to imply, I imagine, that he doesn't know for sure himself. I doubt that my stepson comprehends this motion, or even sees it in the dim light. Our family continues toward the sunset.

If Mr. Scheffer telephones while we're out, will Lynda copy down the message?

When we return, the children vote to watch a dumb TV show. Reg and I sneak into our shoebox-sized bedroom, adjacent to the sun porch, where the color portable sits. We listen to a toilet-paper commercial through the knotty-pine wall.

"Want to make out a little?" my husband coaxes, pulling me onto the bed. I stare up at deer antlers—a depressing sight. I've banned all hunting except target practice in the back pasture. Jenna and Richie have become good shots. Mouse and Lynda dislike the noise. RB III can bring down a tossed beer-bottle cap at twenty paces.

"Shouldn't we wait until after the kids go to sleep?"

"Jenna stays up so late."

"She reads."

"Just let me unzip your shorts."

"Why are you pulling your boots off?"

"We can yank that afghan over us if you're nervous."

"Leave your shirt on, at least."

"Take yours off."

Richie calls, "Lolly, may we make popcorn?"

Pause.

"Yes," I reply to the wall. "But use the electric popper. Jenna, help him."

Reg slides down my underpants, unbuckling his belt. With one hand, I clutch the hand-crocheted blanket that belonged to his grandmother. It falls over my back like a bridal train.

"Sweetie, we'd better stop!" I don't mean to sound annoyed.

He massages my lower back.

"Mom, where's the butter?"

"Second shelf of the refrigerator."

"It's not there," my elder daughter yells from the kitchen.

"Did you put the dish away after dinner?"

"We're trying to take a nap!" her stepfather warns.

I kiss him to shut his mouth. His tongue separates my teeth. Suddenly I discover the old body responding. It's similar to that anxiety-crossed-with-excitement I experienced as a teenager when my parents were due home any second.

"Oh!"

"Good girl!"

Our door knob rattles. Lynda says, "Dad?"

Reg thrusts my torso away. We remain connected further down.

"Wait!"

"Think how this would look in court!"

"Dad?"

"Come on in, honey!"

"No! Get out!" I gasp.

"Lolly!" Reg acts disgusted, rolls away with most of the afghan.

My stepdaughter opens the door a few inches. She seems to scrutinize me from this slit of space. "Dad, Mr. Scheffer telephoned."

I try to explain that we were resting, but Lynda stomps off, calling sarcastically (?), "That's one of the six positions."

Before Reg can dial up Scheffer, his ex rings through. I answer and remain on the kitchen extension.

"On Monday I'm taking Richie and Lynda to Hawaii," Bev maintains. She doesn't plead or beg, but I hear something in her voice—disguised anguish? deception?

"With the surfer?"

"Hey, I realize you were awarded *temporary* custody. But

by law I have reasonable visitation rights, which include two weeks this summer."

"Where were you Saturdays from ten until five for the last fifteen months?"

"Legally I—"

"Don't talk to me about legality! You broke every one of our wedding vows!"

"That has nothing to do with Lynda and Richie."

"You left without so much as a word. Not a 'by your leave' or a 'kiss my ass.'"

"I knew you and your mother would care for the children."

"You took a lot for granted!"

"So did you."

"For six weeks I—"

"I don't care to rehash it!"

Neither of them speak. I fear my husband will hang up. For some crazy reason I want the conversation to continue. It fascinates me. Reg and his ex seem victims of a spider's web. Who's the spider, marriage?

"You originally gave me custody, Bev. It's a little late to change your mind."

"I don't think so."

"The kids and I are getting along just fine. Don't make waves now. After the trial we'll get on a regular visitation schedule—the same as Lolly and Paul."

Bev attacks. "I demand the children for two weeks. Starting on Monday. If you deny me my legal right, I will retaliate and I'm not talking about Weintraub seeking an order to have the court find you in contempt." She smacks down the receiver.

Reg slumps in the desk chair. I crawl onto his lap. He fondles my hair absently. Kissing his forehead, I murmur, "Why don't you let Bev see Lynda and Richie?"

"I'm afraid she'll take them to a state that would not be informed of, or might ignore, the temporary California rul-

ing. Establish residency. Obtain a default divorce. Gain custody . . . then it's bye-bye children. I'd never see them
again. Hell, maybe she's off to Japan!"

"Oh, my gosh! With Hiroshima!"

Reg stares into my eyes as though they were crystal balls.
Is he trying to see into the future? The cowboy laments,
"You know what Mouse told me? My mommy and daddy
have one of those friendly divorces where I get to keep both
of them."

2

"Some homemade dill pickles"

Anneke Van Vetchen saunters across the patio. She's a tall blond Dutch girl with perfect teeth and seven children. Her offspring grow enough yellow hair to provide a Beverly Hills wigmaker with a year's supply.

"Hi, Lolly! Can we come swimming?" Youngsters trail behind this neighbor like the colorful tail of a kite, lugging life jackets, rafts, a plastic boat, an Igloo cooler, and a picnic hamper.

"Sure!" Noticing my thighs burning, I screw the lid off the Hawaiian Tropic. Jan Van Vetchen extends his plump palm. I pour from the bottle. The toddler smears coconut oil onto our Saint Bernard's head. Sissy, who Reg swears is a grown man hiding in a Saint Bernard suit, seems to grin. The commotion startles Governor Brown, a pregnant cat—

named when we were unsure of her sex—which jumps off
the dog's broad back. She's been napping there.

"Titty!" Jan chases.

Governor leaps to the safety of the diving board, where
Jenna lounges reading *Harper's Encyclopedia for Horsemen.*
Anneke glances away, apparently on purpose. Once, this
mother told me: "What I don't know doesn't hurt me." I
watch to make sure my teenager prevents the child from
tumbling into the deep end of the swimming pool.

"Finished the tomatoes, but I still have to can eighty
pounds of peaches. And the cucumbers. Imagine boiling
Ball jars in this heat!" Mrs. Van Vetchen reclines upon a
chaise, unfurling her shapely, bikini-clad body like a paper
birthday-party noisemaker.

Thinking of Ball jars reminds *me* of Sylvia Plath's novel
about suicide, *The Bell Jar.* Staring at my companion's lack
of stretch marks on her taut stomach, I confess, "I counted
out twelve Seconals after the divorce and composed a poign-
ant note. It grew longer and longer, consuming an entire
'Things to Do Today' tablet. Those last words seemed so important to me that writing them became a reason to live."

"I'll give you some homemade dill pickles. Would you
want them?"

I've never met anyone like Anneke Van Vetchen. She
apologizes for knowing how to make catsup. I evidently
seem sophisticated to her, coming from the Pasadena area
and owning a Mercedes, recently retired to the tractor shed.
Out here, wives drive fancy pickups with tape decks and
mud tires.

Anneke's relatives have farmed Dutch Valley for fifty
years. Her burly husband, Henk, runs a four-hundred-cow
dairy. He can't fathom why Reg chops cabbage for my cole
slaw. "No!" Henk protested once. "A great big educated
man who flies his own airplane?"

She questioned our moving. Looking at photographs of
the Milan Avenue house, this natural beauty sighed, "That's

a mansion, Lolly. Why did you leave?" At first I pretended
we wanted to try an alternate life-style. Then I told her how
Reg inherited this two-hundred-acre ranch. Next I confessed
that Jenna and Mouse were mine by a previous marriage.
Finally, I explained about the custody battle.

"We believe the chances of winning are better if we stay
in a wholesome environment. Mr. Scheffer's collecting comparative data on crime rates and drug problems. Gangs of
Future Farmers of America don't paint graffiti on side-
walks."

"What if the judge hates flies, mosquitoes, and cow shit?"

Or worse, he might be like my mother's father, who fled
acres of corn and hogs to better himself by attending law
school in Los Angeles. Grandpa wouldn't return to the country even for vacations. I worry about this at night when I'm
curled close to Reg. He caresses me. I fake snoring, because
my husband won't quit touching until I'm dead to the
world. Once, I protested: "You must rest, darling. Tomorrow is a busy day." His heroic reply was "You're better for
me than sleep."

To Anneke I countered, "It's not safe to walk from the
Music Center to the adjacent underground parking any
more. LA is full of kooks."

"Joe McShane shot up the Red Horse Saloon at the truck
stop at Castaic Wednesday night. One place is as bad as another."

What if Anneke is right? Has our family relocated for
naught? Or truly are we living here so that Reg can play articulate cowboy?

She hasn't informed her parents, the De Jongs, that I'm
"Mr. Bennett's *second* wife." They remember when Reg
played in their pond as a boy and fed the swans. Last May,
rather late in the academic year, I enrolled the four children
in a nearby (twenty miles away) parochial school. The
closest public education requires an hour-and-fifty-five-

minute bus ride. Which doesn't include driving three miles
to the crossroads pickup by 6:30 A.M.

At St. Anthony's, the Irish nuns politely welcomed our un-
likely crew, thanks to phone calls from Anneke and Mr. De
Jong. My friend hasn't informed her father that we're not
Catholic, either. He transported seventeen of us to the
church bazaar last Saturday in his motor home.

Eleven children suddenly swarm the chaises, inspired by
the sound of a potato-chip bag ripping open. Mother Van
Vetchen passes out helpings. After seconds, I wave my junk-
food-starved brood away. Two scrapping youngsters, six-
year-old Rye and three-year-old Henk, climb onto Anneke's
lap. She strokes them, listening to who hit whom, nodding
compassionately so that both assume she's on their side.

I say, "I'm leery of all this pastoral beauty. I've never
known anything but smog."

"You want a potato chip?"

"No thanks. I'm forever dieting."

"Henk thinks you have a gorgeous figure."

"He does?" This sort of information always surprises me. I
never felt I looked that fantastic and concentrated instead on
developing a fun personality. At this point, I'm sick of being
a good sport. I guess I feel comfortable with Anneke because she doesn't believe I am one. She's driven with me on
our dirt roads.

"Henk says you're very glamorous."

When I was young and longed to be thought of as beautiful, people told me I was bright. Now when I long to be
considered bright, people tell me I'm beautiful.

Reg has made me beautiful.

What a gift to give! A gift of beauty. According to
women's lib, I should feel that way by just standing naked
before a full-length mirror. I can't. I saw Paul Whitman's
distorted image of me for too long. Possibly he only reflected
my own bad opinion.

"Really, Lolly, you don't look as though you've had four kids."

I don't remind her that two are stepchildren. I love posing as Lynda and Richie's real mother. "You should talk! I've just been admiring your flat belly!"

"Mom was Miss Dairy Queen three years in a row, and runner-up for Farmer's Daughter," eleven-year-old Hendrika brags as she dispenses Ritz crackers to the boys.

"Oh, donkey poop! That was years ago."

"Sheri told Paul she thinks I have a great shape for someone *my age*."

My neighbor doesn't respond. I don't know what to say. Our conversations tend to be awkward. Either I'm reluctant to expose the real me, or we're groping for common ground.

Anneke blurts out, "Reg is very attractive."

"Our affair was lovely. But marriage has spoiled that." My husband does not tolerate clothes in bed. He contends that mates should sleep naked so they can become comfortable with each other's bodies in a nonsexual way. If being in bed undressed with a handsome man is a nonsexual situation, Mother gave me bad information all through college.

The former Farmer's Daughter runner-up doesn't laugh. She must not realize I'm being facetious.

"Your ex, Paul Whitman, forgive me, but he looks too good to be true. Like an ad in a magazine. I don't trust that. You know what I mean?"

"Paul and Sheri share a Super Max hair dryer. It's what keeps them together."

Anneke eyes me curiously. Or so it seems. I don't think she understands I'm joking. Hostesses used to count on my wit at dinner parties.

"Did you please Paul sexually?"

I'll bet she speculates on our marital breakup. Why not ask if *he* satisfied *me?*

"Did you two get along that way?"

I sigh, "We pretended to."

"Oh?"

"Fifties morality, mentality. Mother claimed, 'If you go too far, Laurel, you won't be able to stop.'" I recall that moment. We conferred in her mirrored dressing room. I rolled and unrolled the cuff of my Levi's, eyeing the crystal perfume bottles that reflected prisms of magic light. "I figured if sex was as great as all that, I'd better sample it. Enter Scooter Barnes—the fellow I went steady with in high school. Unfortunately, I acted too shy and embarrassed with Paul Whitman to admit I knew there was more to lovemaking than his version."

"It's different in Europe."

"You were born in Holland?"

"Americans make too much of sex. It's as natural as taking a leak."

"When Paul and I were engaged, nice girls didn't ask guys to go down on them. I married Reg because he didn't need an invitation."

Anneke opens a can of Coke.

I speak because she doesn't. "On our honeymoon, Paul and I spent more time photographing the Frank Lloyd Wright Butterfly House in Carmel than we did in cottage #7 at Highlands Inn. I had my period. It didn't occur to either of us that we could have sex anyway. We undressed separately in the bathroom and promised it didn't matter. Grace Kelly and Bing Crosby sang in the background."

"You had the radio on?"

My first time with Reg also occurred during the monthly flow. I removed a Tampax on the sly in the Pacific Ocean. Shark bait. Later, he cried, "Lolly, my God, I've hurt you!" I explained that I always bled heavily on the second day.

"Reg said you were an actress."

"He told you that?"

"I've never known a movie star before."

"All I did was major in theater arts in college, teach drama for a while."

"Your husband said you'd been in the movies."

"When you belong to a sorority at UCLA, you expect a studio to announce casting calls about twice a month. Warner's paid a dollar-forty-seven an hour plus sandwiches to try out. I was used in one crowd scene. Margot Haggerty landed speaking parts.'

"Reg said you filmed a TV commercial."

"My uncle was vice-president of Carnation at the time. He arranged for me to advertise their hot chocolate."

Neither of us speak for a while.

"I'm staunchly in favor of women's lib—"

"Oh, I'm not!" Anneke interrupts.

"—equal opportunity and pay and role reversal. However, my choice *right now* is to concentrate on a relationship with Reg and the four children. You might say, career-wise, I'm 'on hold.'"

I sense that my pal doesn't comprehend.

"I'd rather stay at home than . . . than star in a motion picture." I smile. "Besides, I'm practical. I have the opportunity to do one, but not the other."

"I've never thought of you as practical."

An airplane appears in the west. I scrutinize it, playing World War II spotter. It's not a 727 on the descent into Burbank; smaller. But larger than a single-engine crop duster. Twin-engine. As the plane approaches, the roaring noise summons the children like the bell on an ice-cream truck. They rise flying-fish-style from the pool.

"Is that Reg?"

"Yes!" I reply excitedly.

The Beech Baron zooms down to twenty feet above the pine trees. The airplane seems to skim the lanai roof and then pulls straight up, like a fighter.

"Oh, sour owl shit! He's spinning!" Anneke stares skyward, clearly transfixed.

"Come on, Reg! Do an aileron roll!" Jenna screams.

"Don't encourage him!" I protest, although of course he can't hear.

Reg circles back, dives even lower, and trims the tops of the eucalyptus trees along the drive. He dips the wings in farewell, heading north, toward the airport in Santa Paula. I hate to admit it, but watching my husband fly really turns me on. I'm not positive, but I'll bet Anneke feels the same way. She plops stomach down on the chaise, her legs unfolding like an opening pocketknife.

The telephone rings too soon for it to be ol' Throttle Jock calling from the hangar. I don't know whether or not to answer. I'm terrible at handling Bev's threats. Curiosity wins. I silence the annoying bell by lifting the receiver beside the barbecue.

From the pool, the delighted squeals of eleven children playing Marco Polo chorus. I feel like a lead singer. "Hello?"

"Good afternoon, Lolly." Paul Whitman wears his official office voice.

I talked to my ex-husband at his apartment in Newport Beach last night. In case he plans to upbraid me for something I said, I mentally review that conversation. It went like this.

"Hi, Sheri. Is Paul there?"

"He's blow-drying his hair."

"Would you fetch him, please?" Why do I have to speak to my former husband of seventeen years (plus two or three more of courtship equals at least nineteen big ones) through this twenty-one-year-old oracle?

"Yes?" Paul spoke in the angry-sounding voice he reserves for our exchanges if his girl friend is nigh. "What can you possibly want, Lolly? You've called four times already today."

"She did!" I hear Sheri moan. "When?"

"Don't tell her, Paul. What you do at the office is your own darn business. Do you want Fang? Jenna said you

*missed her. I mean, do you think I got more than my share
of the animals, community-property-wise?"*

"The apartment doesn't allow pets."

"What do you call Sheri?"

"No pets."

*"Not even Fang?" Paul used to sleep with the cat curled
above his head like a fur hat.*

Now I quip. "What do *you* want?"

"Paul?" Anneke glances over. How did she guess? I nod
yes.

"Lolly, this is serious. You've got to stop calling me in the
evening. It upsets Sheri."

I remain silent, wiping perspiration from my stomach.

"I don't want you to call the apartment. Is that clear?"

"I thought you said just in the evening."

"It drives Sheri nuts."

"She's jealous of me?"

"Of our seventeen years together. You have to realize
Sheri hasn't had your advantages."

"What's the advantage? Seventeen years with you?"

"I wish you hadn't told her she has the looks and mentality of a cocktail waitress without the class."

"I didn't say that!" Mother did. Mouse must have repeated same. Bless her.

"So what if Sheri didn't grow up in Pasadena?"

"Where is she from?"

"Pico Rivera."

"You're kidding!"

"What's wrong with Pico Rivera?"

"If you have to ask, you wouldn't understand."

"Everyone can't be from Pasadena."

"You're the one who ended up with the membership at
Annandale, a club *my* grandfather helped to found."

"No more calls in the evening!"

"What if it's an emergency?"

"Well, OK. If it's an emergency."

Paul must have forgotten himself. He's using his real voice and sounding like the Paul who sat beside me in the labor room. Sadness stabs me through the heart. Neither of us talks for ten seconds. Outer-space noises blink over the telephone lines.

"You used to be so jealous when Betsy called me at home. My own secretary."

"That was because of the miscarriages. I felt like a failure as a woman."

"Please show some compassion."

"Compassion for Sheri?"

"Oh, this is too much!" Anneke interrupts. She rolls onto one side. Coppertone lacquers her body. "Tell Paul to go fuck a sheep."

"Lolly, it's over. We're going in different directions now. Like a root-bound plant wrenched apart and placed in separate containers to grow into two healthy specimens."

Paul stooped to quoting the *Reader's Digest* to me when we were married. I retort, sick of having watched him drool over big-breasted women for nineteen years, "Jenna told me she and Sheri wear the same size bra."

"Sheri's flatter than you," Paul confesses.

Strangely, I feel sorry for him and change the subject. "Have you talked to Aunt Lou?"

"Why should I, Lolly? She's *your* aunt."

"Marla got divorced."

"No!"

"How's your father?"

"Not very well."

"Sheri said he calls her Lolly."

"You talked to your ex long enough," Anneke criticizes after I hang up the phone. "You act jumpy with him, like a cow in labor."

I sigh.

"I don't read all those psychology books that you do. So I may be wrong. But I think you should *hate* Paul."

Lynda flops down on the foot of my chaise, blocking the sun. If she were my daughter or if we weren't engaged in a battle for custody, I'd ask her to move and turn down the blasted radio.

"Is that Reg's car?"

I listen. Yes, it is—not process servers or kidnapers or private detectives or Bev. Both Reg and Paul drive Porsches. I've had to memorize only one engine sound. A friend of mine, Joyce, married two different Phi Delts. She had to learn only one set of fraternity songs.

My husband's boot heels clunk on the flagstone as he crosses to the pool. I rush to greet him. We meet midway, crush each other in an embrace. Reg cops a feel, as they used to say in the fifties, from my bikini-bare body.

"I'm all sweaty."

"Hope you weren't expecting peace and quiet," Anneke interjects, assuming a supine position—Venus Rising. Karla and young Annele cry over a spilled Pepsi.

"Daddy!" Richie calls from the inner tube.

Jenna waves *Harper's Encyclopedia for Horsemen*. Her stepfather's baggy Flintridge Prep sweat shirt hides her bathing suit.

"Can we go out to dinner?" Lynda begs, reclining on the chaise I vacated. The child covers her hair with my straw hat and twirls my Christian Dior sunglasses.

"I removed thirty-seven frogs from the pool," Mouse announces. "Eleven responded to treatment." She charts frog deaths in a spiral notebook. The chlorine kills them.

"Daddy!" Richie urges, "swim with me!"

"We had a breakdown in the crusher equipment. Ten thousand bucks to repair the damned thing. Five hours of ore production out the window."

"Why did you fly home so early?"

Reg speaks to me in a low voice. "Weintraub, Bev's attor-

ney, (according to her) has given me an ultimatum, forty-
eight hours to deliver the children. . . . Anneke, where
were you yesterday? Why didn't you come swimming?"

"I thought you had company."

"No!" I exclaim. "What made you think that?"

"A couple in a white Camaro stopped at the dairy and
asked directions. From the way the woman was dressed, I
figured they were townie friends of yours."

"Bev!"

"What did the man look like?" Reg unhooks the wire
frames of aviator glasses from behind his ears.

"He was oriental."

"Hiroshima!"

RB III explains. "My ex-wife and her paramour, spying!"

Anneke slaps her luscious thigh. "Oh! I'm such a horse's
behind. If I'd known, I would have sent them on a wild
goose chase up Bell's mountain."

Reg and I exchange glances.

3

"The place to meet celebrities"

Reg still plans to deny Bev the two-week visitation. With house guests from Hollywood, Margot and Lance Haggerty, we nervously wait out the last half of the forty-eight-hour ultimatum. They're unaware of the countdown.

A blue silk toga wraps Margot's sumptuous body. The toga probably started life as a bed sheet. In our sorority days, my friend was famous for turning a pair of red velvet drapes into a strapless formal. The house mother never figured out why the library had one naked window. Today Margot wears gold ankle bracelets.

She drifts across the pool in a rubber boat, chewing ice from her drink. A large hat and enormous sunglasses hide her face. Since the source of Margot's voice is obscured by

flopping straw, her words seem to materialize out of nowhere—a technique utilized by the Wizard of Oz. "Which
means learning your lines in one hour."

"Then, you're an actress?" Reg stares at a trailing oar,
presumably not knowing where to look at Margot. Her daz-
zling beauty blinds like strobe lights. Plus, he acts sensitive
toward how insecure I *used* to feel. I knew a girl who
believed herself ugly until an encounter group stripped her
and "kissed everything." My second husband has done the
same for me.

"I told you six times. Ms. Haggerty plays the lead in a TV
soap!" I had given Reg a complete bio on my old roommate,
who had called the day she received the lengthy letter I
finally wrote.

"I'm a professional enigma," Margot retorts.

"That's wonderful!" I squeal.

"Lolly's my biggest fan."

"I thought *I* was," Lance chides. Having completed fifty
laps of the pool, he stretches out on the deck—his prone,
bronzed body resembling a Greek statue that's toppled over.
He sports UCLA jogging trunks and visor. Earlier Margot's
husband had confided, "The place to meet celebrities is on
the track at Westwood."

"Do you have children?" Reg scoops leaves and dead
frogs from the water with a skimmer. He pauses every so
often to survey the surrounding pasture, a gesture that, for
some reason, makes him seem lonely. Does the cowboy scout
the road for ambushing ex-wives and orientals?

"No children." Margot doesn't mention that she's spent
twelve years charting her temperature on an ovulation
graph.

"She was my maid of honor. I'm sure you met her at the
wedding. You escorted her down the aisle, for cripes sake!" I
appeal to my sorority sister. "You remember, don't you? Reg
was Paul's best man."

Margot clears her throat. Lance frowns at me. I guess it's

impolite to mention that *other* ceremony, although all four
of us were there. It's one thing we share. Why do the three
of them pretend they've just met?

"More shrimp, anyone?" the host asks, dropping the
skimmer behind the retaining wall.

"No thanks, I must stop pigging out."

"That's a delicious cocktail sauce."

"Reg and I like to cook together. I've gained ten pounds."

"You used to be so damn' fidgety, Lolly, you shook weight
off."

"You do look terrific, Mrs. Bennett. This country air
rather agrees with you." Lance yawns.

It takes me a moment to realize that I'm *Mrs. Bennett*.
When asked what my husband does, I still say, "He's an architect." Seventeen years is a long time.

"How did I look before, Lance?"

"Horny," Margot replies for him. "But you had the perfect clothes for it."

"I'll make another round of drinks." Reg exits abruptly,
stage right.

"Tsk. Tsk. You hurt his feelings talking about your first
marriage." The TV star paddles over to the pool ladder,
hoists herself out of the boat without splashing a drop of
water on the toga. Joining Lance and me, drink in hand, this
barefoot actress tilts her head so that the Sassoon cut
swooshes forward dramatically. I think about how she domi-
nates the scene. I'm used to her stepping on *my* lines.

Margot seems to stare over the oleanders across the citrus
grove to The Lazy J Ranch, on the far side of Willow Lane a
mile or so away. Seen from here, the crossfencing paints
white outlines on rectangles of gold barley. It looked even
prettier in May, when the fields were green.

"How big is this ranch?"

"That's a vulgar question! It's like asking how much
money one earns."

Lance shoos away a yellow jacket. Insects are drawn to

the water. In the early morning, bees arrive to drink. They
cover the pool like a noisy black-and-yellow quilt.

"Two hundred acres, which is small, as ranches in this
valley go. But, to quote Reg, 'If you own farm land in Southern California, you're actually in the real estate business.'"

"What's growing?"

"We have a few oranges. Some barley. Alfalfa. Mostly
permanent pasture."

"Jesus, you mean Reg is actually a *farmer?* That's right
out of a 'Little House on the Prairie' script."

"The main crop is for his Black Angus. I guess he's more
of a rancher. That's how he sees himself, anyway." I don't
admit that a hired foreman manages the place.

"Do you sell the cows for steak?"

"Don't talk about it!" Lance pleads.

"Mouse hasn't figured that out yet. When she does,
there'll be heck to pay."

"Can't you keep them as pets?"

"It is too damn' tranquil!"

"I long for rush-hour traffic," I kid.

"You're better off out here."

"Freeways!"

"I was tired of seeing that same picture of you and Paul
in Jody Jacobs' column. *Also attending: that innovative architect Mr. Whitman and his charming wife Lollypop.*"

"Crowds of people driving purposefully here and there.
Horns blaring. Honk! Honk!"

"You needed a *real* challenge. You've succeeded at everything without half trying, even anthropology in college. I
don't think it's good to have it so easy." Do I detect envy in
Margot's voice? Confusion? She fiddles with a gold charm.

"I didn't succeed at my first marriage."

My old confidante and I stare through each other's dark
glasses, peering inside as if we were Easter eggs with windows. We used to have similar setups. I turn away first.

Margot touches my shoulder. "There are lessons you must learn."

I move back. She steps forward. A sloppy cha-cha-cha.

"Somehow Reg is good for you. I notice a change. You act contented. Before, it seemed necessary for you to convince me you'd made the right decision regarding marriage and family versus career. You haven't asked me once if my agent had any calls for haggard women thirty-five and up."

"Remember when you shot that Betty Crocker ad! You asked me what to wear. You wanted to know if you should bake a cake in Chanel slacks!"

"Reg is a heck of a nice guy," Lance sums up. "These yellow jackets don't sting, do they?"

"No sweat, Lance. They're props."

"Not that your other husband wasn't. Damned attractive fellow, Paul Whitman. Never said a great deal."

"Lolly was too much for Paul."

That makes me feel guilty. It is somehow my fault that I was too much for Paul.

"You don't act hysterical any more."

"I was hysterical only the last two years."

"Longer."

"What do you miss most?" Lance asks.

"The Bistro on Thursday nights. That yummy chocolate soufflé."

"Ah, maid's night out."

"I sat next to Peter Sellers once," I recall.

"We saw Warren Beatty last week."

"You breast-fed Mouse until she grew big enough to climb onto your lap by herself. How old was she when you stopped? Almost two? And you had a thing about providing an enriched environment. You pasted colored geometric shapes on everything."

"He sat at the next table."

"Followed by the kids' hamster period. Those yellow plastic tubes crisscrossed the kitchen."

"I was hoping Beatty'd have smallpox scars or something. But he didn't."

"You spent too much energy on your children. I'll never forget that sit-down dinner party when Paul kept extending the cocktail hour, waiting for you to come downstairs. We finally found you sound asleep between Jenna and Mouse in a twin bed with the Dr. Suess still in your hand."

Margot acts distressed. I sense that my divorce from Paul upset her because she carried our so-called "perfect marriage" around like a talisman. It is as though she's struggling to figure out what went wrong. I think this friend longs to blame me. Maybe on some level I encourage this?

"I can't remember a damned thing that Paul Whitman said. Do you, Margot?" her husband asks.

" 'With a blueblood transfusion he fit right in at the Jonathan Club.' "

"That was my line!" I protest. "With a blueblood transfusion *Paul* fit right in at the Jonathan Club."

"Gawd, I hope we last," Lance announces sullenly.

"*Scenes from a Marriage* depressed him," Margot confides.

"You two seem happy."

"Happiness is overrated," she snaps. I recall when her name was Margaret Ann and she rushed down to the Newman Club to confession three times a week—long before she had anything to confess.

"We enrolled the four children at a parochial school in your honor, Margot. The nuns are from Ireland. Fantastic women! Darling!"

"Jenna is startlingly lovely."

"She's a carbon copy of Paul."

"The one with the glasses showed me her frog hospital and graveyard. It's the same thing. What do you call her? Rodent?" Lance inquires.

"Aren't Lynda and Richie cute?"

"What a blond helmet of hair on the boy! The girl reminds me of Brenda Starr, from the funnies."

"Lynda resembles her mother. At least, they're both redheads."

"Do you mind if I snort some coke?" Margot inquires.

"Not now!"

"All right. I'll smoke a joint."

"Out here, all that's available is homegrown. What did you bring?"

"Stop drooling! It's just Maui Wowie. You want one?" She extracts a silver cigarette case from her tote bag.

I shake my head no. "Please be cool. OK? We've got this court trial coming up. Things are tense. Especially this weekend. Reg is taking a stand by denying his ex-wife a two-week visitation."

"Great plot! Reminiscent of *Kramer vs. Kramer.*"

"Right. But the minute Dustin Hoffman remarries, Meryl Streep will scream for custody again!" I rant, "No mother wants another woman to raise her child. It's a romantic notion—the father as a single parent—but as soon as *he* finds a second wife . . ."

"Lolly, that's fantastic! Have you contemplated writing the screenplay? I could put you in touch with 'Swifty' Lazar."

"You've got to be kidding, Lance. She barely passed Subject A," Margot tattles.

"I'm talking about real life!" I insist.

"Who produced that?"

"The French director?"

"You're thinking of *A Simple Story.*" Margot and Lance speak directly to each other.

"Don't you two believe in anything but films?"

"It's what we have instead of God."

"Anyway, Reg's attorney encourages him, but I'm a complete wreck. My husband would have a fit if he knew you were turning on in broad daylight."

Margot offers the lighted joint. I glance in both directions like a child crossing the street, then inhale quickly.

"The smog's gotten so bad in Hollywood I refuse to breathe anything but filtered air," Lance advises as I have a coughing fit.

"Isn't Reg into drugs?"

I can barely talk. "Once in a while we'll share a joint before making love. I've convinced him pot's an aphrodisiac."

"I need it for the Big O."

"That's Diane Keaton's line, Margot," I chide.

"Gawd, that time in your sauna when that idiot director pulled out what was supposed to be a *fake* hand grenade."

"He was a banker, Lance, *passing* as a director," I correct.

"All those naked people fleeing across your yard."

"Talk about a *lawn* party!"

"Tore the hell out of the redwood," Lance remembers.

"Your life used to be nothing but outtakes."

"Hurry, Margot. Smoke faster. The children will be back any minute."

"Where are they? I haven't seen them lately."

"They rode their horses over to pick up the mail."

"I know! Paul Whitman talked about his car. You could always ask him how the Porsche was running."

Reg returns, bearing four drinks on a wooden tray and a newspaper folded open at the crossword puzzle. He's changed into a Levi's shirt, which hangs unbuttoned, and old jeans—I mean peg-legged 1950s-vintage. Water slicks back his gray-blond hair. He used to apply Brylcreem. I wish my husband had worn the polo shirt and shorts I put out for him, or the blue velour lounging robe Mother bought.

Passing behind me, Reg touches my hair. I want to explain to the Haggertys how good this feels; also, when we lace our fingers together. It's unlike anything I've ever experienced before. I think Margot noticed. She studies her tapered orange fingernails.

"Once, I filmed in this vicinity. Could that be possible?"
Lance addresses Reg.

"Anything's possible." RB III passes out gin and tonics.
"Want a hit?"

I gag on my lime slice.

"A beer commercial."

"They stable the West Coast Clydesdales at The Lazy J."
I'm hoping to distract Reg, who is staring at Margot's hand-
rolled cigarette. "Their feet measure twelve inches across.
Don't they, darling?"

Margot sidles over to Reg. Her arm floats skyward. The
drink hovers there. "Never trust a man who doesn't work
crossword puzzles."

"Huh?" Reg mutters.

"It's just dialogue," Lance explains. "She salvages it for
use at appropriate moments."

"Love is a four-letter word," the actress replies.

"Do we all share the one bathroom? I didn't notice a
shower?"

"We're building a dream house on the hill by the hay
barn. Putting in a tennis court."

"After the judge hands down a decision," Reg says as he
sits on the retaining wall.

"Where is the closest movie theater?"

"A town called Fillmore. The Bijou's *still* showing *The
Sound of Music.*"

"We haven't seen that yet," Reg admits. "Maybe next
weekend. Do you want to go, Lolly?"

"I've seen it," I apologize. "Six times. Including one night
on TV when the four children and I watched."

"I couldn't stand living more than fifteen minutes from
Mann's Chinese. Have you noticed? *Everything* opens
there."

"What in the world! It sounds like an Indian attack."

"The children are back."

They trap their horses in the corral. My older daughter

races the others across the patio, throwing mail toward the round table. As the youngsters cannonball into the swimming pool, water swells over the coping, creating the smell of wet cement. Lance and Margot watch as if studying monkeys at the LA Zoo. Richie's fourth-grade class can't ever return there, because everyone but Sister Maura threw hamburgers at the gorillas.

"That's my surf mat!" Lynda claims.

My stepson protests, "I tapped it first."

"Come on, Sissy, come on, old girl. Jump in!" Jenna coaxes.

"Does the Saint Bernard have fleas?"

I shrug. "The chlorine kills them."

"Mommy, can I take Mrs. Frisby for a swim?"

"Who?" Lance asks.

"Mouse's pet rat. The animal enjoys the cool water. She paddles around happily on the first step. Sometimes she'll venture out a bit."

I recognize Bev's handwriting on a letter addressed to Reg. He opens the scented yellow envelope with his pocketknife. My husband apparently swallows the contents as one does a tough piece of meat.

"You always hoped for more children, Lolly."

"I understand you're in the steel business." Lance tries to draw my husband into conversation.

"Perhaps Richie and Lynda are the ones you lost, reincarnated into other bodies."

"Reg may lease his mine to Kaiser for oodles of money!" I brag, wondering if what Margot says might be possible. I feel a new connection to Lynda and Richie.

"You knew Paul Whitman?" Lance continues doggedly.

Reg nods.

"He drives a Porsche."

RB III stuffs the letter and pocketknife into his pants pocket.

"You fly an airplane?"

"He had to ride his bicycle to the airport to take flying lessons, because he was too young to have a driver's license!"

"Oh, Lolly!" Talk about making an entrance!

Margot and Lance turn.

Anneke, her long body exposed—except for three pink triangles of cloth—poses like a *Playboy* centerfold. She pushes a stroller. Three children cling to her bare legs. The older kids and their Great Dane leap into the pool.

"Oww! Oww!" Lance jumps to his feet. "I've been stung!"

"She's magnificent," Margot appraises. "A perfect Daisy Mae! How unfair to have such competition out here in the sticks. Aren't you jealous?"

"I hadn't really thought about it." I gave my jealousy to my first marriage, like giving at the office.

"She must be six feet tall! What a figure! Are all those children hers? Couldn't be."

"Oww! Oww!"

"Did you can the peaches? Lance, dangle your foot in the pool. The cold water will help."

"Could she move that rat?"

"Made jam. Jelly. Syrup. Pickled the rest. Here." My neighbor hands over two jars of pickled peaches.

"Anneke, meet my sorority sister, Margot, her husband, Lance."

"Terrific name! I wouldn't change it. How do you spell *On ick a?*"

"I recognize her from television!"

"Don't you have anything for stings?"

"'Day by Day'!"

"I use snakeweed," Reg offers.

"You're Helen!"

"I film commercials!" Lance pouts.

"I watch it every day. Even when I'm in labor."

I remember that last week Lynda told Anneke the six big

positions. Miss Dairy Queen had replied, "They forgot the one we use while I'm in labor."

"Anneke lives four miles south of us. Her husband owns a dairy. I'm sorry, Lance."

"I've never met anyone who actually watched the show."

"Pearl does."

"She can milk a cow!" Reg brags.

Anneke confides, "I think that abortion was the right thing. But oh how I bawled!"

"Makes her own cottage cheese."

"Your children are Dutch Cleanser ads. Do they have an agent? Such beautiful faces!" Margot enthuses.

"I think it's swelling."

"Hendrika, don't hold your brother's head under the water!"

"He splashed me!"

"The blonde with the braids is perfect. Is that Hendrika? The names are fabulous! Don't you think, Lolly?"

I count three with braids. Four. Five. Six. "Anneke, someone's missing."

"I could die if I'm allergic!"

"The baby!"

Suddenly Reg jumps—clothes, boots, and all—into the middle of the pool. The other children and the adults freeze like in the game of statue maker.

I sight my two daughters as well as Lynda and Richie in line for the diving board, silently mouthing thanks to a God I abandoned years before. The involuntary reflexes linger. Margot, with her Catholic upbringing, still crosses herself when she hears an ambulance siren.

Anneke remains incredibly calm. Possibly because, like the Avon lady, disaster knocks routinely on her door. One week, she spent three days at the Emergency Room: Karla fell from a horse and broke her arm; Peter sliced his hand with a saw; Henk ran a pitchfork through his leg.

Reg surfaces, swims to the ladder, carries Jan Van

Vetchen up the steps, positions the child's body on the deck, and administers mouth to mouth resuscitation.

"Is he dead?" Lance asks squeamishly, limping to his wife's chair.

I glance at Margot, who, curiously, recites the Hail Mary. I can't tell if it's a put-on or not. With expressive hands clasped to her breast, she's perfect for the role of suppliant. I have the feeling she's lost a youngster or two on "Day by Day."

Because of my recent association with St. Anthony's school, I'm familiar with the prayer. I commence mumbling along in some Pavlovian response, coming on, to quote Jenna, "Like a hot-shot Catholic." Anneke hears, nods as if to say we're doing the right thing. She repeats the words devoutly in a loud voice. Her head is bowed, blond hair skirting her face. One by one, the bewildered children pick up the chant, including Reg's and my four. Mouse kneels. The nuns would be proud.

"I don't know the words," Lance apologizes to me. His leg is swollen to grapefruit size.

The chorus of voices float heavenward on the pureness of the country air: "Holy Mary, Mother of God, pray for us sinners now and at the hour of our death."

Touchingly, the children—my car-pool choir—break into song: "Jesus, we adore You. Lay our lives before You."

"A gripping moment," Lance whispers. "I'd give anything to have it on film."

I wipe my eyes. Even Brownies singing "God Bless America" at the Scout Day picnic cause me to cry. Indecision cripples. I don't know whether to stand with the others, or rush to my husband's side.

Then Jan wails, loud screams that denote life.

"Oh, thank God!" Margot exclaims.

"I do. Regularly," Anneke replies, hurrying toward her child and Reg. She embraces my husband in what appears to be a spontaneous gesture, picks up her seventeen-month-old. Fifteen minutes later—life jacket firmly buckled—Jan frolics in the pool as if nothing had happened.

"He wanted to pet Sissy," Reg explains.

"This is the third time since June Jan's been pulled out of a pool. I guess I should look into swimming lessons." Shrugging, Mother Van Vetchen oils her body.

I crave another drink. Tying bikini straps at my neck, I casually gather up the debris: a dish smeared with clam dip, an empty cracker basket, a platter of limp fruit, popcorn bowls. Reg follows me into the kitchen, swiping remnants of food.

The door bangs shut.

"What did Bev say?" I eye the liquor cabinet. "You're dripping water all over the floor!"

"Same old stuff. She wants Lynda and Richie delivered without fail to her apartment Monday. For a two-week visit." He pulls off a boot, dumps the water into the sink.

"Oh, honey. Let her see them!"

Reg shakes his head no.

"At least call Scheffer."

"He doesn't want to hear about it."

"At a hundred bucks an hour I'd think—"

"What I plan to do is probably in contempt of court. If he knew, my attorney would have to advise me thusly."

"Contempt of court! Isn't that serious?"

"The issue's complicated. First, Weintraub would have to get the court to issue an order to show cause. Meanwhile, Scheffer'd seek to slap Bev with a restraining order. Then I'd either be held in contempt or I wouldn't. It could take months."

"Wow!"

"Or if Bev kept the children until the trial—which I'm sure she's planning to do—then she'd be in contempt. You have to weigh the advantages. *Physical* custody means something to me."

"You mean like possession is nine tenths of the law?" That is the extent of my legal knowledge.

My husband nods yes.

"You truly believe your ex-wife would skip the country with the kids? Fly to Japan?"

"I wouldn't put it past her."

"Do they have passports?"

"Yes. We'd hoped to travel in Europe. Of course, we didn't, because Bev left. But before she did, the four of us went down and applied at the Department of Immigration. Had our pictures taken. I never picked up those passports."

"Call and see if Bev did!"

"Don't throw that pineapple away."

"OK, so in your own mind you're behaving prudently. Simply taking precautions?"

Reg reaches around my shoulder for the discarded fruit. I turn so that I'm against him. Suntan oil and his wet Levi's shirt stick us together. His closeness surrounds me like warm water in a bath. It's more comforting than gin. "You were very heroic saving Jan."

"It was nothing. Hey, what's the matter, Lolly?"

For some reason, my body trembles. The approaching legal showdown scares me to death. Grandpa, the dearly departed criminal lawyer, would *freak* if he knew I am going to participate in a courtroom battle. That thought pesters like a mosquito.

Lover Boy kisses my forehead.

"You're treating Margot and Lance abominably. Be nice to my friends."

"The guy's a fag. 'Owwl'" RB III imitates our unfortunate guest.

"No he isn't. He's an actor."

"And she's too phony for words."

"Margot's my best friend."

Reg doesn't answer.

"Why don't you like her?"

"I'm sorry if I seem preoccupied."

"Can't we *try* and have some fun? We haven't gone out or had people over since we moved here. This custody issue eats away at us like maggots. We never talk about anything else. Let me read Bev's letter. Shoot, why'd she sign it *love?*"

"Do you know what's scary about Margot? Her phoniness is real."

I say nothing.

"You were heading in that direction, Lolly."

I feel like smacking him, which is interesting. I've never wanted to hit one of the children. "Do you really not remember Margot? You sat next to her at Paul and my rehearsal dinner."

"I sat beside a very sweet girl named Margaret Ann who was so shy she couldn't look me square in the face."

"Oh! I'm sorry to interrupt!"

Reg and I jump apart.

"Come in, Anneke. Wasn't that a close shave with Jan!"

"He needs to poop."

My husband tousles the child's head, visibly affectionate. "Hi, Jan-boy."

"Thank heavens Reg used to be a lifeguard."

Miss Dairy Queen and the cowboy look at each other. She says, "Yes." This simple word sounds seductive as all get-out.

I grab a can of mixed nuts from the cupboard. When I turn around, I catch Reg ogling Anneke's ass. A crazy panic suffocates me like a boa constrictor with his prey. I can barely breathe. I feel more frightened than when I discovered Paul's Sheri. Yet, what I told Margot earlier is true. I'm not jealous. Suicidal maybe, but not *jealous!*

"I'm going back to the pool."

"Are you OK?" My husband hurries after me.

"Why didn't you stay and talk to Anneke? She probably wanted to thank you *privately* for saving Jan."

"No big deal."

RB III grabs my hand. We walk in silence to the patio. Margot talks on the extension phone by the barbecue. She's trapped the receiver between shoulder and ear. Her arms flap, seagull-like. "How in the world should I know! . . . There's a kid a minute drowning in the pool!"

"Spaced out!" I inform Reg, squealing on Ms. Haggerty.

Covering the mouthpiece, the actress stage-whispers, "Someone named Bev. Wondering where her son and daughter are. You'd think a mother'd keep better track of her kids. It's dangerous around here."

I smile goonily.

Margot pushes the button that disconnects the call. She taps her forehead as if testing for a ripe melon. "I've got to give up dope."

"Seeing pink elephants?" Reg inquires.

"No. Hearing Japanese gongs."

4

"Lolly loves Reg"

"Want me to call the Auto Club?" I asked, wishing I'd jumped into something better after the last swim than cut-off Levi's and a customized tee shirt advertising "Lolly loves Reg." Why didn't I blow-dry my hair instead of pulling it into a ponytail?

My husband's ex-wife wears a white safari suit and gold sandals with high heels, which puncture the soft ground like hypodermic needles. A tiger-striped bandana conceals most of her bright red curls. Bev flicks cigarette ash into a cupped palm, probably having previously heard millions of times Reg's lecture on fire safety. Our barley fields are highly combustible in August despite the unseasonal thunderstorm late this afternoon.

Rain turned the dirt entryway to pudding. This soggy ground captured Bev's car the way the La Brea tar pits used to trap dinosaurs. We suspect that she's here at the ranch spying on her children.

RB III currently shovels mud from under the tire of his first wife's Camaro. Eventually, Reg stands back to inspect the hole he's dug, jabs the blade into a fresh mound of soil, leaving the handle sticking up like a grave marker.

Bev poses to his right; I'm on the left, sitting cross-legged in the Jeep. The three of us form a triangle similar to those horrid drawings of ovaries that illustrated the *Personally Yours* pamphlet distributed by Modess. Years ago, my husband's ex-spouse confided to me that she learned to screw from the instructions for inserting Tampax.

"That ought to handle it," Reg says, boldly climbing into the car on which he is probably still making payments. He revs the engine, eases the vehicle forward. "Get in. I'll take you to the highway. Lolly can follow and bring me back in the Jeep."

"No thanks!" Bev retorts. A compatibility quiz in the current *Cosmopolitan* warns against men who *do* for women rather than showing them how.

"Why don't you want me to come along? Is some stud stashed in the bushes on Willow Lane?" Reg accuses.

"Maybe!" His ex acts rebellious, like my teenager vowing to buy junk food with her allowance.

"The surfer? Or have you moved on to bigger and better prospects?"

"Anyone would be better than you!"

"Not bigger!" I cry.

"Some authority!" Bev taunts, adjusting a loop earring. "It's incestuous, you know, Lolly, your marrying Reg. Not to mention *stupid*. Didn't all those years with Paul Whitman teach you anything?"

I'm not good at impromptu insults, especially since I'm accustomed to treating this woman as a friend. I gave her a baby shower when she was pregnant with Lynda, and baked a stork-shaped cake. The plastic beak and feet remain in my cookie-cutter box.

"I demand to have the children tomorrow for a two-week visitation."

"So your lawyer says." Reg slides from behind the wheel and leaves the engine running.

"Either you hand the kids over or, I swear, I'll kidnap them!" Bev drives off too fast, swerving erratically over the slick surface. She must slam on the brakes, because next the Camaro's tires spin in place, burrowing mole-like in the sludge.

"I'm taking them to Hawaii!" Bev admonishes out the window as the wheels dig deeper.

"You're not going anywhere for a while." Reg leans on the shovel handle, looking exactly like a Grant Wood painting.

I'm sorry Margot and Lance have already gone. I'm sure they'd have loved to witness this scene. It would look terrific on film.

5

"To truly appreciate the privilege of custody"

Anneke and I slump with little Jan between us on the spectator benches at the water slides. I continually survey the crowd and surrounding area for Bev, Hiroshima—the Japanese boyfriend—anyone who looks like a hired kidnaper. Suspicious figures lurk behind the oak trees. The last time I checked, they turned out to be children avoiding the long hike down the hill to the restrooms by taking a country leak. Once, I caught Richie. Spotting me, he quickly pulled up his bathing suit.

Three hours and fifty dollars ago we arrived with a picnic lunch. Extra watermelon floats in the Coleman ice chest beside me, around which ten pairs of flip-flops stack, and beach towels mound. Although clouds streak the sky like a

child's finger painting, the afternoon sun feels hot. Anneke
and I have stripped down to bikini tops and shorts. I wear a
cloth visor to counteract the glare and smear myself with
Coppertone.

My husband did not deliver the children to his ex-wife
this morning, a tactic not exactly approved by our custody
specialist, Mr. Scheffer. I hope Bev isn't provoked into some
drastic action. I just called the attorney's office from a pay
phone at the front gate to ask what to do if Richie and
Lynda's natural mother accosts them here. He was in court.
Reg can't be reached either. The dear man's off buying one
more used Kenworth truck for the mine. The last semi he
purchased died somewhere near Blythe.

I'm sorry that we ventured out to the water slides. But I
was going crazy at the ranch, trapped there with the children like sitting ducks, especially since I'm now convinced
my husband's ex is up to no good. I called the Department
of Immigration in LA. A Mrs. Beverly Bennett *did* pick up
the children's passports.

"Relax, Lolly!" Anneke says as she wrestles with Jan for
her sunglasses. I watch a dark-complexioned man follow
Lynda down the center slide. My stepdaughter rides the turquoise mat on her belly like a tired surfer, oblivious to danger. How can I caution Lynda and Richie to beware of their
own mother?

"Reg maintains that he's not denying visitation but pre-
venting abduction," I tell my friend. Her lack of response
compels me to ramble on. "Bev could skip the country or go
to another state, where the California ruling won't necessarily hold. States are supposed to respect each other's decisions, but I'm told they don't always do so. Reg was awarded
temporary custody at a preliminary hearing, but nothing is
finally settled until *after* the trial. If his ex bugs out to
Japan, it's good-bye forever."

My head aches from this. I check out the man beside me,

envisioning Lynda and Richie, Singer-sewing-machine rich, living in Tokyo.

"Reg would rather face a contempt-of-court charge for not providing reasonable visitation right now than have Bev spirit the children away with the trial date imminent. She's gone months without seeing them in the past."

"Contempt? Is that serious?"

"Bev would face the same charge if in fact she took off with Lynda and Richie. But she'd have them. Don't you see?"

"Give the glasses to *Moeder*, Jan."

"Mr. Scheffer seeks a restraining order to prevent this visitation because Bev swears her attorney is filing an order to show cause to have Reg held in contempt. Meanwhile, what kills me is I'm supposed to carry on as if everything is normal. I wonder if it's safe to sit in the open like this? I wish Reg had stayed home today."

Anneke still does not reply. I interpret her silence as criticism of my extraordinary situation. I don't like it any better than she does.

"There's not much practical guidance in custody cases. Nobody wants to get involved in a family feud, not the judges or the police or social workers. Domestic relations is called the court of the insoluble. Either parent can pretty much get away with murder." I cross my fingers against this unfortunate choice of words. "Did you read about the woman from Elsinore who went to jail rather than tell her ex where their daughter was?"

Three rows away, a fat lady eats popcorn. The smell of hot butter makes me hungry despite the fact that I ate five discarded tuna sandwich halves at lunch and the crust of two peanut butter-and-jellies. I also finished both Mouse and Richie's lukewarm milk. At home, our Saint Bernard usually saves me from this fate. I should have brought Sissy to scare off Bev. Once in a while, the dog *doesn't* wag her tail when I command, "Attack!"

"Mr. Scheffer maintains that biology doesn't guarantee an individual will be a good parent. He believes the father can be the true nurturer of the child."

Staring past the fat lady, I spot a head of curly hair.

"Bev!" I hiss, pointing nearsightedly. This is my eleventh potential culprit in the past hour.

Anneke glances around. "That's Mrs. Hernandez. She got a frizz perm and dyed her hair orange."

"You sure?"

"Mrs. Hernandez! How's it going? I'd like you to meet my friend Mrs. Bennett. Lolly has *four* children at St. Anthony's. I saw your Tommy a minute ago on the fast slide."

Mrs. Hernandez smiles. Bev wouldn't appreciate being mistaken for this toothy matron. Reg's ex is attractive, in a fleshy, southern way. But she would not have fared well on the beaches of my youth. Too pale, too short, too plump. A poor man's Rhonda Fleming. Her drawing cards: slightly crossed gray eyes and a certain tail-swishing walk that Lynda imitates perfectly. My husband claims his first wife was zero in the sack. "Bev always worried about flattening her hair." So did Paul.

"Satisfied?" Anneke asks. "Stop looking for snakes under rocks, Lolly. You'll make yourself sick. Nobody in their right mind would try to lure kids away from water slides. Mine wouldn't leave for a million dollars before their time was up."

"Bev *begged* Reg to take full custody when she left with her surfer."

"She wants the children for the support money. She needs it to live on. My ex-sister-in-law was the same."

"Mother thinks Reg's ex objects to his remarrying." I sigh. "Mr. Weintraub, Bev's lawyer, claims the *other* Mrs. Bennett signed her children away during a period of emotional stress. Now, theoretically, she's got her head together."

"There's Jenna."

"Are you having fun, honey?" I yell. Bev wouldn't dare entice my children away as well, . . . would she?

My teenager pretends not to hear.

"Bev doesn't strike me as the motherly type."

"She doesn't claim to be."

Henk Van Vetchen stands near the exit gate clutching his crotch.

"Hendrika! Hurry! Take Henk potty."

A child cries, "Too late."

"At least he didn't pee in the water this time."

Incurably edgy, I scream, "Jenna! Where's Lynda?"

"Playing the jukebox."

"Get her, and you two watch Rye and Henk for Anneke."

"And Annele and Peter," Mother Van Vetchen instructs.

Hendrika, Jenna, and Lynda thread through the crowd collecting blond-headed Van Vetchens like beads on a necklace. At the top, they hook their mats together and travel down toboggan style.

A whistle blows. The lifeguard orders, "Separate those mats!"

"Maybe we should offer Bev all eleven of them," I joke.

I note that on the next trip down, the three older girls and the younger children ride toboggan style, exactly as before.

"When you first moved here," Anneke confides, "I thought Jenna, Lynda, Mouse, and Richie were all yours. You treat them the same."

"I attended a stepparenting workshop."

"Henk and I went to Marriage Encounter. We ditched the sessions and fucked our brains out. It was so *nice* knowing some kid couldn't barge in."

"I hope the lifeguard doesn't throw the children out. It wouldn't be safe for them to run loose in the park area. At least here they're confined behind a chain link fence. Did you hear his warning?"

"I didn't listen on purpose. With seven kids, the less I know the better."

The whistle blows again.

"Henk's sure the ex-wife's after Reg's bucks."

The lifeguard snarls through a megaphone, "You can't ride down that way!"

"Hey, Jenna! Lynda! Lynda, are you wearing sun screen?" To Anneke I explain, "Lynda burns so. All those freckles." Is Bev spying so that she can brand me a careless mother?

"Richie and Lynda are just a weapon."

The subject exhausts me.

I do a routine check and locate all four children.

Richie muscles into line behind Mouse. Perhaps she saved his place. My ten-year-old tugs at her ruffled bikini. This bathing apparel exposes the raised purple scar from heart surgery which worms over the center of her chest. I wish tank suits were still popular.

Richie and Mouse confer animatedly, then ride double down the slowest channel—a concession on his part, I'm sure. My youngest clings to her stepbrother's back when they crash into the water below. Without her glasses, Mouse probably can't see where the exit ladder is. Richie dog-paddles with his stepsister hanging on. They climb out together and rush back toward the line, hand in hand. If Bev's watching, I hope she notices that.

Richie appears sturdy—angelic with that blond hair. Mouse looks gaunt, frail, wet braids slicked back drowned-rat fashion. Yet my daughter somehow radiates an impishness—a Dickens waif. Maybe it's her tan. She inherited Paul's olive complexion. I imagine these two in angel and devil costumes, a good idea for Halloween! We can plan a barn dance complete with hayrides—to compensate for the lack of neighbors to trick or treat, the children's main gripe about leaving town.

Love for Richie and Mouse fills me like colored water in a

glass decanter. What a shame that one must face losing a child in order to truly appreciate the privilege of custody.

"Darling," Anneke comments when I point to Mouse and Richie, who now share a towel from their rented locker.

I envy my friend's uncomplicated life. This feeling causes me to flex and unflex my feet, which several mosquitoes munch upon despite the Bug Off spray.

The lifeguard's whistle blows. He motions the tobogganers over. Jenna nervously hooks her hair behind an ear, readjusts the St. Anthony's tee shirt. Lynda giggles. Annele and Peter Van Vetchen drift to Hendrika, who also holds Rye and Henk.

The seven accused approach the wire fence.

"We got suspended for fifteen minutes."

"Wait a sec! Come back here!" I cry.

"I have to go to the bathroom."

"Lynda, you look like a lobster! Let me give you some sun screen!"

"Later!"

"Have your hands stamped so you don't have to pay to get back in," Anneke instructs.

"Lolly, can we have money for the snack bar?"

"There's watermelon if you're hungry, Lynda." I turn to Anneke. "Do you think one of us should accompany them?"

"To the bathroom?"

"I know. But?"

"They'll be all right."

I observe the older girls whispering conspiratorially.

"What are they up to?"

My elder daughter and stepdaughter run off.

Ten minutes pass, according to Jenna's Mickey Mouse watch, which I hold for her.

"Where are Richie and Mouse?"

Anneke studies the line of children snaking up the slopes, while I scrutinize those riding down the slides.

"Maybe they went to the bathroom with the others." My friend addresses another of her children. "Karla, go find Mouse and Richie. Check the restrooms. Hurry!"

"I wonder if I should have a look. Bev just might try to steal the children from a public place like this. Not caring how traumatic it would be for them. She often acts rashly, with little thought for the consequences. I swear, I can't go on living this way."

"How could Bev desert her husband and children? Who would leave Reg?"

"It suited her at the time."

"Abandon Lynda and Richie?"

"Mr. Weintraub maintains she found a reliable baby-sitter for them before she split."

"Who?"

"Reg's mother. Haven't you ever wanted to run off?"

"By the time I washed the diapers, stuck a casserole in the oven, bathed everyone"—Anneke shrugs—"it wouldn't be worth the trouble."

"I threatened to leave Paul one night at dinnertime. But I lacked the courage to walk away from the mess. Jenna and Mouse tossed yogurt at each other from opposing high chairs. In a way, you've got to hand it to Bev."

"Lolly! Whose side are you on?"

"I want Reg to have the children, but"—I gaze from side to side to see who eavesdrops—"I don't think Bev is that awful. She's just doing her thing. It's not her fault that society forced her to marry and have children before she was ready."

"Ready! I had my first at eighteen!"

"You don't know what it was like in the fifties. Our mothers told us conflicting things: 'When are you getting married?' 'No man is good enough for you!'"

"Bev acts like a mare in heat."

"Unfortunately that doesn't make her, by law, an unfit mother. I'm afraid Reg must prove Bev is a prostitute, alcoholic, or on drugs. That's the *tradition*, at least. And recently, a prostitute was awarded custody. Unless proven guilty of negligence or a crime, the mother is considered the more suitable parent. *Despite* the fact that a new joint custody law says the child should go to whoever can provide the best home!"

"Does Reg have a chance?"

"A policeman won custody last month in LA."

"Where is Bev living?"

"Near Cal State. Hiroshima's a student there. In an *adults-only* apartment."

"One of those swinging-singles places?"

"Here comes Karla. Did you see Richie and Lynda?"

"They're in line for the bathroom."

"See!" Anneke exclaims.

"Were they conversing with strangers?"

"No."

"Relax, Lolly."

"You're *positive*, Karla?"

"I'm pretty sure Lynda knew *her*."

"Who?" Fear prickles under my skin like a subcutaneous injection. I leap to the ground and race down the hill toward the restrooms, cutting around oak trees as though in a slalom race. I practically step on a couple sleeping with newspapers covering their faces. The woman wears Mexican sandals exactly like the ones Bev sent Lynda from Tijuana while vacationing there.

The restroom lines wind back sloppily about fifty feet. I spot Richie almost at the men's entrance chatting with Peter Van Vetchen.

"Richie!" I hug my stepson. He hugs back. "You're brown as a berry from riding the prairie!" I kiss his sweet shoulders, quoting the lad's father.

"Lolly, can me and Peter ride double down the fast slide?"

"Can Peter and *I*?"

"No way! He wants to ride with *me!*"

"Sure, honey." I move on.

Lynda and Jenna are not outside the women's restroom. Elbowing my way through the door, I try not to act frantic. The inside smells of urine, wet cement, Pine Sol disinfectant, reminding me of Intensive Care.

Lynda braids Jenna's long hair before the steamed-up mirror. I clutch both of them to my breast.

"Hi, Mommy!" Mouse emerges from a closed toilet stall.

"Oh, my darlings!" I kiss Lynda's forehead, then Jenna and Mouse. The two older girls turn away in protest, but not so far that I can't stroke their arms. Nothing could feel better at this moment. Mouse stays close. We embrace. I slide my hands along her ribs.

"What's the matter, Mommy?"

"I love you all so much. Can you understand that? *So* much." Tears gush out.

A day camper edges away.

"Yes." Jenna sounds resigned. Neither of us know how to deal with adolescence. Sometimes she lets me squeeze her hand when we sit together in the car. Our fingers mesh tentatively like young lovers. Then I spoil it by hanging on too long.

"I love you too, Mommy," Mouse professes.

"You're so *emotional,* Lolly," twelve-year-old Lynda complains. "Can we stop and buy pizza on the way home?"

"I'm making meatloaf for dinner."

"Oh, barf!"

"Lynda, who were you talking to? Karla saw you."

"Nobody."

"A minute ago?"

"Oh, that creep from school. She tried to butt into line."

"Let's walk back up the hill together."

"I have to brush my hair."

"You look beautiful. Come along." I touch Lynda's head

the way her father touches mine, hoping to continue this daisy chain of love.

"We'll be OK, Mom," Jenna says. "Don't *worry*. We have to wait for Hendrika and Annele. They're still going."

Reluctantly, I exit with Mouse in tow. I don't see Richie. He must be safe in the men's room. I hope he remembers to wash his hands.

Walking back, my younger daughter and I communicate with finger squeezes, and by bumping into each other and taking a long time to separate. Being with this child calms me. I don't even look over my shoulder to see if Bev follows. The couple under the newspapers still sleep, although the woman stirs. It's possible she glances at me from beneath the sports page. Amazing how those shoes look identical to Lynda's!

Mouse hands me her glasses for safekeeping. I inquire, "Where's the case?"

"In Richie's and my locker. I'll pick it up when I get my towel."

We kiss good-bye at the entrance. As an afterthought my ten-year-old adds, "Richie saw his mom."

"What?"

"She was with Hiroshima."

"Honey, this is important. Start over and tell me everything."

"Richie and I couldn't decide whether to go down the slow or the medium or the fast slide. I suggested it would be fair if—"

"Did you see Bev?"

"Yes. Well, I saw a blob shaped like her. I didn't have my glasses on. We were standing at the top of the slide. Richie just happened to look toward the parking lot. He said the Jap had binoculars."

"Do you think Richie misses his mom so much he *thought* he saw her?"

"Richie doesn't miss his mom. He likes you better, because you don't believe in spanking."

"Binoculars?"

The toothpick shoulders shrug. "Can I go now, Mommy? My time's almost up." Bumping into a dog chained beside the post, she darts toward the turnstile. I head for the stands around on the other side. My feet seem to stick as if running in sand.

"Richie's sighted Bev!"

Anneke shades sleeping Jan's eyes with a towel. "Where?"

"In the parking lot."

"Wait for Jan to wake up, and I'll investigate with you. I'm dying to see her again."

I try to sit patiently. "Anneke, I can't stand it. I'm going to check. Reg would freak if I came home sans children."

"I'll wake him." Anneke shakes her child gently. Jan awakens crying. We pull him to his feet. He stumbles. My friend finally carries the toddler down the hill.

None of the children are lined up outside either restroom. We tromp into both, Gestapo fashion, stare underneath, yank open doors.

"They're gone."

"We must have passed them coming down!"

"Horse apples!"

We race back up the hill. I'm panting. Burdened by Jan, Anneke still beats me to the top. I see Jenna pushing through the turnstile after Hendrika and Annele.

"Jenna! Where are Lynda and Richie?"

She shrugs.

"Where are they?" I scream.

"I don't know." My daughter sobs. People turn to see if I hit her.

I clasp my hands together, speak sweetly, "How can you not know? You were with them ten minutes ago."

"I don't know where they are *now*. They went with their mom."

"Their *mom?*"

Jenna refuses to look at me. "It's not my fault."

"Tell me."

"Richie was eating a snowcone. Why don't *you* ever buy snowcones?"

"Go on."

"Lynda and I walked over. Bev and this oriental guy jumped out from behind a tree. She has sandals just like Lynda's."

"Bev hid under that newspaper!"

"Lynda got a snowcone, too. Her mom wouldn't buy me one."

"What happened!"

"Bev asked Richie and Lynda if they wanted to go out to dinner. You can't blame them, Mom. Your meatloaf isn't the greatest. It's full of wheat germ."

"Bev promised to buy Big Boy pizza?"

"Plus you'll probably cook that disgusting broccoli Anneke gave you from her garden. Why don't you believe in fast food, like normal people?"

"Bev was with Hiroshima?"

"I don't think Richie wanted to go. Bev had to drag him off. He asked me to tell you to take his grape slush out of the freezer so it won't be frozen solid."

"Did Lynda seem glad to see her mother?"

"Not especially. You shouldn't have cut Lynda's hair. They were arguing about that. Also, Bev was furious about her sunburn. You should have made the kid wear lotion."

Anneke thrusts Jan upon Jenna. "Come on, Lolly."

We scramble across the highway to the parking lot, dashing in front of a Peterbilt tanker.

"Bev has a mud-spattered white Camaro."

Sun glints off the rows of parked cars lined diagonally like loaves of bread baking in the heat. There must be a hundred vehicles.

"Lolly!"

I swirl around. An unfamiliar yellow Datsun pulls from a parking space. Lynda waves from the open back window on the passenger side.

"We're going for pizza. Tell my dad. TTFN."

"TTFN?"

"Ta Ta For Now," I explain to Anneke.

Richie's face presses to the rear glass like a pickle in a jar.

"Lynda! Richie! Come back! I love you. So does your father!"

My husband's ex-wife's eyes meet mine. She seems to be appraising my scantily clad body. I cross my arms over my chest. Bev, actually, cups her big boobs, jiggles them, then flips me the finger.

"Wait!" I implore uselessly. "You're in contempt of court! Or you will be if you take the children to *Japan!* We know you picked up the passports!"

"Whose passports?"

"The kids'. I called the Department of Immigration!"

"Hell, I did that a long time ago. Back when Reg and I were married. He used to pass out mimeographed sheets each day of stuff Lynda and Richie and I were supposed to do. Doesn't he give you lists?"

"Just reminders. You know, to pick up his shirts and return the overdue library books."

Bev snorts, "You're such a sucker!"

"No, I—"

"Tell the asshole he's going to pay!" Bev's words jar me like the punch line of an ethnic joke.

Infuriated, Anneke—I've never seen her so visibly angry—throws a succession of dirt clods at the car. "He's too good for the likes of you!" I guess my friend refers to Reg. She screams, *"Hoer!"*

I assume that means "whore."

"Lolly, I think I left my electric blanket on." Richie either blows me a kiss or pops bubble gum.

"Lolly, can I—" Bev shuts her daughter up with a smack

across the mouth. I wince. Then it looks like Reg's ex reaches around and closes the back passenger window or forces Lynda to. The children peer out at me like goldfish.

The Japanese student suddenly pulls a baseball cap low on his forehead and steps on the accelerator. The Datsun leaps forward frog-like, turning south on the highway. "Shall we give chase?" I ask defeatedly, knowing that by the time I reach my new VW bus, unlock it, and follow at 65 mph—top speed—Bev, and my stepdaughter, and stepson will be miles ahead.

"If I had Henk's rifle, I'd shoot the tires. Or *her*." Anneke throws one last dirt clod.

I've been fearing this event for so long that it seems anti-climactic. It was the same with Paul's affair with Sheri. "Did you see the look on Richie's face?"

"The license plate is QMZ 432," Anneke consoles.

6

"A legal no-man's-land"

Seventy-two hellish hours have elapsed. I constantly picture Lynda and Richie's noses pressed against the back window of that Datsun. Will we ever see those precious faces again? This crisis isn't bringing Reg and me closer. Crowbars of unspoken accusations force us apart. Evidently my husband thinks the water-slide abduction could have been prevented. How? Nobody suggests *he* should have stayed home from work.

Reg is prepared to pay his ex-wife's ransom, whatever the price. But not if she asks him to forgo the custody suit. While waiting to hear from Bev, we discuss the kidnaping like serious bridge players lamenting a badly played hand.

"Do you think she's smuggled the children out of the country, to Japan?" I ask.

"God only knows." Reg replies in a hushed voice.

Fear numbs our home more effectively than novocaine. Jenna and Mouse tiptoe about, reluctant to turn on the TV, perhaps afraid to remind their stepfather that they're still around. It shocked them to see him cry. Mouse lent my husband her Get Well Ivy (left over from heart-surgery hospitalization). The plant grows out of Raggedy Andy's head. Jenna wrote an unsigned poem on horse stationery:

> Ode to Reg
> Gladness.
> Badness.
> Sadness.
> Madness.
> Life.

Curled here in the fetal position on the leather sofa, anguish congeals within me like Jell-O. Reg and I stare past each other out the sun-porch windows. He believes I'm manic-depressive, a diagnosis explained at great length in a droning voice that almost puts me to sleep. When my eyes close completely, I envision a nightmarish scene of Bev torturing the children.

"You go up and down like an elevator," my husband accuses. "Euphoric when we seem on the right track, suicidal when our leads turn into dead ends."

I guess Reg would rather contemplate my mental condition (I'll admit to near hysteria) than worry about his children. I worry. Bev used to leave them napping in an empty house while she traipsed to the beauty parlor.

Referring to an earlier discussion about our lousy phone service, I mutter, "Either you reach a false busy signal or a bell noise—like cymbals clashing in a tunnel." The GTE man

who camped here, monitoring calls for six hours, claims
nothing can be done. Area farmers cut the underground ca-
bles discing for winter seeding. "So Bev could be calling
and it's not ringing through."

"When did you last see Dr. Shonburg?"

"It's so frustrating! Depending on *faulty* telephone equipment! Worse than scuba diving with a leaky air hose."

"Six months ago?" Reg guesses.

"Professionally?"

"You quit your shrink, if I recall, because he didn't laugh
at some joke. You must admit that is a bit strange."

I wind hair around a forefinger like a yo-yo string. "You
didn't find me strange then, back when you were dying to
get in my jeans."

"What do you mean *professionally?*" Reg swings around,
pats my rear end perfunctorily, presumably not an invitation. This saddens me almost as much as everything else. I
press against the warmth of his hand.

All last night we clung to each other and made frantic
love. It wasn't romantic, more like two survivors who'd
found refuge in the same foxhole. "Hold me," I whimpered.

Shrugging, I now confess, "I had dinner with Bernie once
or twice. Did you really give Bev a mimeographed list of
things to do each day?"

"Lolly, I'm not trying to pry, but this is important. If
Shonburg enticed you into any sort of sexual assignation
under the guise of treatment, you can sue. A San Francisco
woman recently won a decision against her psychiatrist."

I shake my head like a dog drying off. "No!"

Reg looks away. He presumably studies the purple mountains circling our narrow valley. I count smashed flies on the
window panes.

"I'm going to call the sheriff and demand action." My
husband's voice lacks enthusiasm. He reminds me of Mouse
promising to vacuum under the bed.

"Ask for Sergeant P. J. Thompson. At least he's cute; I mean, sympathetic."

"I want more than sympathy this time."

"The children are with their *mother*, Reg. You can't file a missing persons report. We're considered a 'Domestic Squabble.'"

When I had first approached the cops, on the day of the abduction, everything was routine. As routine as possible with Anneke and her seven children, plus Jenna and Mouse, shrieking about unequal shares of Hershey bars, jabbering firsthand accounts of the abduction, correcting me, interrupting. No policeman in his right mind could have followed the plot.

Patiently the young-looking officer pleaded, "One at a time, please! Somebody describe the circumstances under which Lynda and Richie Bennett actually disappeared."

"Shush!" I warned the others. I then turned the waterslide adventure into a three-act tragedy, finally mumbling, "She trapped them in the car. Hiroshima roared off!"

"Karla has three squares," little Henk sobbed. "I only have two!"

"He ate one of his!" Karla whined.

"Who trapped them?" Officer P. J. scratched his head.

"My daddy has a gun too!" Rye Van Vetchen bragged. "He shoots trespassers and sick cows. Bang. Bang. Bang."

"She's a hoer!" Anneke claimed. "Jan, no! Water's running all over the floor!"

"Wa-lu!" the seventeen-month-old cried, his thumb depressing the button on the upturned Sparklett's bottle.

"A Mrs. Beverly Bennett," I admitted.

"Any relation?" P. J. conceivably tried to ignore the fact that Mother Van Vetchen and I were still dressed in waterslide attire: cut-offs, bikini tops. He focused on my dark glasses.

Silence.

The eleven of us exchanged furtive glances.

"Any relation?" Officer Thompson repeated.

"Real mother!" Hendrika blurted, clearly embarrassed by our evasiveness.

The policeman tore up his report.

Henk Van Vetchen, telltale hands on crotch, peed on the wooden floor.

Reg continues: "Maybe bring in the FBI. Kidnaping is a federal offense."

"A *natural mother* can't kidnap her own children. That's been explained to us by Officer P. J."

"What in the hell do you think Bev did?"

I resist reminding Reg that, earlier, Scheffer quipped that most judges would call the kidnaping charge hogwash. "OK, darling." I scrutinize the foothills. They mound like golden breasts and thighs. Reg focuses on the sawtooth mountains that ring the valley.

A casual observer catching Reg and me gazing westward would think we were scanning the horizon for attacking Indians. We're taking this current staring-across-the-pasture business that seriously.

"They're cutting a road on Bell's Peak."

"That's just the Turner kids with their motorcycle, is all."

"Another ten years and the County will want to pave Willow Lane."

Eventually I speak. "Reg, I'll tell you what the cops will say: 'You have not been granted *final* custody.'"

"Neither has she!"

According to Scheffer, that's the problem. Lynda and Richie exist in a legal no-man's-land. If Reg locates his kids and snatches them back, it will be considered a natural move by some. However, when would it end? The Court's only recourse—should this continue—is to stick the children into a foster home until the trial (a gruesome alternative).

I'm reminded of that biblical story about Solomon. He told two women claiming a baby, "I'll slice the child in

half." The true mother cried, "No! If you're going to do that,
I'd rather she had him." Then Solomon realized who was the
infant's mother.

Our life's more complicated.

"If I only had some clue as to Bev's plans. Has she actually fled the country with Hiroshima?"

"Did you call Japan Air Lines?"

"They can't reveal passenger lists."

"Do you want me to try Bev's mother again in St. Louis?
Or her sister?" I disapprove of these cloak-and-dagger techniques. On the other hand, we can't just concede and accept
the fact that we may never see the children again.

"They'll just hang up on you."

"That's better than having them shout obscenities at
you."

"I'd give anything to hear Lynda's and Richie's voices, to
know they're all right."

"Doesn't Bev have an aunt in Florida? Or is she a
cousin?"

"Lolly, do you think the children are OK?"

"Sure," I say unconvincingly.

"Richie can't sleep without his teddy bear."

Bearie Goldbody rests forlornly against Richie's pillow,
keeping a vigil with one crooked felt eyebrow. His eyes and
other brow came unglued in the washing machine.

"What in the heck *is* Bev up to? I have an idea she's enjoying this. Does your ex have a confidante we could bribe?"

"Hiroshima?"

"The registrar at Cal State told you there were thousands
of oriental undergraduates. And the clerk assured me they
could not come up with a last name in a million years, even
if we provided an address. Bev's address, that is. Besides, it
would be illegal for them to release that information."

"Lolly, I was kidding."

"Oh."

"The surfer!" My husband lurches to his feet.

"Yes!"

"Bev jilted him. Maybe he's mad enough to help us. If I were in his position, I would be."

"Do you know his name?"

"Bag of Dirt. No! Dirt Bag!"

"Dirt Bag?"

"Dirt Bag."

"A nickname?"

"We discussed her lover only once." Reg examines his fingernails. "Bev called home to see how our son was. He had an ear infection when she left. I was relating what the pediatrician said. She interrupted, explaining she had to run. Then my ex called to this fellow, 'OK, OK, Dirt Bag. Richie's sick, for God's sake.'"

My husband lowers his eyes, absently pushes back blond hair that spreads upon his forehead like an oil slick.

"I—I don't imagine 'Dirt Bag' is much to go on."

"How many Dirt Bags are there?" I ask. "Who else can we call? What did Bev's sister say when you talked to her yesterday?"

He shrugs.

"What did she say?" I nag.

"I don't want to repeat it again, Lolly." Pain registers in his eyes like lemons on a slot machine.

"Maybe we could make some sense of it *this* time."

Obviously resigned, he mumbles, "Quote. 'Reg, oh my God! They're not *here*.' Pause. 'You never loved her, did you? Your stuck-up family treated us like dirt. Bevie had to turn elsewhere for attention.'"

"Affection," I correct.

"Right. 'Affection.' Marcie remained silent for a moment. I thought perhaps the long-distance connection had gone bad. But suddenly she added in a different, softer voice, 'I must admit, Sis never appreciated you. And she wasn't much of a mother. She even used a bottle prop.'"

"I can't believe that part about the bottle prop!"

"I know. I know. You nursed Jenna and Mouse for years. You hoped to interest Paul."

"It wouldn't have *killed* him to at least try."

"What's wrong with a bottle prop?"

"Everything! Lack of human contact—"

"I held the children when I gave them bottles."

"You fed them?"

Reg considers, acting embarrassed. I swear he's tempted to protect Bev's image. Somehow her having been less than Supermom is a reflection on him. My husband confides reluctantly, "Yes, I did."

I reach out to him. He backs away.

"Does 'They're not here!' mean 'They're not here yet.' Or 'They're not here, dummy. They've flown to Japan.'"

"The license-plate number was our best shot."

Why? Because beautiful Anneke memorized it? "If Bev thought far enough ahead to *rent* a car, she planned this abduction carefully."

"Or at the last minute her Camaro broke down. She never had it serviced properly or checked the oil. Bev expected *me* to handle that."

So do I.

I pluck yellow leaves from a hanging plant. "I thought that was very clever. Charging the rental on your Hertz Number One Club card. *You* paid for the getaway."

Reg paces. "Bev turned in the Datsun at the Huntington Hotel. Therefore, her Camaro must have been somewhere in the vicinity."

Jerking around, I set the Creeping Charlie in motion. The plant swings like a pendulum above the stereo. "Reg! I've got it! What's unique about the Huntington Hotel?"

"The Rose Bowl teams hole up there over New Year's?"

"The Huntington has a bus to LAX! Everyone in Pasadena leaves from there. Even my Aunt Lou. You buy a ticket at the lobby desk and have a drink in the Ship Room."

"Lynda and Richie are minors!"

"Don't you see? Bev and the children rode the airport bus across town with Hiroshima and flew to Japan. It's so simple! We have to phone the airlines, tell them it's an emergency. There's been a kidnaping. Call the FBI!"

"A natural mother *can't* kidnap her own children."

I shrug. "Try the airport."

Reg rocks back on his boot heels, hands in his pockets. "I already have."

"And?"

"The airlines refuse to give out passenger information."

Later I ask, "You contacted the Disneyland Hotel, didn't you?"

"And the Travelodge near Magic Mountain. But that's so close to us I doubt she'd risk it."

"Where else could Bev take the children? I mean, a place that Lynda and Richie would love enough they wouldn't cry and make a scene about being dragged away. Except, she probably convinced them you relented and gave permission for the two-week visitation."

"Hawaii! Knowing that's the last place I'd look, since it's where Bev claimed she was going."

"They wouldn't need passports. Unless . . . Hawaii, next stop Tokyo. Didn't you fly to Vietnam that way? Hawaii to Guam to the Philippines to Vietnam?"

Our eyes are glued to each other's like when, in a movie, you don't want to witness the screen action but can't turn away.

"They could be in a room anywhere with TV and a week's supply of pizza," I snarl sarcastically.

Reg scratches his chin. He isn't shaving for the duration, or changing clothes. My husband still wears the tan cords and yellow dress shirt he flew home in from the mine. He hasn't slept, either. Unfortunately, we're both able to consume food under duress. I fixed chilled avocado soup for lunch today.

"Maybe they *are* at Bev's apartment. Perhaps we're jumping to conclusions regarding Japan. Our evidence is all circumstantial. Maybe she *did* pick up the passports before. I really don't remember. You know, you might have something, Lolly."

Understated as this is, I eat up the praise. Trying to shrug nonchalantly, my motions look jerky and awkward, desperate. I should take lessons from Margot. On learning about our plight, she telephoned and offered to beg, "Lynda and Richie call home!" in the middle of "Day by Day" as if it were written into the script.

Anneke prays for us, as do the nuns at St. Anthony's. The sisters want to hide the children at the convent until the trial, if we find them. Lance would say, "Great story line! Reminiscent of *Sound of Music!*"

Reg continues, "We've been thinking big." He carries a card stating: THINK BIG. Inside, two elephants copulate. A present from Lynda, who claims to have found it in a package of bubble gum!

"You mean possibly Bev's close by, lying low? The place couldn't have a phone, or the kids would call, *if* they could ring through."

"There are several sleazy apartments and courts around Cal State. Some motels with kitchens. That would be convenient for Bev. She'd have access to her clothes. Hell, maybe they *are* staying at her apartment. I keep coming back to that!"

"We checked!" I protest. "Nobody was there."

"Ahh!" My husband plays B-movie detective. "Possibly we were duped by the drawn shades and unopened newspapers piled at the door."

"They were pretty convincing!"

"Exactly!"

"The manager swore she hadn't seen Mrs. B. Bennett in days. Besides, there's a phone there. I know Lynda would call."

"Disconnected, remember!"

"You think Mrs. Flores, the manager, lied to us?"

RB III stops pacing, clearly stymied. "Women usually dislike Bev."

"Oh, Reg, of course! Mrs. Flores assumed you were an immigration official. You've got that *look*. LA Chicanos are scared to death of feds. What if Bev's keeping Lynda and Richie at her place? She could take them out during the day. There's a theater on the corner showing *Blazing Saddles* and *10*. The children adore those movies."

"Aren't they rated R?"

"There's no sex in *Blazing Saddles*," I swear. "Just cuss words."

"*10?*"

"*Bolèro* is classical music. Ravel."

"I wish you wouldn't take the kids to adult movies, Lolly. At least not until after the trial."

"I'll defend *Turning Point* anywhere! A ballet story. The girls thought the bed scene was a dance. Richie fell asleep."

"*Coming Home*," my husband badgers.

I lack the energy to argue the movie's educational merit sexwise. It should be a training film for marrying couples. Let the bride and groom see what Jon Voight did for Jane Fonda.

"Reg." Jenna slouches in the doorway. A St. Anthony's windbreaker covers the Ocean Pacific tee shirt that hangs down over green cotton surgical pants. Our neighbor in town, Dr. Jaye, brought us provisions from linen supply. I used the gowns as aprons.

"Hmm?"

"I'll go with you to check out Bev's apartment." My teenager and husband exchange glances. Love or compassion or respect or affection or something moves from one pair of blue eyes to the other and back like a dishrag on one of those old pulley clotheslines.

"Sure," Reg replies. "Thanks."

Jenna nods solemnly. "I want to bring Lynda her radio. And her Dittos. She's probably feeling pretty skuzzy without them."

"Let's remember to take Richie his Bearie Goldbody."

"Are you really going?"

"It's better than prowling around here like a caged tiger," my husband replies.

Two hours have passed since Reg and Jenna left for LA. At first, anticipating a call, I traveled from phone to phone to phone like a race driver on a course. Now I'm hunched at the rolltop and am trying to write Mother, a way of killing time. It's actually a thank-you note. We received two sets of monogrammed silk sheets from her the other day. The last time around, my mom brought me Dansk pots and pans. Has she shifted her allegiance from the kitchen to the bedroom?

So far, I have a three-page thesis on what constitutes a good mother. For example: "A good mother serves well-balanced meals with propriety and simple elegance." Actually, I think it all boils down to the fact that a good mother loves her children. Nothing else matters.

The tricky part is defining the word "love." I'd rather be with Lynda and Richie and Jenna and Mouse and Reg than any other people in the world—but not necessarily in that order, or all at the same time, or constantly. Is that "love"? By that definition, doesn't Bev "love" her children?

Or is "love" kneeling beside a sick kid's bed and vowing—if the temperature drops—never again to buy marijuana from the high school boy who pumps gas at the local Mobil station? I didn't smoke regular cigarettes for a year after Mouse's heart surgery. When, in intensive care, she was hooked up to all those machines, I would have sacrificed anything to guarantee her recovery. Fortunately she mended quickly. All I'd forsaken was one pack of Salems a day.

I recall the first night Jenna and Mouse and I spent alone on Milan Avenue when Paul moved out. The three of us self-consciously sipped tea after dinner. Mouse hadn't ever tried the hot drink before. Until then, the girls rushed through the evening meal, eager to be excused. TV was more entertaining than Paul and my daily gossip.

However, on this eventful occasion my daughters and I dallied. Pearl messed with dishes in the kitchen. We heard her singing, "Mine eyes have seen the glory of the coming of the Lord!"

"Burning of the school," Mouse corrected, rattling her cup.

"What?" I poured from a china pot.

"Mine eyes have seen the glory of the burning of the school."

Jenna stirred in teaspoonfuls of sugar, joining her sister in song. They sang along with Pearl—a room away, using different words.

"We have tortured every teacher. We have broken every rule."

"Glory (gory), glory (gory) Hallelujah!"

Jenna and Mouse, "Teacher hit me with a ruler. Shot her in the butt with a rotten coconut—"

I started to laugh. Soon my daughters joined in. We allied ourselves in hilarity, solidifying our revised status? Mouse crept onto my lap. Jenna leaned close. I covered her hand with mine.

Pearl waddled to the dining room door, her large frame filling the space. Slowly the maid moved to me. She gripped my shoulders with strong fingers. The four of us posed in tiers like a lopsided wedding cake.

I finish the letter to Mother, "Or is 'love' a feeling that connects a family, not like puppet strings, or reins, but May-pole streamers dangling from the pole of life."

Once, over the phone, Mr. Scheffer had asked me why I thought I was a good mother—in preparation for court, I imagine. The only thing that came to mind was that I liked to eat raw cookie dough.

I hate questions like that. During an early session, Dr. Shonburg told me to list the things at which I was competent. What could I say besides eating and screwing? I'm not nimble-fingered enough for needlepoint.

"Because Bev felt momentarily inconvenienced by her children, Mother, is she a wretched person?"

I've had non-child-oriented friends before. Alice refused to drive forgotten lunch boxes to school. I used to buy Girl Scout cookies by the carton from her brood. But when Jenna tried to sell this neighbor YMCA toffee, the lady said, "No." I gag on the word.

The telephone rings. Startled by this sound I've been expecting, I scream. As I leap toward the receiver, my letter box and pages scatter.

"Lolly?" a voice whispers.

"Lynda!"

"Is my dad there?"

"No, honey. He's . . . in LA."

"Oh." She seems to wilt.

"Can I help?"

"Do you know where my transistor radio is?"

"Jenna has it!"

"That's not fair! It's still mine. Just because I left—"

"Oh, no! Of course. You see—"

"I have to hang up now."

"Wait! Are you in Japan? Is Richie OK?"

"I mean it. I have to go!" My stepdaughter hisses.

The dial tone buzzes like a lazy fly.

Scribbling on an envelope, I record what I recall of the conversation. A public-address system announced something like "Red cap with wheelchair to gate 24," I think. Unless I've seen that in a movie.

The phone rings again. I whirl toward the bell, still disconcerted like a punch-drunk fighter.

"Hello?"

"They were here!" Reg announces smugly.

"Lynda called."

"When!"

"Where?" I ask.

"Did you turn on the tape recorder?"

Darn. A complicated-looking recording device hooks to the desk phone. "No."

"Oh, for Christ's sake, Lolly. After all our drills."

"I'm sure Bev hung us up!" I scream. "Lynda wanted to talk to you."

"How did she seem?"

I attempt to describe Lynda accurately. "Subdued."

"Drugged?"

"No."

"Was there a coded message?"

"Nothing. It happened so fast."

"Maybe they're on their way back *here*."

"Where are you?"

"Bev's apartment. Her phone's working. She must have paid the bill."

"Inside?"

"She has my mother's tea service on the coffee table. I'm tempted to take it."

"Reg, that's breaking and entering. *Stealing!*"

"I don't think so."

Panic immobilizes me. I open my mouth, choke on words.

"What's wrong, Mommy?" Mouse swipes stale mints from the porcelain dish inside a glass-doored breakfront. She's just dashed in from outside, shedding foxtails on the carpet.

I manage to ask, "Where did you find a key?"

"Bev always uses the same spot. Inside the porch light. I unscrewed the glass fixture."

I try to sound nonchalant. "Is Jenna with you?"

"Yes."

"Darling, do you think that's a good idea? Couldn't my daughter wait in the car?"

"She wouldn't be safe. Not in this neighborhood."

"Mommy, you look funny. Do you want a glass of water?"

I nod yes to Mouse. "How do you know Lynda and Richie were there? Do you have tangible evidence?"

"Jenna found their bathing suits in the dirty-clothes hamper. The ones they wore to the water slides. She recognized them."

"It sounded like the airport."

"What did?"

"In the background. When I talked to Lynda. A PA system said something about a red cap with a wheelchair and gate 24."

"Could have been buses. Trains."

"What would gate 24 be at LAX? Which airline?"

"That's Satellite Two—International Carriers."

"Reg! They're on the way to Japan!"

"I doubt it. Bev's suitcases are still here. The Hartmann luggage I gave her for her birthday three years ago. She wouldn't leave that behind."

How disconcerting for him to have come upon those suitcases! Like finding a dyed Easter egg under the pyracantha bush while picking red berries for a Christmas wreath—you don't quite know what to do with it.

"Her name in gold. She carted that Hartmann luggage everywhere. I paid a fortune for it."

"It could have been gate 42."

"That'd be TWA."

"Your ex could be shipping Lynda and Richie off someplace by themselves, for safekeeping until the trial."

Reg remains silent a moment. Suddenly he exclaims, "God damn, isn't that just like her!"

"Her sister's!" we decide at the same time.

"I'd better fly Oscar Foxtrot to St. Louis."

LOLLY   89

Jenna squeals in the background, "Let me come along! I'll navigate. Read the Jepps."

"Reg," I shriek, "bring my daughter home first. I don't want her flying off across the country on some hare-brained—"

"Lolly, calm down! I'll drop Jenna off at your Mom's. You drive in to Pasadena and pick her up."

Thank Heavens, an excuse to leave this tomb. Reg and I'll pass on the freeway—he returning to Santa Paula Airport, I driving to town.

Mouse hands me a Mayor McCheese glass full of tap water. Last week, Reg removed five dead rattlers from the well. We serve scotch with a twist of snake. I pull my ten-year-old close for a mint-flavored kiss. She waits a respectable amount of time and then escapes to the kitchen. I listen to the rattle of the cookie-jar lid. All she'll find are non-hydrogenated-peanut-butter-oatmeal-fig bars.

Right now, Bev's probably overdosing Lynda and Richie on Oreos.

7

"How to tip in Beverly Hills"

Mother's grand old house in Pasadena seems like a luxury hotel after living at the ranch. Jenna, Mouse, and I spent last night in silky second-floor bedrooms, dreaming, in my case, of cotton candy and meringue, sweet visions with no substance. I awakened with a sense of well-being, stretched lethargically, and slipped through the french doors onto the balcony in my nightie. Then I saw Pearl stooping to retrieve the morning *Times* from behind a camellia bush and remembered the kidnaping.

"Lordy, that's a flimsy gown! You get back inside!" Twenty-two years ago, the maid caught Scooter Barnes undressing me under the grand piano and still acts as if it happened yesterday. "I hung your robe in the closet."

"No wonder I couldn't find it!" Coming home, I've re-
verted to my adolescent self, at least in relation to the permanent members of this household. Mother scolded me for
sassing her at the table last evening. The girls and I failed to
dress for dinner. After dessert, Mouse, Jenna, and I changed
from Levi's to bathing suits and headed for the Jacuzzi.
Pearl picked up our clothes and washed and ironed them
before we could explain that the jeans weren't all that dirty.
This place seems a world apart. Yet, a short while ago I re-
sided in similar surroundings with Paul. As did Reg with
Bev.

How complex!

Is life an intricate geometric pattern woven into the fabric
of individuals like the Persian rug in this parquet-floored
entry?

"Welcome!" I greet Margot Haggerty, who sashays through
the front door after lunch. She is ajingle with gold bracelets
and reeks of Joy perfume.

"I came the instant I could!"

We embrace perfunctorily.

With a wave of my hand, I dismiss Pearl, who answered
the bell. The maid gawks, arms crossed over her ample
bosom, no doubt secretly feeling herself. She moans,
"Lordy, if it isn't Helen from TV! You changed out of that
cute tennis dress!"

"Come into the living room, Margot."

The mammoth black woman tromps after us, lingering
like the smell of fried potatoes even as my friend and I settle
on the velvet love seat. She probably can't figure out how
Ms. Haggerty can simultaneously sob over her homosexual
nephew's suicide on the kitchen portable and pat her satin
cigarette-legged pants into place after sitting Indian style.
Once, when some doctor on a soap opera discovered a case
of polio, Pearl kept me inside for two days. (I know "Day by

Day" plays on the maid's set because I've been in the pantry swiping petits fours.)

"I like your hair!" I tell my pal.

"Disco curls." Margot kneads the dark locks into place. "I cut it right after Ali MacGraw said that at forty she could no longer have long hair parted down the middle."

I hook my long hair (parted down the middle) behind both ears, exposing silver pierced-ear rings shaped like airplanes, Richie's gift for Mother's Day. How callous of me not to have worn them before!

Margot pats my cheek. "The children are all right, Lolly!"

"Reg telephoned from the airport in St. Louis. He flew Oscar Foxtrot there." My voice quivers.

"Where is Bev's apartment?"

"By Cal State. Her Hartmann luggage is there."

"Is it the Halston design? The ultra suede?"

"Reg didn't say. Just that he gave it to Bev for her birthday."

"The other's so-so, the tweed and leather."

"Pearl, you may serve the tea." The maid hovers above Margot like a traffic helicopter over the freeway. She acts as starstruck as a midwestern tourist, one of those awful bird ladies in three-piece knit suits clutching broken-winged handbags to their sides. At the beach they carry wallets to the water.

"Let's drive over there," the actress suggests.

"Where?"

"I want to see if he bought the ultra suede or not. You can tell a lot about a man by the gifts he hands out."

"Mouse!" I call as the child slides down the hall banister. She literally swims in my high school cheerleader's skirt and sweater, discovered in a cedar closet. "Honey, since Pearl is preoccupied, would you push the tea cart in from the kitchen?" The maid appears immune to my sarcasm.

Margot isn't. She flashes me a *don't-be-such-a-snob* look. I remember it well from sorority days.

Beyond the bay window, a gardener fertilizes the lawn. The smell is reminiscent of the ranch. I inhale deeply, sighing.

"Poor baby," Margot consoles.

"No! I was thinking about the *smell*."

Pearl butts in: "Reminds me of the first time I was with a man."

"That's Hiroshima! Disguised as a Japanese gardener! Look, he's eavesdropping!" Quickly, I crawl to the window seat, raise my head like a hungry giraffe. The fellow peers in at me. I make a face at him, motioning to the others.

"In a cow barn." The maid hitches up her white nylons. A run spiderwebs across her beefy thigh. She mumbles a postscript, "Remembering brings a tinge of feeling below." *Sotto voce:* "Won't Freddie be delighted to know that!"

"How was it?" Ms. Haggerty inquires, solicitous.

"White folks make such a fuss."

Still on hands and knees, I place two fingers in my mouth and whistle softly for Pearl's and Margot's attention. "Let's confront Hiroshima!"

"Such a fuss!" The black woman actually rolls her eyes.

"You're the one who used to check my brother's sheets every morning. Randy took to sleeping in a sleeping bag," I accuse, avoiding any mention of Scooter Barnes. "I'm going outside!"

"That's Mr. Hishito's son. Dennis."

"Are you sure?"

Pearl saunters over, whipping a dust rag from her pocket like a gun. She wipes the sill, calls through the screen, "There's prune juice and celery sticks for you in the fridge."

The boy bows and heads around the house toward the servants' entrance.

"Prune juice and celery sticks?" Margot cringes.

"He's a vegetarian."

"I swear that's Bev's boyfriend, spying!"

"Did you get a good shot of Hiroshima? When he drove off?"

"Yes! He was only fifty feet away. The baseball cap didn't quite cover his eyes."

Pearl scoffs, "All orientals look alike."

As if on cue, Dennis Hishito drags in the tea cart, directed by Mouse. The large back wheels squeak in protest. My daughter raids the petits fours.

I accost the alleged gardener's son, pouring him a cup of tea. "Do you attend college?"

Dennis refuses sugar. A boy after my own heart. "Cal State."

"Cal State!" I jump, dropping the silver tongs into the young man's brew. We scramble to rectify the mess. To camouflage my embarrassment, I add, "Did you read in last week's *Nature's Way* that refined sugar causes impotence in white rats?"

Meanwhile Pearl and Margot confer.

"I'll tell you what 'love' is!" The maid's fat arms fly skyward like crows.

"I don't recall anyone asking!" I interject.

"It's a feeling that starts here and spreads down. Then whomp, you don't give no pickled damn about nothing else. Sometimes I've had it with a man while his wife lay passed out on the bed beside us."

"That's sex." Margot raises an eyebrow.

"Do you have a nickname?" I ask Dennis. "*Nagasaki* maybe?"

He blanches.

"Same difference. Love. Sex."

"I couldn't enjoy one without the other."

My friend and Pearl evidently play verbal Ping-Pong. They must think they're auditioning for a sitcom. Margot primly fiddles with the fringe on her silk scarf, the young mistress reprimanding the uppity but lovable black slave.

"Tell me what your friends call you!" I beseech Dennis,

moving in. His rolled-up tee-shirt sleeves expose muscular arms. "Possibly a city the Americans bombed?"

"I never had no choice." Pearl sinks down onto the back of the love seat. These words sound truer than her others. I glance over, but she looks away.

"Come on, Dennis, I want to know your nickname?"

"I'd rather not say, ma'am."

"Tell me!" I demand. "Or I'll poison your supply of prune juice!"

He gulps his tea and backs toward the entry hall. "Dee-nis the penis."

Pearl guffaws.

"Really?" Margot looks interested.

"Wait! Do you know Hiroshima?"

Dennis, obviously shaken, turns and runs. In my opinion, his actions incriminate. I scream, "Hiroshima!"

"His grandmother was killed there," Pearl says.

Margot rises and traipses near the floral drapes. She reads from some internal script. Clearly my friend responds to situations with programmed stage directions instead of involuntary reflexes. Is that worse than my reliance on movie dialogue or Pearl's belief in TV? This close to Hollywood, can any person develop normally?

"But then, what does 'life' mean?" Ms. Haggerty asks rhetorically.

"Life don't mean nothing. It's something you have to do, is all. Like a job. Keep working for those Thursday nights off."

"Pearl, are you *sure* that's Dennis Hishito? Don't you find it a coincidence he attends Cal State? Same as Bev's boyfriend?"

"What coincidence? His brother graduated from there too, Michael Hishito."

"What's with this Dennis and Michael?"

"Their mother's Irish." The maid turns to Margot. "Are you still feeling poorly from the abortion?"

"What abortion?"

"Helen, on 'Day by Day'," I cue my friend.

"Oh, that was several episodes ago."

I half listen to Pearl's response. Disappointment and anxiety tangle my insides, like Scotch tape stuck on itself. "I wish Reg would call back."

"Did you know *her* first husband?" The maid points at me.

Margot nods dramatically.

I watch Dennis out the window. He chops branches from the rosebushes.

"*He* never talked. Even to answer questions. At first, I took his being quiet for niceness. Baked him my special chocolate torte. Six layers. Butter frosting."

"Paul *is* nice," I defend. I'm lonely for him in this suburban setting. Our living room windows faced the purple San Gabriel Mountains, as Mother's do. My ex-husband's and my life-styles meshed better than Reg's and mine. The articulate cowboy sneers at designer labels. If I bought him Ralph Lauren jeans, he'd cut the name off. But the man believes in Levi's shirts. What's the difference?

"Lolly tried to please him when nothing could."

"Reg is good for her," my friend offers.

Pearl fiddles with her dish-towel turban.

"It was bad enough when *she* went off to the country. Took their granddaughters away. But to be involved in criminal proceedings! Her mother's heart is going to break from it. The strain of this kidnaping! Pressure's up. The Missus is on the way to the grave. Which her revered father, Mr. Bedell, is turning over in. I came to California with his wife. Now *she* was a lady, Harriet Hitchcock Bedell. I was a mere girl. Hadn't a real figure then."

"Want a refill, Margot? More sugar? Lemon?"

My pal exclaims, "My horoscope! 'Early morning uncertainty gives way to a heroic sense of purpose.' I suddenly comprehend! I'm destined to find Richie and Lynda!"

"Rots of ruck," I quip.

With fingertips upon closed eyes, the TV star mellows out. "First we must search Bev's apartment."

"Check her luggage?"

This wins me a nasty look. Ms. Haggerty solicits Pearl. "You come with us! Be our cover. Lolly and I'd be suspect by ourselves. That's a pretty raunchy area."

The maid beams.

"No!" I shriek. Margot's really into the role of Nancy Drew, Girl Detective. She fails to realize this is real life. Everything must be relative. That's Reg's main criticism of me.

"Could you change into slacks or something, dear?"

Mouse, who has been quietly devouring the tea goodies, laughs hysterically—obviously at the thought of Pearl's one hundred and seventy-five pounds confined in polyester.

Margot frowns at the child. For not taking the plan seriously, I guess. Perhaps if Mouse grows up at the ranch, she'll be spared media addiction.

"Your uniform's all right. You could have just gotten off work. What do you think, Lolly?"

"Reg wouldn't approve."

"I'll wear my new wig." Each morning as she moseys in from her quarters off the kitchen, Pearl hangs her wig on a hook in the back closet with her shopping bag.

Margot's exit line: "Coming, Lolly?"

I balk. "The tea will get cold."

The small stucco—fifteen-unit—apartment building fronts on a busy intersection near a freeway off ramp. Margot parks her Mustang convertible between a maroon Chevy low-rider and an orange van. My friend and I sport large straw hats and sunglasses, holding Chinese parasols (from Mother's coat closet), incognito. Pearl fills the back seat, undisguised except for the blond wig, which resembles a Marilyn Monroe reject.

Discarded beer cans decorate the dead lawn in the adjacent parkway—a narrow Band-Aid of earth between the scarred sidewalk and blistered asphalt. Compare this to our Americanly Beautiful acres of amber waving grain, equating to wholesomeness; all preserved under a cover of blue sky— like a crystal cake-dish lid. In this section of LA a smoggy grayness washes the air and buildings. *I miss the country.* How delighted Reg would be to know that! It would thrill him as much as my climaxing.

A black boy—perhaps twenty, his skin as light as coffee with cream—comes to sit menacingly on the Mustang's fender. He cleans his fingernails with a matchstick. A scar laces the side of his face, as on a football. His presence intimidates, as well it should—except, that's not a knife handle sticking out of his OP shorts, but a hair pick.

"Boy, move your ass!" Pearl calls from the back seat, where she poses as if on a Rose Parade float. The maid utilizes a black dialect I've never heard before.

Contrary, the young man assumes a supine position across the hood. He says, "Nice place to catch me some rays."

"What?" Margot looks to Pearl for a translation.

"He wants to get a tan," I reply, savvy from growing up thirty-five miles from the beach at Santa Monica. Constant sunshine helped stunt my IQ . . . along with Saturday matinees.

"You look *dark* enough to me," Pearl taunts.

"Do you live around here?" Margot seems to teeter between curiosity and fear. The young man, on closer inspection, is more handsome than frightening.

"Remember what killed the cat?" I warned Margot.

The boy pops up like bread in a toaster. "I had nothing to do with that! No siree. I loved Billy Jean Cat!"

"Billy Jean Cat!" I gasp. Bev's Persian. Reg's ex carted the kitty away in a hatbox.

"Ran into the traffic. Powie!" He unfurls his fingers, simulating an explosion.

Margot presumably feels a momentary advantage, climbs

from the car, and rushes to Scar-face. His dark eyes widen like marbles on the bottom of a fish bowl. She leans close. He ogles my friend's voluptuous honky body.

"Watch yourself, boy," Pearl advises.

Margot twists her scarf around so the ends fall behind. This bares her chest above the turquoise tube top. She removes her sunglasses.

Conceivably suspicious, Scar-face exclaims, "Helen! What you doing off the TV?"

"Channel 2 at one o'clock," Pearl brags.

"You must live in this building, since you knew Billy Jean Cat," I surmise.

He shrugs.

"Boy, tell the lady," Pearl demands.

From her purse, Margot extracts a neatly rolled bill, which she waves in front of this fellow's nose. He seems to comprehend, as I do—from my former life—that it's a fiver wrapped over a joint. Some people use cocaine in a Baggie. That's how to tip in Beverly Hills.

"We're looking for a woman who lives at this address. She kidnaped some youngsters. Their names are Lynda and Richie Bennett. Brought them to her apartment for a short time. We're willing to pay for the information. Aren't we, Lolly? The children's stepmother," Margot introduces me.

His mouth opens as if in surprise, but he turns the motion into a yawn and grabs the money.

"The children's bathing suits were found in Mrs. Bennett's dirty-clothes hamper. So we're positive they were here."

"How'd you get inside?"

"Key in the overhead porch light," I reply.

"I told her that was as stupid as under the mat!"

"What!"

"Nothing!"

"No! What did you just mumble?"

"Would you happen to know a Beverly Bennett?" Margot wants to know. "Her roommate is a Japanese student."

"What did you say about under the mat?"

The actress continues, "Before the Japanese student, there was a beach bum. A surfer."

"With a great tan." At least that's what Richie claimed.

"Bev dumped him," Pearl contributes.

"Who told you that?" Scar-face pockets the money and the joint.

The maid points in my direction.

I shrug. "I got it from Lynda."

Ms. Haggerty queries, "Can we first establish whether or not you're acquainted with Bev Bennett?"

His jack-o-lantern grin says yes to the above.

"Lynda maintained that—"

"Don't believe everything you hear."

"Have you seen her?" I leap from the passenger seat, bruising my thigh on the side of the door, which is open only partially, because of the high curb. It blocks his retreat.

"Hey!" our informer complains as I jump him.

"Is my stepdaughter all right?"

"Is Beverly Bennett on the premises?"

"Do you know Dennis Hishito?"

"Is he in a fraternity?"

"You wouldn't happen to have noticed if her luggage is the Halston design or not?"

"I doubt it. He's oriental."

"You mean Hiroshima?"

Pearl inserts, "His grandmother was murdered there."

"Where?" the black boy's visibly confused.

"What *Lolly* said," Pearl reiterates.

"When did Hiroshima's grandmother die? Man, she sounded alive and well day before yesterday. Screeching clear across the trans-Pacific cable for him to return and run the factory. Seems he's the oldest living son or grandson.

The family can't marry off the maiden sisters until he comes home and settles down."

"Did Bev and the children go with him?"

"Yeah."

"To Japan!"

"No. To the airport."

"Which apartment is Bev's? What's your name?" Margot continues her interrogation while this fellow and I engage in a serious staring contest, no child's game. Two and two is suddenly making four for me. Not for any logical reason. A hunch. Intuition. I look away, and without meaning to I glance at his crotch.

"What happened to your face?" Ms. Haggerty badgers.

"I got hit with a board." We've made eye contact again. Sure! I heard about the accident from the kids.

"Bev's got big boobs." Pearl describes my rival so that Margot, who heads up the apartment steps, can recognize her.

"They ain't that big."

"Come with me, Lolly."

I'm torn.

"She's not home, Lollypop," Scar-face echoes. Except, Margot only said Lolly.

I remove my hat, toss my long mane of hair, smile; who else can he be? "Hello, Dirt Bag."

We shake hands. The surfer compliments, "You ain't that bad-looking."

For some reason, we don't release our fingers.

Margot prances over. I sense she doesn't like being up-staged. "Do you two know each other? Why in the heck didn't you say something, Lolly?"

"Where are Richie and Lynda?" For some crazy reason, possibly because Dirt Bag is Bev's friend and she once was mine, I feel he's an ally. The young man radiates a brand of infectious charm or good will, the way den mothers do. Besides, he's got a fantastic build. I can see why my husband's ex-wife likes him.

"They ain't here!" He yanks me around so I'm no longer facing the street.

"Was that Bev who just drove by? You are expecting her! That's why you're waiting out in front! She's picking you up!"

Margot walks back to the driver's side. "Come on. I'm thirsty. Let's all go get a coke. Why didn't you simply tell me you knew him in the first place, Lolly?"

The strange invitation includes Dirt Bag. He moves toward the passenger seat. I climb into the back, practically on Pearl's lap. "Should we leave? I mean, Bev no doubt will return."

"Not if she saw you," Dirt Bag rationalizes.

Twenty minutes later, the Mustang angles into a slot at Two Ee's drive-in at Atlantic Boulevard and Huntington Drive, one of my old stomping grounds circa 1958. In fact, I'm sure I was here as Paul's fiancée on a double date with Reg and Debbie, the bird-brained, peroxide blonde Reg took out in college. All of which tumbles my emotions like clothes in a dryer. Once in a while, fun is tossed forward as visibly as a red tee shirt.

Dirt Bag sits sideways with his arm along the edge of the driver's seat, where Margot sulks. I'm wedged between Pearl's knees and an armrest. The maid consumes her second hot fudge sundae. Loud music on the radio blends with similar songs from other cars, producing a stereophonic effect that stifles conversation.

Trapped by Pearl, I sip an iced tea as though in a straitjacket. Sweat sticks my arms to my sides. My left leg protrudes from under Pearl's calves on the floor behind Margot. While keeping time to the disco beat with his head and hands, Dirt Bag manages to brush snapping fingers over my ankle and then up across Margot's neck. This gesture apparently revives her.

"You're a dead ringer for Harry Belafonte," Margot yells over the music.

"Who?"

Pearl guffaws. I guess because Margot dated herself.

"Where are Lynda and Richie?" I suddenly feel tired and cross.

Dirt Bag slurps his root beer.

"You can trust us!" Margot leans close, breathy.

"I haven't seen 'em today."

"Yesterday?"

"I told you. We went to the airport."

"You put Lynda and Richie and Bev on a plane to Japan!"

"You're warm."

I'm too exhausted to play. Dirt Bag seems to comprehend. "Hiroshima flew to Tokyo. I loaned him the bread."

"I thought he was rich."

"He bought Bev a fur coat with the money his grandmother wired him."

"A fur coat?"

"He'd seen that in an American movie. With Japanese subtitles. The man paid the chick off with a mink."

"Bev and Lynda and Richie skipped the country?"

"Not with Hiroshima."

"Who else is there?"

"The Moslem singer."

"The Moslem singer?"

"Abdul!"

"Abdul?"

"What's with Bev?" Margo asks. "She run a canteen for the United Nations?"

"When did you last see the children?"

"I took them to the Dodger game last night. Bought Richie a hat."

"Who won?" Pearl asks.

"Dodger Blue. Five to one."

"Did Bev go to the game as well?"

"She went to a recording studio with Abdul. He's cutting an album."

"Where are the children *now*?"

Dirt Bag looks in both directions. "They probably went to hear the Moslem sing without me."

"Who is his agent?" Margot inquires.

"William Morris."

"They're too big to give personal attention."

I burst into tears—either as a manipulative tool or from the strain of the past few days.

"Lolly, what's wrong?"

"Don't you see? Reg flew to St. Louis for nothing. All that expensive fuel! While he battled turbulence over the Rockies and midwestern thunder cells, the rest of us slept peacefully, or rooted the Dodgers on, or hung around with recording stars."

"I thought your husband loved to fly."

"Where are the children, Dirt Bag?" I'm starting to panic.

"I don't know."

"Please?" I place my hands over my heart in a symbolic surrender like a puppy who rolls on his back exposing the vulnerable belly.

"Really. I don't know."

"But you were expecting them at the apartment?"

"Surf's up. I wanted my board. There are twelve-foot waves at Malibu. I'm teaching Richie to hang ten."

"You don't sound convincing," Margot critiques.

"Ah ha!" I grab Dirt Bag around the neck.

The mini-skirted waitress arrives to collect the tray. She notices me strangling our guest. "Oh, there you are, Dirt Bag. I thought we were leaving for the recording studio at one. When you didn't come by with the kids, I came on in to work."

"Whose kids!" I scream.

The waitress counts out the change and exits quickly, giving Dirt Bag some kind of a high sign.

"Whose kids!" I squeeze tighter.

Dirt Bag chokes.

Pearl karate-chops my wrists. "Go, boy, while the going's good."

Dirt Bag eyes the maid. She purses her pale lips, an innertube of pink floating on the dark sea of flesh. Their heritage connects them. Whatever gaiety had inflated our foursome leaks out as if from a day-old party balloon.

"Dirt Bag, does Bev love them?"

"She's their mother, ain't she?"

"Where are they?" I whine, noticing he vacillates between good grammar and colloquial English. I figure him for a lit major.

"He don't know." Pearl motions Dirt Bag out of the car.

I remember the tales the black woman used to relate about her grandfather who was a slave. The maid herself was raped in the woods at age thirteen.

"At first I thought he just fell down on me and had a convulsion. You know, a fit."

"Who?"

"White man. I cleaned for his wife. Your grandmother, she took me away from all that. I came West with her in 1920, the year she married your grandpappy."

Confused, but not averse to speedy exits and evidently sensing Pearl's radar for danger and urgency, Dirt Bag opens the door. He sprints across the parking lot toward two fellows in a car with a Cal State parking sticker on the bumper.

"Why don't you let the mother and her children be!" Pearl sings. She could be belting out a hymn from the back row of the Evangelical Church on Washington Avenue in Altadena.

"Pearl! Whose side are you on?" Anneke had asked *me* that once.

Margot announces, "I have a Noxzema interview at five o'clock."

"We can't give up now! Dirt Bag knows where Lynda and Richie are. Let's follow him."

"In the olden days they did that. Separated the young ones from the mother. Broke up families."

"What with rush-hour traffic and all, I better be on my way or I'll be late."

"Let the mother be," Pearl bellows as the Mustang engine revs. The maid clutches the wig to her head. A breeze bounces the corkscrew curls. Struggling up, I notice Dirt Bag ambling toward a phone booth. Our eyes collide across the space. He turns and runs, hurdling trays full of dirty dishes that are stacked before empty parking slots.

8

"If a man deserted
his family"

Boiled from the Jacuzzi, hastily towel-wrapped, I grab the ringing telephone. Why in the heck didn't someone else answer? The bell sounded at least twelve times. Alcohol flutters through my bloodstream on butterfly wings, the result of drinking gin while submerged in one-hundred-eight-degree water.

"Hello?" I drip water on Mother's lanai floor as Pearl announces from another extension, "Andrews residence."

"Lolly! I was about to give up."

"*Reg!* I've got it, Pearl."

"Andrews residence," the maid repeats.

"Pearl, I'm on. *Thank you.*"

No telltale click. Waiting, I wring out wet and tangled

blond strands of hair. The beach towel unknots, sliding off bare boobies. This would seem more important if I weren't having trouble keeping my balance. Can I be loaded on two drinks?

"Lolly?"

"Where are you, Reg?" I clutch terrycloth ends together.

"Midcoast Aviation."

"Didn't they give us wineglasses with their insignia for a wedding present?"

"The transponder started malfunctioning over Tulsa last night. I'm having it checked."

"What? You didn't mention that when you called before."

"I didn't know what was wrong then."

"You didn't say *anything* was!"

"Nothing serious." My husband must disguise his info, no doubt remembering I'm a neurotic about his flying. Bev wasn't. I maintain she didn't care if he crashed or not.

"You're still at the airport in St. Louis?" Gardenias float in a bowl on the glass table. Their sweet aroma intoxicates further. The soft, white petals remind me of Reg's bottom—protected from the sun by tennis shorts.

Some member of the household lifts another extension and dials a number without listening to see if the phone's in use.

"I'm on," I explain when the clicking stops.

"Lolly!" My father seems surprised. "Nice of you to call. I didn't hear the phone ring."

"Hello? Hello?" From Reg, evidently distressed although it's possibly the connection. Creaking noises rollerskate over the wires. I hear Pearl's raspy breathing. My father lingers; ice cubes clink in his highball glass. At least, that's what it sounds like.

"Daddy, I'm staying *here*. At the house. Remember? Reg flew to St. Louis. He telephoned me *long distance*. It's costing him a fortune."

"Your husband doesn't have the children with him, does he? Mother and I don't think it's a good idea for the six of you to fly together in that plane. If anything happened—"

"Lolly, could we speak privately?"

"Say, you don't believe I meant to intrude on your con-versation?" My father's obviously hurt. "Reg, you there for a Cardinals game, by any chance?"

"Not this trip."

"Of course; they're playing in Boston."

"I'm having some work done on the transponder. The air traffic controllers hard-ass you when you don't show up posi-tively on their radar."

"I was in the service too, you know. World War II."

"Having the Baron checked," ol' Throttle Jock repeats. He apparently wants to keep his mission a secret. Unfortu-nately, I've already told Mother, Jenna, Mouse, Margot, Pearl, and Dirt Bag that my husband's there spying on Bev's sister.

"Lolly, there's no answer at Marcie's."

"Didn't mean to barge in." My father clunks down his receiver abruptly.

"She's either out or not answering her phone. I can't de-cide if I should rent a car and drive over."

"Hello!" Daddy-dear returns. "Say, how long do you think you'll be on?"

"I don't know!"

"No rush! It's just that Mother and I are off to the Music Center. I wanted to whistle up a cab."

"A cab?"

"We've decided taking a taxi is just about as economical as driving. What with the price of fuel and parking. Saves wear and tear on the Cadillac, too. And eliminates the muss and fuss—"

"Marcie wasn't there," my husband breaks in.

"I'll go next door and use the Hooper's telephone."

"You'd better check into the Marriott first." I think what a waste that will be, Lover Boy alone in a motel room. "I hope you'll be able to sleep."

Reg can't sleep without sex. He takes it nightly, sometimes a double dose, the way Paul swallowed Seconal. This is one of the reasons I feel necessary to my second husband. RB III needs me the way Richie needs Bearie Goldbody—someone to hold in bed. I don't believe just anyone would do, which forms a major part of the basis for our marriage. Try to switch a child's familiar stuffed animal.

"I kept dozing off in the lobby at Midcoast today. And then I'd have this frightening nightmare about the children."

He waits. I guess for me to comment. "It's that wretched chili you eat out of airport vending machines."

"In the dream, Lynda and Richie are embalmed with clown faces. It's a gala funeral. At first I don't realize that. I think I'm at a circus or a carnival. Bev is dressed like a tightrope walker. In net stockings."

"Am *I* in your dream?"

"I've thought about funerals all afternoon. My brother's."

I remember. I attended with Paul.

"My father's."

I attended with Paul. Afterwards, Bev drove the four of us by Movieland Wax Museum.

"My mother's."

I remember. Paul attended with Sheri. "It must be from the flying. Being up so close to heaven," I offer feebly.

"Have you called the ranch to see if my ex left a message with the answering service?"

Oh, darn! "No, I forgot."

"Lolly," Reg lowers his voice until it's barely audible. "What do you think the dream means?"

"The dream?"

"Do you . . . do you think the children are dead?"

"No! Dirt Bag would have said something!"

"Who?"

"Dirt Bag."

"Dirt Bag!"

"Dirt Bag."

"Is this the same Bag of Dirt that Bev—"

"Dirt Bag."

"—ran off with?"

"He took them to the Dodger game."

"What in the hell!"

"Bought Richie a hat."

"A hat?"

"A Dodger hat."

"You've seen the children? I've been worried sick—"

"No!"

"Then, how do you know my son has a Dodger hat?" Reg's words sound separated, like ice cubes in a tray.

"I'm not positive it is a Dodger hat. I assumed it was. Dirt Bag simply said 'hat.'"

"He called your parents' house, Dirt Bag did, and said, 'Hello, I just bought Richie Bennett a baseball hat.'"

"No."

"Then?"

"I went to Two Ee's with him."

"With Richie?"

"Dirt Bag."

"On a date?"

"Not exactly."

Pearl coughs.

"Get off the phone!"

"Not until this is settled."

"Oh, honey. I didn't mean you!"

Long-distance silence.

Followed by more long-distance silence.

"He's black as the ace of spades," the maid throws in.

"Who said that, Lolly?"

"Pearl."

"Is there some reason she's on the telephone with us?"

"Pearl!"

The maid's receiver clinks in an exaggerated way, and then I hear her come back on the line.

"What did she mean, 'He's black'?"

"More of a light brown, actually."

"Who?"

"Dirt Bag."

"*Dirt Bag!*"

How can I explain? "Reg darling, don't worry. Dirt Bag is darling—"

"Dirt Bag is darling?"

"—he's teaching Richie to hang ten. And . . . Bev . . . Bev wouldn't *harm* those kids. She's their *mother*, for Pete's sake." I pause. "Billy Jean got run over."

"The tennis player?"

"Your ex-wife's cat."

My husband doesn't reply right away. When he finally speaks, his voice sounds sad and lonely, like a drunk cowboy singer's. "If a man deserted his family, openly ran around with unsavory women, returned months later to claim his children and child support, do you think he'd have a snowball's chance in hell?"

Reg's silly cliché endears him to me. You have to be a brave person to use dippy sayings and wear short-sleeved dress shirts under suits.

"If that same man then *kidnaped* his children from their mother, do you think society would let him get away with it?"

I hear a kettle whistling. Pearl must be boiling water for tea.

"Lolly, do me a favor. Drive to the ranch and stay there." The request sounds sadly routine—as though Reg has asked that or something similar before, perhaps of Bev.

"Can I pass Go and collect two hundred dollars?"

"The coyotes won't come close to the house if you lock the cats in the garage at night. Don't let the kittens wander off into the fields. That's what draws the 'yoties in. Sissy will protect you."

Either Reg or Ma Bell cuts off the call.

"The children belong to the mother!" Pearl reverts to the black dialect she used earlier.

Is she in cahoots with Dirt Bag? I slam down my receiver.

9

"[A father's] one and only function is..."

The VW bus, dubbed The Orange Crate, limps over the ranch road's home stretch on three out of four cylinders. I felt weird cruising around Pasadena without my Mercedes. Townsfolk own 450 SE's like signature jeans. Earlier today, when Margot discovered I'd brought the Volkswagen, she refused to ride in it, insisted we drive *her* car to Bev's.

"Help unload the sponge cake that Pearl sent along," I call as Jenna dashes to greet her horse. Super Star whinnies from the adjacent triangular pasture. Mouse vanishes around the corner of the garage. She's probably off to check out dead frogs. In her absence, they've no doubt clogged the swimming pool's scum gutter.

I hate entering an empty house. Especially one closed up

for several days. Fumbling for the flowerpot's hidden key, I stall. "Jenna! Mouse! Don't expect me to haul your suitcases. Whose tennis racquet is that?"

A suffocating silence and visual clues warn me. My media-marinated mind expects Sharon Tate's bloody living room the day after the Manson family's visit. The kitchen wastebasket lies sideways in its own filth like a toppled drunk: coffee grounds, egg shells, soup cans. Yellow window curtains dangle from broken rods. The screen humps out in a colander shape. Perfect surrealistic art á la Judy Chicago entitled "Twentieth Century Ranch House Kitchen." All that's missing is a woman impaled by an ironing board.

Sweat lathers my forehead, either from fear or the heat of the place—which feels oven-hot, stuffy. I open the louvered door to the afternoon breeze. "Anybody here?" I ask, sounding ridiculous.

I'm brave because it's daylight and I expect protection from the sun god after years of devotion. In my teens I rotated a beach towel westerly as the day progressed, as did everyone "cool" at Santa Monica. Tourists and old ladies hid under umbrellas, which they also turned. The sand became one giant clock, polka-dotted with worshipers who moved a little each hour. I remember explaining this phenomenon to Jenna, aged two. She knelt beside me, building a fort against the seawater. The child squinted heavenward, trying to comprehend.

Paul's girl friend could ride a surfboard before she could walk and surely must know enough to slant her towel. Sheri will educate my daughters beachwise if some mad rapist is hiding out here and murders me in the next five minutes.

This positive attitude regarding Sheri is terrific emotional growth. Six months ago, Reg flew me to Catalina Island for lunch and we encountered fog. I thought, "If I die in a plane crash, Paul and Sheri will inherit the children. That will serve the four of them right."

"Anyone here?" I repeat.

An unidentifiable sound breaks the silence.
Automatically I scream.
Thump. Thump. Thump.
"Who is it?"
Silence.
This noise clearly originates in the bathroom. I creep
down the hall. The door's ajar. Why aren't Jenna and Mouse
rescuing me? Or Reg? Darn him. Everything is *his* fault.
He dragged us out here to live on his grandfather's ranch:
my husband's own blessed mother refused to. In town I had
a burglar alarm, for Heaven's sake. A thousand dollars'
worth of electronic security. Except, the children and I (but
never Paul) accidentally set the siren off so many times the
police ignored us. Officer Rucker said we qualified for the
Cry Wolf syndrome.
Something moves in the dim light.
I scream again.
Then: "Meow!"
"Fang?"
"Meow!"
"Governor Brown?"
I kick the door open, playing B-movie cowboy.
Governor saunters over to press against my legs; her pregnant belly lumpy like Lynda's bread dough. I lift the cat to
the cradle of my arms, stepping forward. "Oh, Gov! Have
you made a mess! I thought the *kitchen* was a wreck."
The bathroom's a complete shambles. Towels wad on the
floor like toads. The chrome bars hang askew. Toilet paper
unrolls in streamers. Hand lotion and an ear ring tree,
knocked from the back of the john, clog the bowl. The contents of the medicine cabinet fill the basin. The cat apparently tried to jump onto the shelves.
"Hey, Gov, what are you looking for? A safe nest for your
kitties?"
A streak of movement causes me to glance toward the
bathtub. A rat darts to and fro through a maze among

tipped-over bottles of Clairol shampoo, conditioner, and cream rinse.

My mouth releases nonstop screams bred into me through sex-linked genes.

The cat lunges from my arms, dropping bomb-like on the rat. The chase commences or, I should say, resumes. Has this crazy Tom and Jerry routine been going on ever since I left, or has this havoc been wrought in the past few hours? Four months ago, I would have fainted. Now I simply slip out the door, closing it tight, knowing that thanks to natural predation . . . the cat will eventually win.

In self protection, my mind wanders: *This is nothing compared to the time I stepped on a snake in the bedroom. Or that spring afternoon Reg and my hillside picnic became a tryst and a startled Angus chased me across the pasture, obviously incited because I wrapped up in a red paper tablecloth. Reg, who'd sprinted on ahead, hollered instructions from the other (safe) side of the barbed-wire fence. He figleafed his hands over his nakedness.*

"Lolly, for God's sake, drop that red cloth and run! Who in the world will see you out here in the middle of nowhere?"

On cue, Sister Kathleen, the principal and baseball coach of St. Anthony's Grammar School drove in with Jenna, Mouse, Lynda, Richie, and the rest of the team, fresh from their victory over Sacred Heart.

I regard these toughening-up experiences the way Reg does IQ tests. Like, what in the heck do they really prove? Mother calls from town to tell me how lucky I am to find love in midlife and to live in such a wonderful place. But she won't stay overnight.

Now dizzy with the heat and confusion, I grab a cold—actually half-frozen—Budweiser from the refrigerator, which on summer setting produces beer popsicles and petrified lettuce. Can I possibly leave the disheveled house for Mini-Maid, the husband/wife cleaning team, due in three days?

One morning in Pasadena, Mouse spilled an entire syrup bottle between the counter and the stove. I pretended the accident had just happened when Pearl waltzed in.

The sound of children fighting revives me. I look out and see Anneke parking her pickup truck under the pepper trees. Assorted Van Vetchen children hop down from the back.

"Lolly!" my friend calls toward the porch. I saunter outside, still traumatized.

Three beers later—we put it away with gusto—I relax on a chaise by the pool, basking in the pink twilight and the warmth of friendship provided by this uncomplicated woman.

"You're not used to hardship, is all," Anneke says. Under her supervision, the four eldest children (including Jenna and Mouse) have cleaned the house and now ride horses as their reward. Hendrika disposed of the dead rat. Four other youngsters play on the sun porch with Lynda's—she's not here to object—Victorian dollhouse. Jan sleeps in a playpen.

It's that time of day before the pre-dinner rush, which mothers cherish. Time seems golden and suspended in the honeycomb of daily activity.

The beer helps, of course.

"Remember when I opened the dishwasher and a mouse ran out? Reg, the turkey, quipped, 'Aren't you glad you have the kind of mice who do their own dishes?'"

"Out here you have to expect inconveniences. Cope."

Does she imply that I'm unable to? These words prick my thin skin, but I let it pass. Anneke glances over. To see if I heard? Margot's suspicious nature contaminates.

"Take life in stride."

"It's useful if you're big on snakes, rodents, scorpions, black widow spiders, and cockroaches."

"They don't bother me."

"Reg certainly admires you," I bait Miss Dairy Queen.

Anneke nods.

I'm sure she figures Reg should have married someone
strong and capable like her. "My husband thinks I'm a
candy-ass." Why do I set myself up?

Anneke nods again. "A person of refinement shouldn't
have rats in her bathtub." She reaches over and squeezes my
hand. For an off-balance moment, I trust her as before. Take
that, Margot Haggerty.

Following a circling hawk, my eye travels to where our
dirt driveway meets Willow Lane. I note two figures coming
up out of the draw, which floods in winter. At first I assume
they're the Saint Bernard, Sissy, and our mongrel, Fred,
who is currently in heat. Don't question the masculine
name. Carolyn Keene never explained why Nancy Drew's
girl friend was called George . . . and I read the entire series
hoping to find out.

I surmise Fred has been calling on the sheepherder's dogs,
who are too well behaved to desert their flock even for an
aromatic bitch. The two wanderers progress more quickly
than the dogs usually travel, somewhere between the speed
of a jack rabbit and a grazing donkey.

"Look, Anneke. Are those dogs on our drive?"

She shades her eyes.

"Or wetbacks?"

Reg tells tales of wetbacks killing for food and water and
shoes. They wear through their soles crossing the mountains
between here and LA. Out riding right after harvest, Jenna
and I surprised five men and a boy. There was no place for
them to hide. The mowed rows of barley resembled a flat
bolt of gold corduroy. I handed over our picnic basket,
speaking perfect C+ Spanish. They grabbed the food and
ran. I wanted them to at least say, "Thank you." "¡De nada!"
I called angrily. Never before had I seen such panic in human eyes.

Anneke says, "We'll have to feed them. Do you have
refried beans and tortillas? I'll make burritos."

"Won't they rape us or anything?"

My friend gives me a quizzical look. "Not wetbacks! That's Lynda and Richie!" I climb onto the retaining wall and peer over the oleanders.

Mother Van Vetchen stands on her chaise.

The figures disappear for a moment where the road dips, then two heads bob up at the crest of the hill. Sun streams off Richie's blond hair like a religious picture. Lynda wears a Cal State visor. The children continue toward us and, possibly because they believe themselves unobserved, they behave naturally, kick a stone between them.

The dogs pick up the scent and trot out from under a bush, barking hello.

I hurdle the oleanders, landing hard enough to jar my back, and run through the patch of barley stubble between the pine trees in our front yard. Crossing a field in a bikini is a mistake. Prickers imbed themselves in naked flesh. Dozens of insects feast on me. I bat away huge grasshoppers. Weeds cut long scratches on my thighs, and rocks stub my bare feet. I stumble several times on the uneven ground.

"Lolly!" They trudge over the final hill. I embrace both my stepchildren. Then several bear hugs later, I hold them at arm's length. "Oh, good heavens!"

"Dirt Bag said he met you," Lynda announces sheepishly.

"What in the world!"

Richie grins. "Chicken pox."

Reg's daughter explains, "We couldn't go to Vegas because we might have exposed the whole nightclub. Besides, he's never had them."

"Who?"

"Abdul."

"Vegas?"

"The Moslem singer got a job there."

"He owns a pet snake."

I comprehend all at once. "So, since you two would

have complicated the Abdul Adventure, your dear mother
dropped you off here!"

"We told her you never went anywhere."

"Is my grape slush still in the freezer?"

"Mouse drank it!"

"Unfair!"

"She claimed you used *her* Frosty Cup."

"We have our own Caladryl." Lynda's visibly pleased,
proud. "*Mom* bought it for us."

My neighbor and her seven children, Mouse, and Jenna
rush out. The group encircles the no-longer-missing persons
as in some kind of primitive ceremony, plying them with
kisses. It occurs to me minutes later: if the Van Vetchen
brood contract the disease one by one, Anneke won't be rid
of the pox for five months.

"Bev wasn't even sure I'd be home!"

"She called your parents'. Pearl said you were on the way.
Mom and the maid had a long talk."

"Scooter Barnes! Scooter Barnes!" Richie taunts.

Around 3 A.M. the telephone rings. I answer in the kitchen,
where I'm fixing orange juice for Richie. He needs it to
down his aspirin.

"Is Reg there?"

I recognize Bev's voice. Someone sings scales in the background. In my sweetest middle-of-the-night voice I reply,
"No, he isn't."

"What the hell!" She sounds cross.

"He'll be in *later*."

"Later! Do you know what time it is? Where is the son of
a bitch?"

"Flying home from the Midwest. A *business* trip."

"Marcie was there. My sister just didn't care to see him.
Which is surprising. I always figured they wanted to screw."

"No kidding!"

A bomb of anger must explode inside Reg's ex. "I return the kids and their father's not even there. Typical!"

"I expect him shortly!"

"Pearl promised you'd *both* be home."

I push Governor from the counter. The cat attempts to climb into the bread box.

"Why doesn't he stop fighting me? My attorney maintains men rarely win custody. It would save us both a bundle on fees. You know, at one point Reg *asked* me to take the children back. When his mother died."

"Yes!"

"But his terms were ridiculous! My dear ex-husband insisted I be a cub-scout leader. Mom Bennett was some God-damned big-shot den queen or something equally sick."

"Scouting is an important aspect of—" I'm glad she interrupts.

"Richie hated cub scouts. He used to ditch the meetings."

"There's no troop out here. Just 4H."

"I know. Weintraub plans to use that against you. Lack of organized activities."

"But you said Richie didn't—"

"It's all a bunch of legal hype. That's why I wish Reg and I could resolve the issue ourselves."

"I—"

"He is so God-damned stubborn. I can't believe you married him. Really, didn't all those years with Paul Whitman teach you anything! I wish Lynda and Richie were here. Abdul's a sensation!"

"Margot said your friend should go with a smaller agency."

"We're working with Flip Wilson. He's at Caesar's Palace. Flip's got a red Porsche with his name painted on the back, just the way it looks on TV. With the arrow. Frank Sinatra bought me a drink. Tell the kids I got Frank's autograph for them. It says, here, let me read it, 'Lynda and Richie, you're sure lucky to have such a pretty Mommy.'"

"Neat!"

"They'll get a bang out of it. Listen, if either of the children's blisters become infected, have them seen by a doctor. Is there a pediatrician close by?"

"Ventura."

"How far's that?"

"Forty minutes."

"I don't want Lynda's *face* to scar."

"No, of course not!"

"God, Lolly, how can you stand it there!"

Lynda calls from the bedroom off the kitchen. "Who are you talking to?"

In an aside I say, "Your mom."

"Can I tell her hello?"

"Lynda's coming to the phone, Bev."

"God, what's she doing up at *this* hour! The kid's sick!"

Lynda grabs the receiver out of my hand. "Hi, Mom!"

From the squeals and giggles, I assume Bev tells her daughter about Frank Sinatra's autograph. I wonder if Reg's ex would get one for Jenna and Mouse.

I medicate Richie, tuck Lynda in bed, and the phone rings again.

"I've been reaching a busy signal for twenty minutes. Who've you been chatting with so late! It's almost 4 A.M." Reg doesn't wait for my reply. "I'm at Santa Paula Airport. The goddam transponder still isn't working right."

"When will you be home? I didn't know your mom was a den mother."

"Twenty-five minutes. Heat some soup for me, would you?"

"Why don't you stop somewhere and eat? I don't want to rattle pots and pans. I just got the children to sleep."

"Why so late?"

"They're restless. Being sick and all."

"Did Mouse catch Karla Van Vetchen's cold?"

"Chicken pox."

"I could swear you told me she'd had that. Something about breaking out at her third birthday party."

"Not Mouse! Lynda and Richie!"

"Lynda and Richie?" his voice cracks.

"Oh, darling! I forgot to tell you. The kids are back. Bev couldn't take them to Vegas because Abdul's not immune. I promised her, as soon as they scab, you'll fly them over to see the Flip Wilson show. She offered to get you and me tickets as well. Boy, I'd like to go!"

"Make that a double scotch and water."

Reg and I rehash the return of the kidnap victims as the sun rises. We haven't been to bed. He's exhausted, but for some reason I'm running in high gear. I haven't stayed up all night so much since college midterms. Shadow patterns cover the pool like a lace tablecloth. (One of Shonburg's marital questionnaires listed this multiple choice: As a couple: 1. we get high together, 2. attend football games, 3. watch the sunrise. Now I can say my husband and I do all three. I scored zero with Paul.)

Somehow, with Lynda and Richie safely home, sleeping soundly, I fall apart. It's as though anxiety had glued me together. Currently, Reg paces in frenzied circles similar to a cornered thoroughbred, "Some nerve! Bev's got some nerve! Drops the kids off like a milkman delivering half and half! Expects me to be here! Chicken pox!"

"I wonder where they got it?"

"And you, Lolly! You tell the woman who just kidnaped my children that I'll deliver them back to her as soon as they've scabbed!"

I shrug.

"So they can see some flipping show!"

"The Flip Wilson show."

"Crazy! She's crazy. . . . You're crazy!"

"Maybe you just have a penchant for marrying crazy women!"

"Crazy!"

"Reg, honey. You're shouting. Please, you'll wake the four children."

"You *are* crazy, Ma," Jenna calls from the playroom loft.

I refill my glass with scotch and snake water.

Reg asks for seconds.

"Prevent Richie and Lynda from seeing that show and you'll come across as the number-one bad guy. If you don't believe me, ask Scheffer."

"I will!" (Later in the day, the lawyer votes in favor of Flip.)

"It would be fun for the four of us to fly to Vegas."

My husband shakes his head as though there's a rattle inside that he can't find.

At 8 A.M. our family gathers solemnly for the homecoming breakfast. Caladryl paints my stepchildren's faces.

Mouse asks, "Why have you heated the butter and the syrup? It's not Easter Sunday."

"We're celebrating!" They don't seem to buy my cheerfulness. Richie asks to be excused as soon as I serve his plate. "Can I eat in front of the TV? Cartoons are on. Mom let us watch them every morning."

"Lucky!" my ten-year-old exclaims.

"I'm coming too." Lynda rises, grabbing the syrup pitcher and a waffle.

Jenna chews stoically.

Mouse cries into her china plate.

"Let them go," Reg advises. We stare at each other across a ruined meal.

"You just can't compete with Bugs Bunny," I say.

My husband folds his linen napkin. "Neither my son nor my daughter said they *missed* me."

"I noticed. It was Abdul this and Dirt Bag that. Not to mention Hiroshima!"

"I feel like the father of the bride at the reception."

"What do you mean?"

"My one and only function is to pay the bills."

10

"Ice cream at two
in the morning"

Unable to sleep because my head aches, I toss about our bed like Reg's Beech Baron in choppy air. Ultimately my husband awakens.

"Want me to rub your back?" he asks, yawning. This is a euphemism for—a prelude to—sex.

"OK."

"You don't sound very enthusiastic, Lolly."

"I'm sure I have a *fever*. I must be coming down with a summer cold. I've got a backache. My stomach hurts."

Reg coaxes, "Do you think you could manage on your knees?"

Afterwards, Lover Boy brings orange juice and holds me.

"I can't get over how glamorous Bev looked in Vegas. All made up and with the spotlight shimmering upon the sequins glued to her red hair. Don't you agree? Really pretty."

"I didn't notice."

"Those purple gauze pantaloons were spectacular! That beaded bra! Wow! Although personally I thought the gold piano was a bit *gauche*."

Reg flew his children and me to Vegas last week. Jenna and Mouse stayed with Anneke, where Paul picked them up for the weekend. My friend also baby-sat a sister-in-law's infants. Thirteen children crowded her spotless kitchen when I dropped the girls off.

"Oh, Anneke, can you manage?"

"What's two more?" she replied. "Jenna and Mouse, come have some speculaas. They are Dutch cookies."

It turned out that Abdul performed in a motel lounge off the strip, not Caesar's Palace. I misunderstood. He worked with Flip Wilson (along with hundreds of others) at a muscular-dystrophy telethon. Anyway, Bev and her recording star escorted Lynda and Richie to the black comedian's dinner show.

Reg and I watched over the four of them from another table like nannies in Central Park casting a protective eye. Then, the following night, we sat with the children during the Moslem singer's act at the Ezee Inn Motel. Billed as Ms. BB, Bev accompanied him on the piano.

When the show ended, I sensed Lynda's reluctance to leave. We stood in front of her mother's black-and-white glossy photo at the entrance to the bar.

"Can't we go back to their suite?" my stepdaughter begged. "Mom said some people are coming over for hors d'oeuvres."

"Suite?" I couldn't believe this place had one. It looked like a hot-sheet joint to me.

"Well, room."

Even Richie acted sorry about leaving. He said, "Abdul promised he would let you hold his snake, Daddy."

Reg did not answer. He leveled his Stetson so it rode two inches above his eyebrows and headed out. I shepherded my stepchildren into the neon-lit night, pleading, "Come on guys. I'll buy you an ice cream cone."

"Do you think Daddy has gas pains? His face looks like it."

"Let's hurry and catch up with him."

"My dad's just jealous because he can't sing as well as Abdul. 'Home on the range' in the shower is all."

"Your mother looked fantastic!"

"I hope I inherit Mom's boobs. Poor Jenna, there's no hope for her. Did you know my dad prefers big-breasted women?"

"A triple decker! Any flavor."

"Lolly, you shouldn't bribe us with ice cream at two in the morning. It wouldn't sound good in court."

"Bev played very well," I murmur, sneezing, still trapped in the cage of Reg's arms. I hate being sick. Maybe I'd better down a bunch of vitamin C, ward this thing off.

"I heard that Moslem has a student visa, so he can't work legally. His wages are being paid directly to my ex-wife. I could cause trouble."

"Are you going to?"

"No. It's the first paying job she's ever had."

11

"As though Reg smelled defeat"

"Why didn't Mouse and I get to see the Flip Wilson show?" Jenna perches on the edge of our double bed. "Why did you shunt us off to Newport? It's not fair."

I prop myself up with pillows. "I told you. Bev only had so many complimentary tickets. Besides, I didn't shunt you off. It was your regular weekend at Daddy's. I thought he was taking you to Disneyland."

"He had to work. A client was in town."

"Did Sheri stay with you?"

"She went sailing with friends."

"Left you and Mouse alone!"

Jenna shrugs.

"Oh, baby, I'm sorry." I touch my teenager's cheek. My

insides shrivel up with her disappointment. I hate losing *control* more than I hated losing Paul. "We'll do something special, real soon."

"That'll be the day."

"Maybe fly to Catalina Island for lunch."

"Who?"

"The six of us."

"Why not just Mouse and me for once?"

"We'll do something. I promise."

Jenna rolls up the sleeves on her Levi's shirt—she and Reg dress very much alike. "When? The twelfth of never?"

"As soon as I'm feeling better."

I wasn't coming down with a cold. Nothing that simple. No, Anneke's children didn't contract chicken pox. I did— which means I must not have been immune to the germs floating in that last inch of lemonade Richie always left in his glass. Our dogs refused to drink juice.

CHICKEN POX! My reward for TLC. The thanks received for providing Lynda and Richie with baking-soda baths . . . for dabbing Caladryl on gooey blisters . . . for playing endless games of gin rummy and changing bed linen . . . for fixing hot chocolate at midnight and ginger ale with ice cream at 7 A.M.

"Chicken pox!" I peer into the bathroom mirror. Eighteen red-rimmed blisters blossom on my neck and face, not counting those which crowd the inside of my nose and ears, and under my tongue. It's too sickening to look at. I rest gingerly on the edge of the tub. I discovered pocks polka-dotting my behind and other private parts while inserting a Tampax.

"Boy, you're really out of commission," Reg sympathized. "You've not only got the pox, but also the plague."

I pick at a rather unsightly pustule on my calf. "It's not fair!"

My skin is—was—my best feature: smooth and peach-colored with sweet blond fuzz. During adolescence only a half dozen zits erupted. Girl friends hated me. I never washed my face and lived on candy. Hence the nickname Lollypop. My conversion to health food occurred during my first pregnancy. Like any convert, I'm a fanatic.

In fact, I became so adept at mouthing Milk Duds I could recite an entire Latin translation without Mr. Elrod's catching on. My brother informed Scooter Barnes, "Hey, Barnes, don't let Lollypop give you head, you'll attract ants." I didn't comprehend that statement for about eighteen more months. By then, Randy was away at college, where I couldn't kill him.

Years later, when my first marriage disintegrated, I flirted with a Pasadena doctor at a Junior League dinner party. I didn't realize he was a dermatologist. His wife had the worst case of adult acne I've ever seen. During the salad course, Dr. Robert Ashley ran his finger down my bare back and whispered, "You have the most extraordinary skin!" At the time, I considered this a cop-out. The man simply couldn't think of anything complimentary to say about any other part of me, despite the fact I wore a very revealing dress. So I refused to meet him for lunch.

Reg used to adore my skin. "The best thing about it," he'd say, "is that it goes all over." My husband won't admit it now, but the pocks repulse him.

I've felt terribly grouchy lately. I wonder what the suicide rate is for chicken pox? I itch until I can't take it any longer, twisting and moaning, writhing around. Then I scratch, stopping after the blisters ooze and bleed. Currently, balanced on the edge of the tub, I examine my chest. There must be forty spots, including the tip of each nipple—pocks ride piggyback. Will deep pits scar my body like potholes in a highway?

Stirring baking soda into the tub, I slide in. Soon the prickly lukewarm water irritates like bee stings. I wrap in the only available towel, which sports a picture of Spider Man, and braid my grimy hair. Three blisters mar the part. In an effort to look festive, I tie Mouse's plaid ribbons on the plaits.

Speaking of my youngest, the little doll crept into our bedroom about midnight last P.M., making her way through a house lit only by a Mickey Mouse nightlight plugged into the bathroom. She claimed it didn't matter, she couldn't see without her glasses anyway.

"Mommy?"

"Hum?" I replied sleepily.

"May I hop in bed with you?"

"Umhum." A redundant request, since the child had already snuggled down beside me, clutching Charlie the Bride Dog.

"Jesus, Lolly, no! I'm stark naked!" Reg protested. Wearing a Milk Drinkers Make Better Lovers *tee shirt—a gift from Anneke, allowed because of my sickly condition—I shielded my daughter from his bareness.*

"Did the Blue Monster Man return, Mouse?"

"No. The Blue Monster Man stayed in town. He rents the attic where we used to live, on Milan Avenue."

"No kidding!" from Reg.

"Why did he decide to stay there?"

"Blue Monster Man needs parents' unhappiness. That's like his oxygen."

"Daddy and I never fought! Ever!"

"But you wanted to."

Silence.

"Does it upset you when your mother and I argue? Lately, we've both felt anxious because of—"

"No."

"No?"

"You two are like me. You yell and get it over with. Then you hug and kiss. Woo woo woo!"

"*Jesus!*" *from Reg. In the night he isn't as articulate as usual.*

"*Do you—*" *Mouse hesitated.* "*Do you think Bev will try to kidnap Richie and Lynda again?*"

Her stepfather sat up. He flipped the light switch, which also activated the radio. Willie Nelson warned, "*Mammas don't let your babies grow up to be cowboys.*" *My husband's sleep-tousled hair resembled a golden storm. He draped the floral sheet over his chest.* "*I don't think Bev will kidnap Richie and Lynda again. We had a hearing and the judge agreed it would be in the best interest of the children to leave them at the ranch until the trial next month.*"

"*Richie said they had to lie on the floor of the car, because when Bev pulled up to her apartment Mommy was talking to Dirt Bag.*"

I wince.

"*Bev kidnaped Richie and Lynda because I denied visitation. I won't do that again. If she wants them for a day or two, a special event, we'll arrange it. Like the trip to Las Vegas.*"

"*I wish I could have gone.*"

"*What does anyone see in that place?*" *He seemed baffled.*

"*If Bev asked for her kids over a weekend, how do you know she wouldn't keep them like before?*"

"*Because her lawyer told her she couldn't. It would make the judge angry and it might influence him to grant me custody. Bev wants custody as much as I do.*"

"*She doesn't act like it.*"

"*Maybe not, but she enjoys the part of mothering that's fun. And she's good at the fun stuff.*"

"*She stole them from the water slides! Lured them away like how the witch got Hansel and Gretel into the oven.*"

"*Mouse, are you afraid Bev might kidnap you?*"

A long pause ensued. "*Sort of.*"

We hugged her.

"Honey," Reg consoled. *"Bev won't kidnap anybody. It was my fault. I denied visitation. It was strategy. Like in a chess game. Lynda and Richie were pawns. I was wrong to play games with them. I see that now."*

I hated hearing my husband talk this way. He sounded like John Wayne acting heroic for the sake of the troops. It was as though Reg smelled defeat. I think that verbal slap on the hand from the judge was a lethal blow. Yet, Bev didn't seem to be affected in the least. *"Reg, we truly feared she would skip the country with the children!"*

My husband sighed, absently fiddling with Charlie the Bride Dog's wedding dress. He reached for the Hang Ten bathing suit he keeps under the bed in case of fire. *"Come on, Mouse. I'll lead you back to your room."*

After retying one of the ribbons three times, I wander toward the kitchen, overhearing laughter. Reg lolls poolside with Anneke Van Vetchen and assorted children. The voices of my husband and friend drift inside, like a song from a city neighbor's radio—you hear the music but can't understand the words.

"Ha! Ha! Ha!" Anneke's accent tinkles like a wind chime. Her body, I muse, moves similar to one as well—flowing effortlessly, all dangling parts separate but connected.

Followed by Reg's deep chuckle.

More giggling.

Complete with Spider Man and ribbons, I sneak to the window.

This gorgeous Dutch girl stretches out face down, the untied straps of her bikini top hanging off the chaise longue like drapery pulls. Reg leans over from his chair and holds a tube of Coppertone upside down. He squeezes out a series of dots on her back—a meticulous cake decorator doing rows of rosettes. Then my husband connects the lotion drops with his fingers. I imagine how great that must feel. To him as well? Lover Boy probably is incredibly horny, thanks to the chicken pox. Our quickie this morning wasn't much of an oasis after a three-day dry spell.

Anneke raises up slightly, giggles again.

Maybe she's ticklish.

Margot Haggerty warns inside my head: "A perfect Daisy Mae. Aren't you jealous?"

No. Anneke is my true friend. I let jealousy ruin a first marriage. According to the shrink, Paul reacted as I'd scripted him to: I accused my first husband of being unfaithful so often that he finally thought he owed it to me.

I've grown through these experiences—which is why I'm a rational and mature second wife. Ha! An iron poker hangs from a brass stand beside the fireplace. I want to use this blunt instrument on Reg. Which Dr. Shonburg would find interesting. I never wished to hurt Paul. Only Sheri.

Reaching forward, I trip, stubbing my toes and knocking the brass stand over. It clanks noisily against the hearth. Broom, tongs, shovel fall out like Pick Up Sticks. As I right myself, my towel unknots and falls to the floor.

I dart to the bathroom. My naked body flashes red pocks and white skin, similar to strawberries and vanilla ice cream in the blender. The door locks with difficulty. (Reg removed the knob from the outside once when Richie inadvertently trapped his arm in the toilet tank. It's too incredible a story to relate here except to say the boy attempted to retrieve a plastic sailboat he'd flushed down, thinking that was where it would end up. Anyway, the bolt has never been the same.)

Moments later, children knock on the door. I order them to pee in the bushes. Lynda threatens, "Wait until I tell that to the judge!"

I counter, "I'll say who gave me chicken pox!"

Eventually, however, I'm caught. Richie pleads, "I have to go number two."

Due to my illness, I haven't been on bathroom patrol. There is not one towel left in here. They must be drying on the diving board, or in mildewy heaps on everybody's bed, stuffed under the sofa, used as liners for Governor Brown's basket. The cat's due momentarily.

"Richie, I'll come out. But please don't look. OK? I don't have my robe."

He promises. But then he stares. "Ugh!" My stepson screams. "You look grossening."

"No worse than you did, pal." I wrap my arms around the bareness.

Richie snickers. "I didn't have half that many on my stomach."

"Lolly!" Reg saunters in from outside most likely looking for cold beer. "You shouldn't parade around naked in front of the boy. What would the judge think?"

I lunge for the bedroom door, which I slam behind myself.

My husband's entrance speech. "What are you doing?"

I rummage ferociously through drawers looking for something non-scratchy to wear. Tee shirts, underwear, scarfs, leotards, knit caps, mittens float momentarily around me like New Year's confetti, then drop to the floor. I grab Scooter Barnes's football jersey, old number 27, which stacks on a chair along with my cheerleader uniform and two prom dresses Mouse collected from Mother's cedar closet.

"Where did you find that?"

"What?" I pull the jersey on over my head.

"The San Pasqual jersey."

"It was my brother's." Reg won't know that I'm lying.

"Randy was number 63. He used the same number when he played at Stanford. I've visited the shrine."

"The shrine?" I stall for time.

"His bedroom at your parents' house."

A giggle slips out like a fart. I decide the best defense is an offense. "Who did you give your football jersey to? Horny Thorny?" I refer to Reg's high school sweetheart Amanda Thornton.

"I hadn't discovered girls when I played ball for Flint-ridge Prep."

"You're certainly making up for lost time this morning."

Reg moves in on me, attempts to touch my body, but there is no place that is pock free. Frustrated by lack of grab-ass, he pulls a braid. The ribbon unties.

"I want to live in town." I crawl over the bed to avoid the cowboy.

"Why won't you tell me whose jersey that is?"

Because I've learned any intimate detail you share with a husband will be eventually used against you. "I miss the ballet."

He intercepts me at the bedroom door. "We have tickets to see Mikhail Baryshnikov at the Hollywood Bowl next week!"

"I simply cannot be expected to carry another bucket of water to the washing machine for the rinse cycle. And don't advise me to call a plumber. I've telephoned every service man in Ventura County. No one will drive out this far. Especially when they hear about the dirt roads. I've just given up. I bathe in cold water."

"Bathe? What's that got to do with the washing machine?"

"Same hot-water heater!" I snarl.

Reg's shoulders slump.

We stare at each other.

I think: Why did he waltz into my life? I was surviving very well. (Wasn't I?) Then he had to fuck my brains out and ruin everything. I should have listened to brother Randall. He told me this joke about the monkey who hung his tail over the railroad tracks. The train whizzed by and cut it off. Ol' monk turned around to see what happened. The caboose lopped off his head. The moral: don't lose your head over a piece of tail.

I dream about my house on Milan Avenue, with sunny bedrooms, flower gardens, and Pearl to clean. I should have stayed. Rented rooms or something. Is Blue Monster Man really inhabiting the attic?

"I can't hack it here, Reg, I really can't."

"That was Scheffer on the phone a while back. He's set up sessions for all of us with a court-appointed psychiatrist."

"No!" I clutch myself. "I won't be seen by anyone! I'm a complete mess!"

"You'll be OK by then. Your face is starting to scab already."

I scratch my thigh. "I mean emotionally."

Reg looks at me quizzically. I swear he remembers that day many years ago he visited me in the hospital after a miscarriage. Neither of us speak. Then we chew around the subject like an olive pit.

"The psychiatrist, a woman, some Dr. Kravetz, insists on interviewing every member of the household. You and me and the four children."

"Not Jenna and Mouse. They've suffered enough—missing out on Flip Wilson."

Reg shrugs. "So don't make them miss out on this!"

"No! I mean yes!"

"I agreed we would be seen as a family unit."

"Will Bev be taking in her household? Dirt Bag. Hiroshima. Abdul?"

"No. They don't have to go. Just Bev. And then the six of us."

I lower my eyes. What I said about not being able to hack it is somewhat true. I help my husband fight for the custody of his children and sacrifice mine in the process. Meanwhile Bev does what she darn pleases (including forcing me to play nursemaid) and is adored for it. Even Reg admires her for landing a paying job. What's my reward? Chicken pox.

Everything I attempt out here fails. I pump the well dry filling the swimming pool. Compared to Anneke, I'm a dud. The pathetic part is, right now, I don't even care. I just want to move back to Pasadena, where my skills are appreciated.

What skills? I start to cry. "If Anneke is so gosh-darned resourceful, making stupid cottage cheese and all, you'd think she'd be able to apply her own suntan lotion."

Reg seems to absorb this statement like those highly touted paper towels. He backs away, abandoning me to sobs and nose wiping. "If your goal is to be a jealous wife, you should have stayed married to Paul. It would have been easier on Jenna and Mouse."

"You didn't have to rub clear down to her crack!"

"Lolly, this is the truth. Anneke asked Hendrika to apply the lotion. The kid refused, saying, 'Let Reg do it.' At that point what could I do but offer? For the life of me I could not think of a tactful way to refuse."

"Same thing happened to Paul. Sheri was out there on the coast highway hitching a ride, and he simply couldn't turn her down."

"Don't judge my behavior by his."

I scowl.

"Lolly, you're my wife. I love you very much. More than I've ever loved anyone. More than Bev. That's why she's so angry at me. You and I have something most people don't know exists. Either that's valuable to you or it isn't."

"What we have is called sex!"

"Don't knock it!"

My chin trembles. I refrain from saying anything sarcastic. I've been leery of smart-aleck answers in serious conversations since I visited Paris. I saw the guillotine blade that cut off Marie Antoinette's head. Her only mistake was quipping, "Then let them eat cake."

"I feel a responsibility for, a commitment to our relationship, Lolly. I've never felt that way before. I love you and you love me back. That means we have a great deal to offer. To ourselves. To the four children. That's why I pursue the custody issue."

"Daddy?" Richie pushes the door ajar. "You promised to go swimming with me."

"I'll be right out."

"Anneke wants to borrow your air compressor. For the rubber boat. Everybody's waiting for a ride. It's taking her too long just blowing. Even though she's doing a good job."

I snap. "I'll bet. It's probably her specialty."

"Lolly Bare!"

I turn away. Reg spins me around like a fan blade. He holds my hands in his. Eventually our eyes meet. My husband looks exactly like the pilot shot down over Berlin in an old World War II movie. The type who appears so darn earnest and kind and gentle and nice that the German girl hides him in her barn.

He's so silly and corny and straight and old-fashioned and all-American—stands at attention whenever "The Star-Spangled Banner" is played—tall and blond and tanned and it feels awfully soothing where his fingers currently touch my shoulders, pocks or no. I've said it before and I'll say it again: better than anything has ever felt . . . if I can't trust the cowboy, who is there?

Reg kisses my splotchy forehead. "I love you, Lolly."

"I love you."

We come together slowly in a romantic embrace.

"Oh, excuse me!" Anneke has followed Richie into our bedroom.

"Give up on the blow job?"

"I . . . the children act hungry. It's after twelve. I . . . would you mind if I made hot dogs for everybody?"

"I'll do it!"

"No, Lolly. You lie down. Rest while you can." Mother Van Vetchen hitches up her bikini, nudges me gently toward the bed. I'm just one more child to care for. "You're looking better! Would you like me to put Caladryl on your pocks? I do believe it relieves the itching somewhat. Here, lie down on your back. Let me pull up your shirt."

Reg returns to find Miss Dairy Queen rubbing cotton balls across my bare chest. Let him be a little jealous. I say, "Did you notice the ones on my nipples?"

12

"Like the cat's cradle"

Ours is an uneasy relationship, Lynda and mine, based on my hoping the child will accept me as a surrogate mother and her believing there's no reason she has to. We acted wary of each other at first. Ironically, she and I share many traits, which is both an asset and a liability. The two of us vie for Reg's attention, although I'm growing comfortable enough with myself to stop competing. Usually.

In a way, Lynda provides me with joys Jenna denies. When my stepdaughter first started her period, she squealed, "Lolly!" I rushed to the bathroom and was unabashedly told the news. We danced around, hugging each other. My own teenager never mentioned the fact she menstruated. I knew a month later. Jenna wrote "Maxi pads" on the grocery list. Evidently, she'd used up her "emergency" supply, which I had stuffed beneath Winnie The Pooh pajamas after the school nurse's lecture in fifth grade.

Today I help Lynda buy something decent to wear to the shrink's. Decent by Reg's standards, since he objects to jeans, which seem acceptably *haute couture* to me. Didn't some designer maintain that Levi's are America's only major contribution to fashion? I rarely don anything else, although my stepdaughter's Dittos do appear a bit raggedy and worn thin in the seat.

In the past several hours, I've watched her try on a dozen outfits: bathing suits, overalls, tennis shorts, leotards, "sweats," jackets, coats; all the while searching for a *dress* to wear. Now we're stopped before a sporting-goods store. The mannequin in the window surfs a cardboard sea.

"I don't think your dad would approve of calling on Dr. Kravetz in a wet suit!"

"Guy! That's *gay!*" My stepdaughter utters this popular slang expression. Everytime she says it I want to strangle her.

"Come on, Lynda!" I'm eager to start back to the ranch before the Labor Day-weekend traffic hits Highway 126. I would have coerced one of my own daughters into settling for something hours ago.

"If we'd eaten lunch at a fast-food joint, we wouldn't have had to wait around for a table. *That* wasted the entire morning."

"What do you want in there?" Our noses press against the glass.

"Roller skates."

"You have roller skates."

"Not Disco Skates."

"What's wrong with yours?"

"They're not tennis shoes with polyurethane wheels. Everybody has them."

"I can just see you skating across the pasture."

Lynda brandishes The Look. It means "Boy! are you weird." Unlike Mouse and Jenna's "Boy! are you weird," it also says, on some level, "Must I fight you for my father? You have two husbands, but he's the only dad I've got." Will the shrink blame me for her attitude?

Impulsively, I caress Lynda's thin shoulder. She jerks away. To make it appear that I touched her accidentally, I lean down to adjust my espadril strap. "We missed you and Richie a great deal while you were 'away.' And *worried!*"

"Why did you worry? We were with my mom."

That's precisely why we worried.

"Do you like my mom?"

The strange thing is I do. I admire her zany behavior but despair over the hurt Bev's actions left in their wake. Sometimes I think she's an alter ego, acting out my secret desires. It's usually about 7 A.M., when I'm hearing four affirmative verdicts re the grossness of the oatmeal. Now I tell Lynda, "Sure!"

"She doesn't like you."

"Let's try the place next door. The Miss Fit. That's a catchy name."

"I hate broccoli," my stepdaughter replies.

Conceivably, she suspects we're having it for dinner again.

"Don't you think The Miss Fit looks cute?"

"I'd rather go to K-Mart. They've got a much bigger selection. Why can't we?"

"I think The Miss Fit looks perfect."

Lynda crosses her arms, sword-like. "I want to go to K-Mart."

According to the stepparenting classes, power struggles are to be avoided at all costs. I cross my arms, sword-like. "There isn't one in Santa Paula."

"We bought that rubber boat there."

"In Simi Valley."

"You hate K-Mart. You think the clothes are cheap."

True. "You usually end up getting what you pay for."

"My dad goes to K-Mart."

"For spark plugs. Not wearing apparel."

"My mom bought a jacket and a bathrobe there. She says you're a snob."

This scares me. I sounded like Barbara Bedell Andrews a moment ago: "You get what you pay for." I devoted my youth to not being a snob, using Mother as the classic case of what I didn't want to become. This rebellion took the form of dating boys whose dads worked at gas stations. Mom's reaction: "He seems nice enough, Laurel. It's a shame his father wasn't in a fraternity."

Don't I love Reg because he has the Pasadena Prefers qualifications, yet one would never know it? He comes off like an intelligent cowboy. And it tickles me that this turns Mother on. I've heard her brag, "Reg married Lolly in a pinstripe suit and *boots!*" She asked me once if he wore "shorts" under his Levi's.

Yet Bev's analysis may be accurate. Lately not only have I started echoing Mom, but she's coming on like my dearly departed grandmother. Do daughters truly become their female parent?

"Why do I have to buy a dress, Lolly? Can't I wear jeans?"

"Your dad thinks it would be better if we girls showed up in something other than casual pants. It's a question of respect."

"Can't my mom take me shopping? I mean since she has to return to LA for the appointment anyway."

"I'll bet you'd like her to!"

Right out of stepparenting effectiveness training.

"Well, can she?"

Yeah, Lynda, she could if she gave a darn.

My stepdaughter seems to sense my unspoken reply. "Guy!"

"Let's try The Miss Fit!"

"Your hair looks *dead* that way! Why don't you have it styled?"

"Miss Fit, here we come!"

"I'd rather go to K-Mart."

"I'm sure you would."

"My *mom* would take me to K-Mart!"

"I'm *sure* she would."

"I'll go inside with you, but don't say one word about vitamins leeching out in the cooking water."

During lunch the waitress and I discussed the proper preparation of fresh vegetables.

"Before he met you, my dad just fed us TV dinners. After Grandma Bennett died."

I twist my gold wedding band.

Lynda speaks in an aside. "Have you seen Mom's ring? The one from my dad? It's covered with diamonds. The day after she was crowned Miss Marine Corps, he took her to Hall's Jewelers. That's a real fancy store. You sit on velvet stools and a man brings stuff out on a tray."

"Are you sure it isn't a restaurant!"

"Guy! Your sense of humor is completely *dead*."

"Do you like the jumper in the window?"

"Dad made pancakes from that mix where you add water. You're such a health-food nut. Nobody can stand what you fix. My mom said people used to make fun of the stuff you served at birthday parties. Did you really force a group of kids to eat tapioca pudding instead of ice cream? Poor Mouse and Jenna."

I feel as though she's jabbed a switchblade through my heart. It's ridiculous, but I could cry. How *awful* if my daughters were embarrassed. I was just trying to do the right thing. Don't react, I warn myself. Don't react! "Didn't you like that delicious albacore we baked last night? The fresh corn on the cob? The homegrown squash? The potato salad? Peach cobbler? That was real cream I whipped. Right out of some Van Vetchen cow."

"I like the kind in the can better. That you squirt. It has more flavor."

I gasp.

"Your potato salad isn't as good as my mom's."

"Does she marinate the potatoes first, like I do? Use a ratio of four eggs to one potato?"

"She buys it at Colonel Sanders."

"I thought you loved my french toast. You had five slices this morning!"

"I'd rather eat Sugar Pops."

I push open the door to The Miss Fit.

Like pedestrians at a red light, Lynda and I halt together before an outfit displayed attractively on a mannequin. The ensemble includes a long, puffy-sleeved, peach-colored, satin blouse and a tiered skirt trimmed with numerous grosgrain ribbons.

"How darling!" I enthuse.

"Oh!" Lynda's stunned.

"But much too birthday-partyish for a visit to a shrink! Like the Mexican girls who wear velvet skirts and lace blouses to school on free dress."

"I want it."

"Honey, we don't even know if it's available in your size." I finger the price tag. Forty-five dollars for the cotton skirt. Forty for the blouse. Plus tax.

"That'll fit."

"Here are some cute wraparounds."

"But I want this!"

"Oh, Lynda!"

"Guy, don't have a wet dream!"

"Lynda!"

She clearly senses my exasperation, moves in. "You said I could pick out whatever I pleased."

We cram into a bright red saloon-doored dressing room on the mezzanine. Heat rises and becomes trapped here. The air conditioning from downstairs doesn't seem to have any effect. I hold my purse, Lynda's tote bag, a shoe box containing her new platforms, and the transistor radio, and feel like a coat rack.

My stepdaughter's jeans, tee shirt, and tennis shoes litter the floor. She steps over them carefully as though they were land mines. The store's Muzak wallops a disco beat to which Lynda gyrates before the three-way mirror, poking me with every arm swing.

I zip up her skirt in the back, fasten the button. Since Jenna, Mouse, and I grow long and lanky, I'm not used to Lynda's petite body. The child resembles a perfectly sculptured Barbie doll.

"Do I look OK?" Lynda sounds very unsure. I was that way before her father convinced me, actions speaking louder than words, that I was a terrific piece of ass. Is his love strong enough to save me *and* his daughter?

"Precious!"

"I don't want to look precious!" she moans.

"How about if we buy this for Cotillion and find a wrap skirt to wear to the shrink's?"

"You're trying to bribe me!"

Yes. "No!"

"Do you have enough money?"

"If I write a check."

"Isn't your checkbook money from Paul? That's for Mouse and Jenna." My stepdaughter turns. In the three-way mirror her reflection complies, skirt twirling. "I want to wear this to the shrink. What's a shrink like? You went to one before. Didn't you? My mom says you were whacko to marry my dad."

"Dr. Kravetz merely wishes to talk to you. Help you explore your feelings. Be your *friend*." I speak to her mirror image.

"How gay!"

"Lynda! . . . The psychiatrist will ask you some routine questions. No big deal."

"Like would I rather live with my mom or dad?"

"I don't think Dr. Kravetz will be that direct."

"What would you have said when you were my age? If a shrink asked you?" Lynda swings around to face me, skirt ribbons flying like an airport windsock.

We're inches apart. I count the reddish freckles on her pert nose. "How can I answer that? My dad went to an office every day. He wouldn't have been around to care for me. Our situation is entirely different. My dad lacked the freedom your father has. Which your father's worked darn hard to achieve, by the way. He can stay home just about whenever he wants because of how he's arranged things at the mine."

Exhausted by this speech, I slump into the wall.

"My mom swears she would have returned eventually if Dad hadn't *married* you. Even if his mine didn't produce ore. It was just her luck that he struck it rich *after* their divorce. When they were together, everything Daddy touched turned to shit."

That doesn't sound fair to me either. I don't envy Sheri Paul's success; I had more than my share of it.

"Mom said she would have come back," Lynda repeats.

"You believed her?" A cruel question.

Lynda shrugs. "She did last time."

Last time! Bev left before? What kind of a deal was that? This woman moved around as she pleased; meanwhile Reg and his mother baby-sat for the children? No wonder my husband's ex-wife hates me. I ruined a great setup.

Then a concern throbs that I can hardly allow myself to feel, like ignoring a barbwire cut when fixing fence a mile from the house's first-aid kit. *What if I'd found this out after that first night at the beach? Would I have stopped seeing Reg?*

No.

Why not?

The sex blew my mind.

Did he have others as well? When she went away previously? While he was dating me?

Oh, of course! I am so naïve. A Pollyana from Pasadena believing in a screen version of "The Lolly and Reg Story." Cast Robert Redford and Jane Fonda, advertise it as another remake of *A Farewell to Arms*.

Reg *must* have had others. No man could be that good— on premarital sex alone.

Then Lynda brings me back with the accusation, "You'd freak if Jenna and Mouse wanted to live with Paul and Sheri."

I can barely breathe.

"Wouldn't you?"

"Yes!" I blurt, panicked and claustrophobic in this tiny cell. I lunge forward, wanting to run. Where? Anywhere. But there's no place to go. Lynda shoves the chair back. It bars the swinging doors.

Is the temperature ninety degrees in here? I sweat profusely and smell. I raise my arms to fan the pits. This action is repeated three times in the mirror.

Bev's snide remark of last July travels around the inside of my head, like a well-aimed pin ball: ". . . Reg married you instead of hiring a housekeeper."

What should I do? Can I survive another divorce? Must I return to the marriage mart?

The marriage mart? *the Gloria Steinem in me demands to know. Why not a glamorous acting job? I have a degree in theater arts from an excellent university. Some experience. Connections. Except, didn't Margot say her agent had stopped looking for middle-aged hags?*

Besides, isn't marriage what I do best? Marriage and mothering.

Are they low aspirations?

Or is it just that it takes very little to make me happy?

In fact, aren't I content with the role of Reg's wife?
Mother of these four kiddos? Worse! I enjoy it!

Hysterical, I gaze at my triple reflection: not too bad. The
black tube top and coral necklace with the dark print skirt
seem stylish on the angular bod—pot belly shows only when
I'm hunched over in a bikini. Besides, the life guard at the
water slides ogled me, sagging stomach and all.

I throw my shoulders back, stand erect.

*I'd be OK out there in the big bad world except for one
thing. I love Reg more than I've ever loved any person in
my life. I feel connected to him: physically (Oh!), mentally,
emotionally, spiritually.*

This makes me stagger.

*Did Reg's other women refuse to do floors and windows?
I try to remember the conversation we had last week, when
I was sick with the chicken pox. My husband said, "I feel a
responsibility for, a commitment to our relationship, Lolly.
I've never felt that way before. I love you and you love me
back. That means we have a great deal to offer. To ourselves. To the four children. That's why I pursue the custody
issue."*

Was he lying?

No. Reg is an honest man. I always marry honest men.

The saleswoman peers in. "Adorable! But you're so pretty,
anything would look nice. You have your mother's profile.
The exact nose."

Lynda and I exchange sick looks.

The woman departs.

My stepdaughter and I are suddenly bound together in an
intricate way . . . like the cat's cradle that the girls weave
with yarn or string over their hands. I say, "Funny about
that. You inherited my nose."

"Lolly, do you think Mom cares if I live with her or not?"
Lynda's voice lacks its former brashness. My stepdaughter
sounds the way she did when she asked if she looked OK.

Sweat trickles across my forehead. I wipe it off and knock one of the hair combs askew.

"Does she want me around, or am I in her way?"

Pause.

I edge toward the door. It wobbles.

"Lolly! Someone can see in!" Lynda yanks me forward. "Well, does Mom want me around?"

I jump away, stepping on a tennis shoe. Lynda clings to my arm. Our actions are captured in the mirror. We look like modern ballerinas performing a *pas de deux*.

Pause.

"I'm sure your mother loves you very much."

"Does she want me around? It doesn't matter with Richie. He's always cheerful, so he can stay anywhere. But . . . does she *want* me?" Lynda squeaks out the last four words.

Oh, sweetheart, do you have to ask? I have a super idea. Let's run away together. Screw Mr. and ex-Mrs. Bennett. Pick up Richie and Mouse and Jenna and split.

"You knew her, Lolly. Tell me. Does she?"

I sigh. "Of course your mother wants you around. So does your dad. You're the most popular kid on the block."

"I'm not in her way?"

I don't trust myself to speak, shake my head no. Have I just granted Bev custody?

Lynda reaches behind and yanks down the skirt zipper. We stand very close together. I help with the button.

My stepdaughter whispers, "Thanks, Lolly."

I nod as if she means for the dress.

13

"Other mothers lead normal lives"

I swear Dr. Kravetz covers up mounting hostility toward me with a sugar-sweet smile like spreading thick frosting on a cracked cake. I have no inkling of what I've done wrong. This causes me to squirm on the hard, armless chair. Noticing that my blouse is unbuttoned, I try to fasten it. Meanwhile, the shrink waits for an answer.

The good woman must weigh almost two hundred pounds. Pearl's rival? Am I destined to go through life battling fat adversaries? A muumuu, topped by a white doctor's jacket, drapes her body. The pale face and neck—one indistinguishable mass—rise from the Hawaiian print like a breaching whale. In the desk opening, she knocks her knees together. This action causes the hula girls on the sea of lap material to dance, the palm trees to sway.

Watching my fingers fumble with the thread loop, Dr. K.'s glare seems to intensify.

What have I done now? Closed up my blouse? The shrink doesn't want to see my boobies, does she? Heck, maybe Kravetz does. When we shook hands, she did squeeze extra hard and hold on for an awkward length of time.

"You believe," the doctor repeats, pencil poised, "that the creature in the bathtub was a rat?"

We've dwelled on this ridiculous subject for ten minutes—something I mentioned in passing to point out how frantic events became when Bev kidnaped Lynda and Richie. Dr. K. has sidetracked me into a carnival hall of mirrors where distortion serves as truth. "I'd just driven all the way back to the ranch—"

"Then, the ranch *is* some distance from town?"

Oh, shoot! That's one of Bev's complaints. She claims it's impossible to make the round trip on one tank, which would hinder her weekend visitation.

"—on three cylinders after a fruitless search for the children in the LA area. I wasn't much in the mood to classify rodents. Maybe it *was* a mouse."

"Interesting. You say that you were worried *despite* the fact your *step*children were with their *natural* mother?"

Lynda reprimanded me for the same thing. I recently read (probably in *The Farm Journal*) that with the onset of labor, some gland secretes a hormone that actually produces the nesting urge in females. Does the substance accumulate in the bloodstream, like alcohol? One drink, after a binge, can make a person drunk. That might explain why, with all my miscarriages, I seem more susceptible to motherhood than Reg's ex-wife.

"Of course I worried. Bev and Hiroshima *abducted* the children, for Heaven's sake."

"Hmm."

"It was *normal* to worry!"

"Hmm."

"You think I created mental anguish for myself as a form of self-punishment?"

The psychiatrist studies her notes, flipping pages in a ritualistic manner that entails wetting the forefinger of her right hand. "Let's talk some more about Governor Brown."

"I don't think he's going to marry Linda Ronstadt."

"Your cat?"

"Oh! *Her*. I told you she gave birth day before yesterday." I have the feeling my answer to this silly question is somehow relevant, but not knowing why, I don't understand exactly what to reveal. Perhaps Dr. K. merely hopes to frustrate me. I know shrinks do that sometimes in mental-status exams.

The psychiatrist snaps her swivel chair forward. I fear that her gigantic body will be propelled toward me like a rock from a slingshot, so I shy away. Why can't this shrink be as wonderful as the woman therapist in *An Unmarried Woman*? Doesn't she realize the last couple of years have taken their toll on me? I'd love her professional sympathy. No one else has offered any. Both Anneke and Margot maintain, "You're much better off with Reg, Lolly."

The psychiatrist taps perfectly manicured magenta fingernails on the desk. Numerous rings burden her chubby fingers. "Yet you allege there are no kittens?"

"The coyotes!" I explain again.

"What makes you so sure the cat gave birth?"

I shrug, exasperated.

"Is this conversation upsetting you, Mrs. Bennett?"

"It upset me when Reg said that either coyotes or owls killed Governor's kittens. I cried for days."

"How long?"

"A couple of hours?"

"Hmm."

"I was sad, appropriate to the occasion."

"Did you, in fact, ever see the kittens?"

"No!"

The doctor leans closer. Her lipstick matches the finger-nail polish and smells like grape. Jenna wears those flavored kissing lip glosses also. "Very interesting."

"But I'm positive they existed, if that's what you're driving at."

"You think I'm driving at something?"

"I don't know. Are you?" What's bugging this tub of lard?

"Hmm."

"What are you thinking? That, because of my miscar-riages, I believe in pregnancy but not live birth? Something like that?" I grin, helpful.

She writes jerkily, filling one page and the side of another. I swear there's a smirk on her face. It wasn't this way at all with Dr. Shonburg. He liked me, even lusted after my newly divorced body. I went out with him so he wouldn't think I was anti-Semitic.

"Governor Brown was fat one day and skinny the next," I explain, wishing to dispose of the subject but unable to find a verbal trash can.

"Fat! Ha!"

An unfortunate word choice. "Pregnant."

Dr. K. pops a Cert into her mouth.

Maybe she'll OD on breath mints.

How do I get myself into these crazy situations? Other mothers lead normal lives. They're assets to their husbands, give great parties, raise bright children, have affairs with golf pros on Tuesday mornings after they have their hair done—lead a typical existence.

Where did I go wrong? Why am I slouched on this straight-backed chair in a pale institutional-green cubicle undergoing the third degree from a court-appointed com-pulsive eater? And meanwhile my blouse peekaboos open because of this dang' abalone-shell button and flimsy loop.

"You are convinced, Mrs. Bennett, that your cat was pregnant?"

"Yes! My brother Randy is a veterinarian."

"Your brother examined the animal?"

"No! But—"

"Hmm."

"Governor Brown mated with three wild cats, including a Manx. Sixty days later, her belly swelled up like a balloon. Not totally scientific, I grant you, but on the ranch, small-animal hospitals are not readily available. Heck, Reg swears Mr. McGinnis still castrates his sheep with rubber bands."

"Interesting that you should mention *castration*."

"Mouse and I counted at least four kittens inside Governor's tummy. If you're careful, you can find the little arms and legs."

"Mouse? Is this the same one from the bathtub?"

"My daughter, Mouse."

"You have a mouse for a daughter?"

"That's her nickname."

Dr. K. refers to a sheet of paper. "Jennifer Catherine Whitman. Age thirteen. Elizabeth Jeanne Whitman. Age ten."

"We nicknamed Elizabeth 'Mouse' as a baby, because she was not quiet as a———."

"I see."

I smile.

"You called the female cat *fat* when you obviously meant to say pregnant. Do technical terms embarrass you?"

"No." A Freudian slip. I resist retorting, *Did you hear about the LA disc jockey who phoned Bullock's Wilshire and asked the lingerie department if they had any Freudian slips?* (Bernie Shonburg thought it hysterical.)

Dr. Kravetz continues, "For instance, what term do you use to describe heterosexual intercourse?"

"Fantastic!"

No response from *Herr Doktor*. Is she scribbling that my

affect is inappropriate to the content of my thought? Why does the shrink stare at me in such a funny way? Does she think I'm lying? Or is she trying to trick me into saying that I openly discuss sex with the children? Which, of course, I do. How *else* would I learn anything?

"That was a little joke, Dr. Kravetz."

"Then, you do not find heterosexual intercourse, as you put it, 'fantastic'?" The shrink actually blushes, and then I feel blood rush to my cheeks. "I'd like to discuss your miscarriages in more detail."

Darn. I thought I'd passed them off rather casually earlier.

What did my husband tell this lady in their hour together? Why wasn't I allowed to speak with him before coming in here? Was it feared that he would brief me? Was it necessary for ol' Lollypop to be shunted off to that stark waiting annex with three-year-old copies of *Business Week*? They're enough to drive anyone crazy.

Where are Jenna, Lynda, Mouse, and Richie? In some playroom, I realize. But where? Doing what? Playing charades with autistic children?

"Were these miscarriages traumatic experiences for you?"

I think, "Oh, yes. Yes they were. I'd love to rid myself of that constant lump in my throat by sharing those pent-up feelings with you. I wouldn't risk it with Shonburg—he could only prescribe so much Valium. Which I refused to take anyway. I wanted to feel sad. Or Paul. Paul, in his own way, hurt more than I did." I shrug.

"Let me see." Dr. K. scans another set of notes. "Did you in fact say, quote, 'I feel as though I am dying slowly from the inside out'?"

Tears suddenly well up in my eyes. What blackmailer reported that? Oh, no! Bev!

I have total recall, like instant replay during sporting events. When I miscarried thirty-three months after Mouse was born, Reg's ex visited me in the maternity ward. Several people dropped by. I guess because I was listed in critical condition for a few days due to a hemorrhaging problem. Or maybe they knew Paul stayed away? I used to believe it was because he felt it best to spend his free time with Jenna and Mouse.

"Lolly! How in the hell are you!" Bev plopped onto my bed late one afternoon. She removed her high heels. "Jesus, you look awful. Let me have a cigarette and I'll fix your hair. I've got some mascara in my purse too."

"Nice of you to come."

"Anything to get out of the house." Bev used my water glass as an ashtray. "Listen. Reg is going to stop in on his way home from work. Carnations are your favorite flower, aren't they? My husband remembered that you carried them at your wedding? I guess he ordered the bridal bouquet."

"I never knew!"

As Bev rattled on, she renovated yours truly: combed hair, applied makeup, poured herbal-essence body splash. When she pulled my torso forward to remove the hospital gown—change me into the frilly negligee she'd brought as a gift—I fainted. I came to with Bev screaming obscenely for a nurse. Having an ear for the dramatic, I replied, "I'm dying slowly from the inside out."

Mrs. Bennett continued speaking as two RNs propped me up with pillows, took my pulse and blood pressure. "Detain Reg as long as you can. OK? I don't intend to be back to the house before ten tonight at the earliest. I hired a sitter so I could visit you, and I plan to make the most of it."

I prayed hourly to be able to hold my children soon and couldn't comprehend why this woman, who didn't seem to have any definite plans for the evening, wanted to stay away from her household.

"The great escape, as it were."

"Escape from what?" I asked feebly.

"Oh, God, I forgot. I'm talking to Supermom. You're probably even sorry about the miscarriage. I was delighted to have one."

"I didn't know."

"Neither does Reg. Actually, it was an abortion!"

(It took me a long time to realize that Bev is not necessarily cruel or malicious, just insensitive, but in a good-hearted way. That's going to work *for* her in court.)

Before I could figure out how to respond, my OB arrived. Dr. Sam Wilson, ogling Bev openly, announced in a monotone, "Because of the lab results on the current blood work-up you must be hospitalized at least one more day."

"What in the hell does that mean?" Bev interceded for me. "Can't you assholes ever talk in plain English? You'll scare the shit out of Lolly with that kind of mumbo jumbo."

I sensed no one had ever talked to young and handsome Dr. Wilson in this manner. He was a dead ringer for TV's Kildare and acted his part as if from a script. LA County Hospital probably offers a semester in media medicine.

Bev crossed and uncrossed her glamorous legs, which dangled over the edge of my bed like fishing lines. Perhaps they were. She clearly hooked the medico. Stunned him at least.

"Look, this place is dead. Is there a bar close by where somebody free, white, and twenty-one could get a drink?"

"Monty's," Dr. Wilson replied, seemingly showing off he knew where the "in" hospital crowd hung out. Big deal. Everyone in Pasadena knew that. I could tell by the OB's polyester suit he was from the Midwest or someplace equally stupid.

They exited together—I supposed, to go their separate ways. I pleaded, "Can I leave tomorrow?" Bev shouted over her shoulder, "Don't embarrass Dr. Kildare here by running out of blood or anything, Lolly."

"Dr. Wilson," he corrected.

Paul telephoned at dinnertime. Neither of us knew what to say to each other.

"I'm sorry I lost the baby. Our son." I pushed away the tray. Untouched whitefish floated in a watery cream sauce.

My then husband said good-bye abruptly. Somehow, during that hospital stay, the pulled-too-taut rubber band that held Paul and my marriage together snapped.

Reg arrived after I'd been given morphine and Seconal. I'd been dozing, and when I opened my eyes, he was waiting beside the bed holding long-stemmed carnations, a mirage.

"Am I dreaming, or is that really you, Reg Bennett?"

"Hi." He clutched the flowers in one hand, resembling the Statue of Liberty.

"How're you doing?" I asked.

"How are you? Your . . . your hair looks different. Fancy."

"Your wife teased it into a bouffant style. What do you think?"

"Fine."

"You don't like it." Tears leaked from the corners of my eyes. I turned away, pulled the sheet up so that Reg couldn't see where milk from oozing breasts wet the nightgown. At that moment I longed to cram my two daughters' plump young bodies back inside mine, making the three of us one—a trinity I could believe in.

"What's the matter, Lolly?"

I didn't trust my voice.

He coaxed, "Tell me about the baby."

I mumbled, "We planned to call him Chip. Like Chip off the old block."

Reg handed me a small gold handkerchief. The brown-yarn hand-stitched hem was obviously the work of little Lynda. Paul hid gifts from Jenna and Mouse in a drawer.

Now I push aside the complicated memories of that day

which kaleidoscope in my mind and confess to Dr. Kravetz, "Yes, I said that. I'm dying slowly from the inside out." What I don't admit is that the dead baby did not require a funeral because he wasn't quite seven months old. I'd hate to be the garbage collector on *that* route.

The shrink pops another Cert into her mouth. "Let's review our discussion of your schooling?"

"I told you I was varsity cheerleader, which for some reason got us going on the book *Passages*. How I read it when Paul was seeing Sheri. I know! I said you were acting like I was some blond *shiksa*. Reg isn't even Jewish. He's more WASP than I am. His mother's ancestors arrived on the *Mayflower*, his father's sailed with William Penn."

"That's important to you?"

"To my mother."

"Did you and your husband attend the same university?"

"No, Reg and my husband did."

"I thought that Reg is your husband."

The smile slides from my face. I hook straight hair (I brushed the curl out of it earlier before that small mirror in the annex) behind both ears in two nervous gestures, scratching the back of my head. Reg refers to Paul as "Lolly's *real* husband." "Of course. I meant that Reg, and my ex-husband, Paul Whitman, both graduated from Pomona College, in Claremont."

"Do you feel that you are still married to Paul Whitman?"

"Seventeen years is a long time." My ex shadows me. I set the toilet paper to roll from the bottom, leave the car in neutral instead of first gear, *butter* the salami sandwiches. But Paul doesn't enter Reg and my bedroom. Well, maybe after I've smoked a joint . . . and then it's just his face. *The disapproving voice whispers inaudibly to Reg, who grins like Tab Hunter*. The person I actually fantasize about is Scooter Barnes. What would Dr. K. make of that?

"You referred to Mr. Whitman as 'my husband.'"

I pleat the cotton skirt over my knees. "A natural mistake.
I'm nervous, I guess."

"Nervous?"

I am convinced that this woman really dislikes me. At
least feels ambivalent. Am I acting paranoid? No. I may be
slightly schizo, semihysterical, but I'm not afflicted with par-
anoia. Truly, just the opposite. I always assume everyone is
on my side.

My sweating palms leave dark ink-blot shapes on the rust-
colored wraparound. "I think this situation is conducive to
anxiety."

"Anxious as well?"

"What happened to the good, old-fashioned Rorschach?"
Does she write that in a clinical interview Lolly Bennett
was found to be uncooperative?

"Do my questions make you angry?"

"Our sixty minutes are almost up and we've yet to discuss
my capabilities as a mother. Mr. Scheffer claimed you'd be
interested in my child-rearing techniques."

"Did the attorney brief you?"

"No! Well—"

"Do you approve of masturbation?"

"Ginot said it's fine but you don't meet many interesting
people along the way."

"Would you encourage the practice?"

"I wouldn't chop off guilty fingers."

"How do you feel about nudity?" She's writing rapidly.
The pen scratches ta-ta-ta like machine-gun fire.

"What *about* nudity?"

"Did you appear before your stepson in the nude?"

Richie blabbed! To whom? Casually to his mother? *"You
should have seen Lolly. She had chicken pocks all over."*

"Yes, but—"

"Do you feel that sexual tension might be created by per-
mitting your thirteen-year-old daughter to share a bedroom
with Mr. Bennett's son?"

"Richie's only nine years old! Besides, Jenna's so modest she wears sleepers over a bathing suit in a bundle bag."

"Do you think that her modesty may be induced by her stepbrother's presence?"

"Don't you remember how you acted when you first sprouted breasts?"

"How do you feel about homosexuality?"

"What about homosexuality?"

"I'm asking you."

"I wouldn't purposely raise a kid to be one. But I know a lot of fine people who are. I dated a guy, an actor, at UCLA who later came out of the closet. We still exchange Christmas cards."

"Were you attracted to a male homosexual?"

"I didn't know. He was darling! I—"

"Why? What drew you to him?"

"His turquoise blue eyes, I guess. I'm a sucker for blue eyes. Blue eyes and Mary Jane shoes on little girls."

Dr. Kravetz removes her glasses, flashes me a blue-eyed look. I feel she hopes I'll say something like "Yours are nice."

"One possible explanation for your attraction might be that because you were unsure of your own sexuality, you chose someone who obviously was also undecided."

For some idiotic reason I feel myself flushing. That ditty Lynda brought home from St. Anthony's plays inside my head. "People think that we're just friends. Actually, we're lesbians."

"Have you ever had a homosexual experience?"

"I just told you. I went out with Dale at UCLA."

"Hmmm."

"Oh, you mean with another woman! Some of my best friends are lesbians." Unfortunately, I chuckle, thinking of another of Randy's jokes. "I'm not laughing at you, really, Dr. Kravetz. . . . There's this awful story my brother told me. About the three biggest lies? Some of my best friends

are Jewish. (Oh, sorry!) The check's in the mail. And I won't
come in your mouth."

The doctor's eyes narrow.

"No, truly, I had a sorority sister—"

"Please, describe the experience."

"No! I mean, I had a sorority sister who turned out to be
a lesbian. She was my roommate. Not Margot Haggerty.
Freshman year. Doreen Churness. Actually, we shared bunk
beds in the pledge dorm. Not shared. Doreen slept on top. I
was underneath. In the bottom bunk. I hate being on top. I
am always afraid I'll roll off. The bunk bed. Not with a man.
I like it then!"

During this tirade, Dr. K. has leaned back as far as her
chair will maneuver. It's pressed against an op-art wall
poster that looks suspiciously like male genitalia. Is she
sneering at me?

"Do you consider your second marriage to be a sound
marriage in spite of your jealousy toward Anneke Van
Vetchen?"

Oh, Reg! Did you have to mention that? "Yes. I was totally wrong about my friend. Anneke's an exceptionally
sweet person. Is exactly what she seems: kind, helpful, gen-
erous, sincere. It's not her fault she's a sex symbol. There
isn't a mean bone in her body. I like her very much. Adore
her. *Love her!*"

"Ah ha!"

"Reg and I are determined to provide the four children
with a wholesome and enriched environment. We're like old
trees who wind their roots around saplings until the young
trees can stand on their own."

"Don't you believe Mrs. Beverly Bennett is prepared to
do the same?"

"Bev deserted her children. Doesn't that act speak for itself?"

"Not necessarily. The *natural* mother obviously wishes
them back at this time or there wouldn't be a custody issue."

"Don't you find it incongruous that when Reg and his first wife were together, when the four children were toddlers, Mrs. Beverly Bennett *often* left Lynda and Richie with me? So how can she object to my caring for them now?"

"Perhaps that seemed to be a rational solution then."

"Rational! She would dump the kids off saying, 'Keep them, would you? Bob called and asked me to play tennis.' Once I objected, 'But Paul's taken the day off. We're leaving for the beach!' Mrs. Bennett replied, 'Don't let Lynda burn. She's very fair. Not half Indian like your two.' To add insult to injury, I later learned that Bev didn't even appreciate what I did. She told Reg I was 'a pigeon.'"

"Hmm." Dr. K. rattles pages.

"Don't you suspect that, on some level, child-support funds are attractive to Bev? That she's discovered she can't keep herself, and Abdul, and Hiroshima, and Dirt Bag on alimony alone?" I raise my voice.

"It might also be possible that Mr. Bennett seeks custody to *prevent* his wife from receiving child-support funds, as a means of controlling her?"

"Oh, shoot!" I would have screamed and kicked the floor except that people who act like that around here are hauled off in straitjackets. "Don't you mean *ex*-wife?"

Dr. K. sucks on the remaining Cert.

I sigh. Is a sigh actually a cry for help, as Dr. Shonburg maintained? I'm tempted to ask. "What are you going to recommend to the court? Or are you supposed to say?"

"If I told you and you did not agree with my answer, how would you react?" Kravetz coughs.

"I wouldn't try to seduce you if that's what you mean."

"One option might be the reunification of the primary family." The shrink leans forward. She must be testing to see if I'm oriented to time and place and purpose of evaluation.

"Let me ask you something, Dr. Kravetz. Why, unless I truly believed that Reg is the better parent, would I help him seek custody? Realistically, wouldn't Jenna and Mouse and I fare better without Lynda and Richie underfoot?"

"Underfoot?"

"You know what I'm trying to say."

"Possibly you see the Bennett offspring as substitutes for the babies you lost, as surrogate children." The shrink collects what appears to be my file, closes the folder.

Margot has suggested the same thing.

"Dr. Kravetz, do you really feel a woman who once professed, quote, 'I discovered I have more natural talent for playing the piano than I do for motherhood,' should be granted custody when the children's father has a knack for parenting?"

She reopens the file. "Was there really a rat in your bathtub?"

"I give up. Was there a rat in my bathtub?"

She rewards me with a nasty look. How unshrinklike!

"Doctor, I'm rescinding my consent for Jenna and Mouse's psychiatric evaluation."

The shrink smiles Cheshire-cat-like, "I have already interviewed them."

"You agreed to see me first. You promised!"

"Are you disappointed that I was unable to keep my word due to scheduling conflicts?"

I've risen and clutch my hands at my sides. The darn blouse button pops open again. "When did you see them?"

"While you waited in the annex. After I had observed you through the two-way mirror."

I shriek, "No!"

Kravetz nods.

"Let me guess. *Elizabeth* did not respond well to her name. Therefore, despite the Stanford-Binet of 193, you've concluded the girl's a nitwit?"

"You have a sardonic sense of humor, Mrs. Bennett."

"It's 'leave them laughing when you go and if you care don't let them know.'"

"Pardon me?"

"Something I picked up from Mama Cass." Why did I use a fat reference to an obese lady? What's wrong with Mac Davis? He recorded "Both Sides" as well.

"Hmm."

"I don't feel these sessions have been conducted in a professional manner. I'm sorry to say, I smell a rat."

The doctor wags a plump finger at me. "There's our old friend in the bathtub again."

For a minute, I believe her to be human. Trust her. Emotion surges through me like the dishwasher when you push the button for POTS AND PANS. She grilled ol' Lolly and I've come through with flying colors. "A+ and funny, too," as a college professor scored one of my English exams. I smile.

"I will escort you to the lobby."

I allow her to propel me by the arm.

When we enter the large room, Reg, looking harassed, buys Lynda and Jenna candy bars from a machine. That must be a last resort. Richie wards Mouse off with a potted palm. Later, in the car, my daughter explained, "We were playing lion tamer."

Then I spot Beverly Bennett. My rival's apparently arriving exactly on time for her second appointment with Dr. Kravetz. From three points of a triangle, Dr. K. and I, Reg, and his ex converge: white cells rushing to the point of infection like in one of those health movies they showed at junior high.

Bev is disguised as Sally Sorority: sweater, skirt, owlish glasses.

"Hello, Lolly! Thanks so much for watching the children while I was in Vegas. I'm back now. For good. I'll do the same for you sometime."

"Let me wait until all four of them have leprosy or something equally catching." I pick at a chicken-pox scab.

"Reg!" Bev extends both hands.

He jams his into his pants pockets.

"Miriam, nice to see you again. Hope you're free for dinner."

Miriam (Kravetz) giggles.

"Mommy!" Richie charges over.

"Hi, there, big boy!"

He purrs like a kitten undergoing the rough-tongue treatment.

Lynda stays close to Reg. "Did you dump Abdul?"

"That's none of your business!" To me, Bev's voice sounds harsh, but Dr. K. nods as if the child's mother had given an appropriate response to an openly hostile, snot-nosed question. The shrink says, "Mr. Bennett, I would like to speak with you privately for a minute in order to verify some information."

My husband and I exchange panicked looks as he exits.

A wailing ambulance siren draws the four children to a street-front window. Bev and I are left standing together like extra girls at a seventh-grade dance.

"Let me buy you a cup of coffee," Reg's ex offers.

We amble toward the machine. I'm terrible at prolonged hatred and soon reply, "Those glasses look cute on you."

"I think they make me seem more serious."

"How's Abdul? We enjoyed his act. Did you see Frank Sinatra again? If you ever have the chance, Jenna and Mouse would like his autograph, too."

"Abdul and I are splitsville."

"No!"

"He's being deported. He wanted me to return to Iran with him. But I couldn't see myself behind the veil."

I laugh.

"I converted for him. That's enough."

"You converted?"

"I pray continually that Reg be reincarnated as a Moslem woman. The trouble with you, Lolly, is you limit yourself. You're nice-looking, you know. But all you have to show for thirty-some years is two stinking marriages. You've gone from the frying pan into the fire. Paul Whitman. Reg Bennett. They've got interchangeable parts."

For a moment, like watching a falling star—*before* it vanishes and you're not able to believe what your eyes saw— I hear the words this attractive woman utters.

"You've got such a hang-up about children. So much guilt. Abdul believes that in a past life you were a teacher who lost the sixteen youngsters in your care because you were too chicken to shove them out a third-story window when the building caught fire."

"Wow!"

"Look, if you ever want to rock out, give me a call. We can fly to San Francisco for the weekend."

"What would I do with the four children?"

"Leave them with Paul's girl friend."

"Sheri!"

"Why not?"

I must admit the idea intrigues me. She'd age ten years in a day. "Bev, you're not serious. We couldn't subject her to those monsters."

"*Everyone* would appreciate you more when you returned. Hey, Dirt Bag thinks you're cute. I gave him your phone number."

I want to inquire further, but I see Kravetz and Reg marching back.

"What do you think of Fats?" Bev asks.

"Who?"

"Miriam."

I confess, "For some reason she evidently hates me."

Bev shrugs. "I told her you were a lesbian."

"What!" I feel kicked like a soccer ball.

"Have you had the stove repaired? God, I hated that drafty ranch kitchen. We used to spend the Memorial Day weekend there every year."

"The *broiler?* No."

"Mrs. Bennett?"

Bev and I both turn. Dr. K. beckons to her.

A week later.

"The telephone!" I cry as Reg opens the ranch door following our morning jog. My husband rushes inside, leaving the screen ajar. Sissy pushes through. His wagging tail knocks a bowl of fruit from the corner buffet. Grapes squish underfoot as I cross to the refrigerator.

"Yes?" RB III motions that I should bring him a can of beer and whispers, "It's Scheffer. He's received Kravetz's report."

"That was fast!"

"I see." . . . "No, go ahead. Read it."

He downs the Coors, dents the can into a V. Eventually Scheffer must finish; my hero replies, "Could you go through that once more?"

"What?" I pry.

"You're saying Bev is *unstable?*"

"Goodie!" I exclaim.

"But I'm *paranoid?*"

"Paranoid?"

"OK. OK. *You're* not saying. Kravetz is." Reg balances the receiver between his shoulder and ear, repeats to me, "Since I couldn't control Bev during our marriage, I wish to control her during our divorce." He returns to Scheffer. "I don't quite comprehend that paragraph about Lolly. Could you go over it again?" . . . "Oh, Christ! No! Kravetz dragged me aside in the lobby to ask if we kept a rat in the bathtub. Or if we had any dead kittens lying around."

I grab his arm. "What did you say?"

Reg shakes his head no. "That bad!"

"Thanks a lot!"

"Lolly, keep it down."

"Keep it down? You crucify me and I'm supposed to keep it down. I told you about that rat! And *Governor Brown's* kittens died! You said so!"

"Another Governor Brown, Mr. Scheffer."

"You crucified me!"

"What's the prognosis on a person 'out of touch with reality'?" he asks the lawyer.

"Out of touch with reality!"

"Is there time to seek a second opinion?" . . . "I see."

Suddenly everything comes clear. Dr. Kravetz is a lesbian. She got angry at me because she thought I was too and wouldn't respond to her advances. My darn blouse! Miriam believed I flirted, then rejected her! I scream, "Dr. Kravetz is a dyke!"

Reg hold his fingers to his mouth like a librarian.

"And Bev! She's a bisexual liar!"

Reg covers the mouthpiece. "Lolly, Mr. Scheffer can hear you!"

"A God-damned, flaming, motherfucking dyke!"

"No, no, Mr. Scheffer. That wasn't Lolly. A neighbor who just dropped in. Not a neighbor, exactly. A stranger. Car broke down on the highway. Then, the shrink recommends custody with the natural mother?" Reg says to the learned counsel. "How will that affect our chances in court?"

"Good!" I sprint toward the door, slipping on a plum. "The only thing *better* than custody with the natural mother would be *reunification of the primary family!*"

FALL

14

"Good mothers beget good mothers"

Daily, Mouse slashes calendar numbers with a purple crayon. Three days left before the trial. Yet, to the casual observer, we seem calm. It's like Anne Frank eating strawberries as the Grüne Polizei drew near. Of course, that's probably *why* she gorged herself. The approaching court date is the reason I'm pigging out on hot buttered rum. I found the most delicious recipe in a cookbook that belonged to Reg's grandmother.

Trapezoid shapes of golden sun slant through the windows onto the carpet. This honey-colored light spreads across the faces of the four children, or perhaps their cheeks reflect the fire that dances with leaps and twirls, creaking and hissing like the slap of ballet slippers on a hardwood

practice floor. I said we make a nice picture. One must look
behind the canvas.

Richie vows Sissy chewed his good shoes. The boy no
doubt figures he won't have to meet the judge without them.
But those look like scissor cuts to me, and my garden shears
are missing. Besides, the Saint Bernard's taste runs more to
Jockey shorts.

At this moment, Jenna, Lynda, Mouse, and Richie, uni-
formly dressed in St. Anthony's blues, write homework as-
signments and eat popcorn from a communal bowl. The
smell of melted butter, the spicy odor of hot cider, the burning pine, and an apple crispness to the air affirm that fall is
well underway.

At his rolltop desk, Reg works the crossword puzzle from
today's *Times*. A while ago he asked the kids, "What's a
two-letter horizontal word for vertical?" I curl on the leather
sofa under an Indian blanket with Buckley's spy novel
Who's on First. On loan from Margot. Panic has turned me
into a compulsive reader. Books keep ol' Lolly Bare up until
all hours. My husband thinks I'm avoiding sex. Am I?

At least I'll face Weintraub with a stockpile of quotable
quotes. Rules usually dictate my reading. I can choose only
from what's in the sun porch's game cupboard. Forty years'
worth of vacation time killers stack there. I'd forgotten all
about *To Kill a Mockingbird*. Jenna's almost finished with it;
the rape fascinated Lynda. Or possibly the courtroom
drama.

If we lived in town, the youngsters would study in iso-
lated upstairs bedrooms; Reg would abandon us for Mon-
day-night football. Despite the new antenna, what we see
on that channel are shadowy figures who swim through a
purple haze. Fine tuning only garbles Howard Cosell's
voice. At the ranch, we're coerced into the kind of closeness
that park rangers achieve around an open campfire by asking the audience to sing "This Land Is Your Land."

Mentally I compose a note to Margot, who telephoned

yesterday to announce that she's been subpoenaed. "Dear
Margot, The six of us gather before a blazing fire, and it's
such a lovely moment I'd like to press it in the book pages of
my mind so that afterwards I'll have proof that flowers grew
on this custody battlefield." How's that for someone accused
of barely passing Subject A? Reg maintains that waiting for
court is similar to sitting in a dentist's office; but he says we
can't permit our anxiety to be worse than the drilling.

"Reg, how do you spell ambivalent? *A* or *e* at the end?"
Mouse's question scratches the silence like a fingernail
across a chalkboard. She expects him to know. On a religion
paper the child claimed, "My stepfather is good at language
arts because his mother spoke Latin."

"Did the dictionary omit the word?" He sounds weary.
Horny? I'd better finish Buckley by bedtime.

Richie gets into the act. "Daddy, does 'rapped' have two
p's?"

Mouse, presumably sensing that Reg feels Richie needs
help—which now can't be offered without smacking of prejudice—replies, "Double the consonant after a short vowel."

"I know that, Four-Eyes, but does rapped have two *p*'s?"

"Shut up, Dick-Head!" My younger daughter shoots her
stepbrother with an orthodontia rubber band discarded by
Jenna. He twists Mouse's arm into a hammerlock.

I pour myself another drink. This sounds idiotic, but I see
their fighting as progress. Before, Richie would hit only
Lynda. Try to sell that program to a judge.

"Reg excels at everything!" I attempt to divert the children, feeling nauseous. I'm not used to drinking all afternoon—my body ODs on brown sugar.

"I beat him at Scrabble last night!"

"*Re-native* didn't count, Mouse!"

"Jenna used 'renege.' It's the same thing, only with Indians."

"Not everything." RB III tosses the newspaper into a

wastebasket. "After I discovered airplanes, I barely passed
freshman physics."

Jenna caps her pen. She's apparently genuinely interested,
in contrast to when I expound on topics such as where to
place the soup spoon. Maybe because her passion for horses
rivals his passion for flying. My passion for him returns suddenly. I really prefer making love during daylight.

"Then the most important thing Pomona College had to
offer me was a bedroom near Cable Claremont Airport,
where I parked my Cessna 140."

Jenna interrupts. "You're better than my dad at English
and math."

Which surprises me. She usually is supportive of her father. My elder daughter continues, "Remember when we
calculated the time necessary for a rocket to reach escape
velocity? No one else in the class answered correctly. Even
Sister Ann wasn't sure."

"Daddy draws super pictures of George Washington,"
Mouse defends.

"What can you do, Lolly?"

I'm jarred just like the time Dr. Shonburg asked what I
was good at. "I marry great men." Margot said it better:
"The thing about Lolly is she marries well." I picture myself
in twenty years on a shopping spree with Paul and Reg looking like that photo taken in Paris of John Derek with Bo and
Ursula.

My answer must embarrass Reg. He hastily adds, "Lolly
taught drama for five years at University High School."

Interesting he'd be proud of that. The nice thing about a
second marriage is that you're easily impressed with each
other. In the same vein, you compromise readily, not having
a lot at stake yet.

"Are you an actress, Lolly?"

We'll find out on the witness stand. "Margot and I played
in *Hamlet* at UCLA. She was the queen. And I Ophelia."

"Get thee to a nunnery." Reg shows off his knowledge.

"That was a euphemism for whorehouse!"

"You a nun!" My stepdaughter cracks up. She glances from me to her father. I feel she's flirting with him. "Lolly's hardly *celibate.*"

"It's one of her new goals."

I gulp hot buttered rum, refilling my cup, yet again, from the Thermos on the coffee table. "Come on! We've missed two evenings, is all."

"Longer!"

"No. Tuesday night—*Catcher in the Rye.* Wednesday—*Peyton Place.*"

"*Appointment in Samarra!*"

"That's a short book. You were up when I came to bed."

"What else is new?" He winks. I grimace. So does Lynda.

"Mom did a TV commercial once." Mouse stretches. "She bought me a ten-speed with the residuals."

"Why aren't you in a series like that lady Margot instead of sitting around here?" A perplexed expression contorts Lynda's mouth like a bulldog's. This question must never have crossed my own daughters' minds. The three girls turn their faces toward me as sunflowers bend in the sun's direction.

Sitting up—it isn't all that easy after a quart of hot buttered rum—pulling my knees to chin, and locking arms around, I think of Margot Haggerty and how the paths of our lives diverged. Diverged? Wow, I must be tipsy. (The other time I drank too much was on a college date with Paul Whitman. I barfed on his leather upholstery. He almost dumped me because of it, sold the car to get rid of the smell.)

In town, I had fears of "missing out." But not in the country. Is it because here there's nothing to miss? Or am I truly "on hold," as I explained to Anneke?

Maybe it's my dormant period. Like a seed blown from an old dandelion, I wait to sprout again. Seriously, today it is enough for me when Jenna says, "Mom, come watch this Bogie-Bacall movie."

Or "Mom, stay a minute. OK?"

My mother did the same for me, and Grandmother Bedell for her. Good mothers beget good mothers as surely as child beaters beget child beaters. Is good mothering a worthy objective? A sufficient objective? All I can say is that Mouse's Pepsodenty good-night kisses satisfy as surely as audience applause.

I suspect that Margot, for all her success, envies me on some level. When Reg and I attended her gala "Virgo" party last month, she showed me off like a prize broodmare. "This is my friend Lolly. She has four *children." I refrained from quipping, "The two-year-old's running in the ninth at Santa Anita."*

Out loud I say, "Two paths converged in the woods and I, I took the one *most* traveled by."

"Robert Frost?" Mouse assumes we're playing Quotes.

Jenna corrects: "It's *least* traveled by."

"You know how Nana and Pops Whitman slaved away at drab jobs, working toward retirement their whole life? Then Pops died the first month in Florida?" I slur an occasional word. Anything I say will sound heavy-handed. I can hear Jenna. "Cut the lecture series, Ma."

"You could be on TV!" Lynda pushes.

"Do you want a career, Lolly?" I detect a slight note of panic in my husband's voice.

"I think one should enjoy . . . his hour upon the stage." I burp—bad timing! "Let's say I'm 'on hold'!"

"It can be very trying to be kept in the holding pattern over an airport."

"Sister Kathleen offered me a job. Teaching drama at St. Anthony's." Am I digging an escape tunnel—just in case? I don't even think I'd like the classroom these days. A friend reports students now dribble basketballs on the stage instead of memorizing lines.

"Would you like to?"

I shrug.

"We can order season tickets for the Ahmanson Theater in LA." Is Reg trying to pacify me?

"There's a little theater group here," Jenna says. "I saw an ad at the community center. They're doing *The Wizard of Oz* during Christmas vacation."

"Oh, Lolly! Let's try out!" Lynda begs.

"Who'll play Judy Garland? You or me?"

My husband nods as if to say, "Whew, that's taken care of."

"Mommy, I didn't get it about Pops Whitman going to Florida to die."

"Oh, Mouse! There's nothing to get!"

"Should you have another drink, Lolly?"

"When I grow up, I want to be what Daddy is." Richie sounds serious. "What *are* you, Daddy?"

The telephone rings. I check my watch. Bev is right on schedule. She's taken to telephoning every four hours on one pretext or another.

Reg answers the call at his desk.

"Hello?" . . . "Sorry. We have plans for the weekend. We're going camping at El Capitan. Returning late Sunday night. You can see the children Monday morning in *court*. Son, it's Mom."

"We're going camping?" Lynda asks as her brother accepts the receiver from Reg, climbing upon his father's lap.

It's news to me. But I second the idea. This state park on a wooded bluff overlooking a pretty stretch of beach above Santa Barbara is one of my favorite spots. If we're lucky, the blue-skied Indian-summer weather will hold. I start planning cook-out menus.

"Hi, Mommy. I fell off the motorcycle again. I have to go now. Here's Lynda."

They treat the receiver like a hot potato.

She listens for a while, whines, "How gay!" and hangs up.

Bev's call effectively hushed the four children. Is her plan
to terrorize? I'm reminded of our interview at St. Anthony's.
The kids acted subdued then, too. After the principal
dismissed them, I faced her alone. I close my eyes, remembering.

"*Have these youngsters ever attended a parochial school,
Mrs. Bennett?*" *The Irish nun looked as strong and service-
able as good linen.*

"*They've attended other private schools,*" *I answered evasively, fiddling with the cuff of my silk blouse. The kids and
I had overdressed for the meeting. The Mexican mother
waiting in the foyer wore a cotton shift and flip-flops.* "*Did
they do well on the entrance exam?*"

"*Extremely high scores.*"

Were the good marks showy, like my clothes? "*They're
coming from excellent school districts. . . .*"

"*Why do you seek admission to St. Anthony's?*"

"*Because I desire the best education available.*"

"*And the closest?*" *the nun accused. She must have
known about the hour-and-fifty-minute bus ride into Fillmore.*

St. Anthony's red-tile-roofed convent, church, and school
—all connected by covered arcades—sprawl mission-like in
the middle of rolling fields only twenty minutes on Highway
126 from the ranch. Besides, I could car-pool with the
Van Vetchens.

Resigned, conceivably, to enroll my family because of Anneke's father's recommendation, Sister Kathleen lifted her
spectacles and rubbed where they pinched her nose. I examined the nun's exposed face. Blue eyes broke through the
pale complexion as patches of sky often appear on a cloudy
day. Several reddish curls slipped from the confines of the
wimple.

As Sister Kathleen Donovan speaks, I try to imagine her
as a child, see the lass bicycling through the streets of Dublin, thick braids flying. She stops at the grocery store to buy

*onions for her mother's stew, dallies to pet the owner's cat.
Puss sleeps on the doormat, undisturbed by the tinkling bell.
Mr. Flanagan calls out, "Katie my girl, you forgot your
change. You'd forget your head if it wasn't fastened on."*

". . . *serve the children of well-to-do ranchers. A far cry
from the poor of Dublin our convent pledged to educate,"
Sister finished as my mind wandered back. She stared outside, possibly at Jenna, Lynda, and Mouse, who dangled
from monkey bars in full skirts.*

*Did she miss Ireland? Were we both expatriates? Except,
I'd moved only ninety miles north. I glanced beyond the
playground to the rolling hills—not like white elephants
(would Sister know the Hemingway reference?) but scoops
of peanut-butter ice cream. Richie's current favorite flavor.*

*"You're stuck here, aren't you, Sister, in this Godforsaken
place?"*

"No place is Godforsaken, Mrs. Bennett."

"Oh, sorry!"

*"I think the Santa Clara River Valley is lovely. Especially
in spring. Then the air smells of orange blossoms. Or even in
winter after the first rain."*

*"Yes! Reg brought me out for a picnic when we were dat-
ing last January! I told him that the seeded barley seemed to
unfurl quickly like plants in Disney's time-lapse photog-
raphy. The bright green fields were so refreshing! I guess
that's why Listermint uses that color for mouthwash."*

*"If you'll forgive my curiosity, Mrs. Bennett. What do you
do on the ranch? You . . . well, you're not my typical parent, I suppose you know."*

*"I watch sunsets. I can study a sunset through the entire
cocktail hour without craving a dry martini. Usually." I repeated exactly what I'd told Margot, who had asked the
identical question earlier.*

*"Anneke Van Vetchen explained a little about your mov-
ing here. But I'm not so sure the country will suit you." The
nun rose to terminate the interview, "Thomas Wolfe said*

*you can't go home again. Although perhaps what is even
more difficult is leaving in the first place."*

Sister's words stained my mind like spaghetti sauce on a
white blouse. The air in her office suddenly seemed close. I
left quickly, muttering a good-bye.

"Lolly." Lynda shakes my arm. I must have dozed off.
"Can we make cookies for our lunches tomorrow? Those
fig-roll things of yours are disgusting."

"Willie Tucker calls them turds."

"I bought chocolate chips," Reg confesses. "The kids lob-
bied to stop at the store on the way home from school."

"Traitor!"

"Can we, Mom?"

"OK. But also make a batch of oatmeal to take camping."

"Are we really going camping?" Lynda wonders.

Mouse asks him, "Have you ever gone before?"

I feel better after my short nap. I envision the six of us
roasting marshmallows over an open fire while the setting
sun bloodies the Pacific Ocean. Camping invigorates me.
Why do I love it and not life at the ranch? Because camping
is temporary.

"Let's pack lightly," Reg suggests. "Take only necessi-
ties."

"You mean like a bottle of rum?"

"My transistor radio," Lynda adds.

The four children bake cookies in the kitchen, which in this
small house is adjacent—perhaps ten feet away. Through the
arched doorway I overhear Jenna confide to Lynda, "I think
my mom's had one too many. I have not been allowed to
cook anything decent since March of 1969."

"Was that the same month she gave that speech on talking dirty?" Mouse asks.

"No. You weren't even born then."

"Mommy said war and hate were the only bad words she

knew. That the f--- word was just an impolite way to describe something natural. Same with the --it word."

I had forgotten the profanity lecture. My daughter's total
recall touches me. Closing my book on a marker Lynda
crocheted, I peer over the sofa back. The children ring the
oak table.

"Lolly said you could use the f--- word?" Richie seems in-
credulous. I can hear it now in court.

"Sure. Well, if you wanted to be impolite."

"Are you allowed to be impolite?" Disbelief.

Mouse evidently is stymied. "Jenna, are we allowed to be
impolite?"

"Mom doesn't come right out and disallow anything. But
we're expected to choose appropriate behavior. Otherwise,
she's (my teenager mimics me) *very* disappointed.' You
have to learn to translate her. Don't be fooled for a minute
and think you can leave your bed unmade."

Mouse chimes in: "Or get a bad grade in math. Mommy'll
tell you to start enjoying long division."

"People always think *your* mom is nice." Lynda seemingly
acts resentful.

"She is!"

And Dr. Kravetz wondered why I love Mouse so much?

Richie repeats, "Well, can we be impolite?" I think he is
still pliable, soft like Play-Doh, hoping to be molded by his
father, not Abdul or Hiroshima or Dirt Bag. There's not
much future in hanging ten.

"No. Mom'd be too disappointed. When she says 'I'd really appreciate it *if*,' that's an order."

"Getting slapped is simpler," Lynda says.

Richie maintains, "Lolly doesn't order me around."

"Yes she does," Jenna advises. "It's just that you're still
fooled by her sweet words."

"I like Lolly," my stepson protests.

"Pst! Reg!"

He whispers from his desk, "I heard." We share the moment, as children do each other's chewed gum.

I motion him to join me on the sofa. We cuddle together and spy upon the kids. It's like creeping downstairs on Christmas Eve, except he sticks his hand under my blouse.

"You're boozed," Reg comments, indulging in what fifties morality labeled "heavy petting."

"Not now. The nap revived me."

"I wish my mom would let us stay here."

"Atta boy, Richie." I speak behind a needlepoint pillow that I hope shields my words.

"Wouldn't she? If you told her you wanted to?" Mouse trades a ball of raw dough for chocolate chips.

"No."

"Did you ask her?"

"She said I *have* to live with her because she's my mother."

"Reg! It's wrong for Bev to talk to Richie that way! Scheffer warned us. That will go against her in court."

"Or the judge will rule it to be normal talk for a *woman*."

"Mommy said Lolly will always favor you two."

I clench my fists.

Jenna licks the spoon, which she then thrusts back into the batter. "I think she'd bend over backwards to be fair. You know, like how mothers always treat guests better."

Richie laments, "My mommy doesn't allow guests. She used to tell me if I had to play with Curly Hodges, do it at his house."

At times I've wanted to say that but lacked the nerve.

I remember back a couple of nights ago. *Reg's ex telephoned later than usual in an agitated state and asked to speak to me. She may have been drinking.* (Look who's talking!) *I could hear a TV blaring in the background.*

"*Lolly?*"

"*Hi, Bev.*"

*"I just found the pictures from the shower you gave me
for Lynda. God, I was a blimp!"*

"Do you have a shot of the cake?"

"There's one of Reg's mother and your mom."

"Oh! Can I have it!"

*"I'll stick it in the mail. What about me holding Jenna?
She looks to be about a year old."*

Who deserves custody of that picture?

*"Also, I dug out my daughter's christening album. Do you
realize you and Paul are her godparents?"*

How complicated! I'd totally forgotten. He and I must
send along a leather-bound Bible next Christmas.

*"Lolly, ask Reg not to take this case to trial. If the mother
and father can't decide where their kids should live, how
can a total stranger? Let me have them. They're my children, for Christ's sake. Could you survive without yours?"*

I try to cover my nakedness with a dish-towel sarong. I'd
been in bed when the phone rang. "No."

Silence.

I didn't know what else to say. I almost asked how
Miriam Kravetz was.

*"Hey, I don't pretend to be mother of the year. But
Lynda's my little girl. She looks just like me, for God's sake.
Every time Reg sees her he must cringe. And, Jesus, Richie's
my son. His first word was 'Mmmmmma.' I love them. My
brand of love may be . . . well, unconventional. But I'm still
their mother. Talk to Reg, please. I can't. He despises me.
Because I wounded his manly pride. Even though I always
said he was good in bed!"*

*"You did say that. I remember. You claimed he had phe-
nomenal staying power."*

"Exhausting!"

I nod.

*"Listen, I'm begging you. Begging. On my hands and
knees. I know Lynda misses me. So does Richie. Don't they?
Don't they miss me?"*

Oh, wow. Here I am again back in The Miss Fit dressing room. "Sure."

"I miss them."

"Who are you talking to?" Reg called from the bedroom. Knowing he listened, I gave a programmed speech. "Bev, we've completely rearranged our lives to provide the four children with a wholesome environment here at the ranch."

"How can you stand that place?"

"Have you seen Dirt Bag?"

"Lolly, tell my ex-husband I'm going to get the children." Her voice, which had been soft before, like cooked squash, toughened.

"OK, but—"

"And I don't care who gets hurt in the process. Understand? Do you understand, Lolly Whitman?"

"Bennett. Lolly Bennett."

Bev hung up.

Now I glance back toward the kitchen. Lynda fiddles with the eyelet trim on my best apron, which the child borrowed without permission. "I hate sharing a bedroom."

Reg winces. But I hear what his pubescent daughter really says. Possibly because we are similar in some ways. Lynda's statement decodes, "Hey, Mouse, do you mind sharing a room with me?"

"If we stay here and build, the new house will have five bedrooms! She knows that!" My husband sounds exasperated.

"My room was so big back on Milan Avenue that I was afraid to sleep there alone. The Blue Monster Man hid in the closet." Mouse apparently doesn't take personally Lynda's declaration about hating to share.

"The Blue Monster Man didn't move out here, did he?" Richie asks.

"No."

The lad nods. "It's safe here. Like King's X."

"Jenna, would you rather live with your dad?" Lynda seems to dismiss Mouse and Richie.

No response. Jenna is not really nonverbal, but has learned the power of the unspoken word. Reg and I exchange glances. None of the children speak. An adult would be unable to bear the silence.

"Would you?"

"It's better for Mouse and me to stay with our mom. Dad has to work every day and needs some social life on weekends."

I cross myself, backwards. Anneke insists it's from watching Jackie Kennedy on TV. Her left would be the viewer's right.

"Bless you, Jennifer Catherine!" I whisper.

"Jenna's a clutch hitter, all right," Reg agrees.

"What if he wanted you to live at his apartment? It sounds like a pretty swinging pad. Right on the beach."

"Daddy has a water bed," Mouse informs, "and an ice maker."

"Or don't you like Sheri?" I'm amazed at Lynda's savvy. Reg now has one hand inside my jeans. I'd score maximum points in a junior-high slam book for Below the Waist.

Jenna concentrates on stirring the batter. "Dad's taking Mouse and me skiing at Park City, Utah, for two weeks this Christmas."

"Do you like Sheri?" Lynda pries.

"Mommy said Daddy wouldn't love anyone who wasn't OK," Mouse admits.

Lynda sighs in a dramatic way. "Children have to come through divorce flexible, with an extended family."

Reg asks, "What?"

"I sent away for *The Children's Book About Divorce*. It's replaced *The Book of Lists* as her secular Bible."

"I hope I don't have to talk in court," Richie says. "I stutter."

"Me either," from Mouse.

"I won't," Jenna exclaims.

Lynda acts knowledgeable. "We have to meet with the judge in his chambers."

"No!" Richie cries.

"I won't say anything." Jenna sucks on the stirring spoon. Does she suspect we're listening?

"The judge'll make you."

"How can he? I didn't confess to Father Sweeney."

"I did! And I asked him if Reg would go to hell for shooting our horses."

"Shooting horses?" Reg whispers.

"You said you were going to if the kids didn't clean out the water trough."

"No!" he protests.

"Yes!"

"What did Father Sweeney say?"

"He asked if we attended church."

"Reg, let's go for a walk." I speak in a normal voice, so the children will hear. I can't take any more. Fighting for equal shares of bowl scraping, under an old Tiffany lamp, Jenna and Mouse and Lynda and Richie resolve aspects of their relationships.

These decisions will hold regardless of any judge's decree. At this very moment, I love the four of them so much that my insides feel as though they'll puff out like the fruitcake we baked in Campbell's Soup cans last Sunday. The aftereffects of hot buttered rum help.

"You know how I can tell you're boozed?" Reg replies, readjusting my blouse. "Because alcohol deadens your senses."

"The cold air will sober me up." It's what he wants to hear.

15

"A far cry from The Bistro"

My mood blackens to match the night. Reg and I saunter silently up the barn road, taking our second walk in the past three hours—this time after dinner. The children's continued soul-searching, while washing dishes, scares us away. Distance has silenced their confused voices. Looking back from atop the hill, the house appears ghostly with amber, cat's-eye windows.

The air feels damp and smells of fertilizer, and the dirt shifts under foot like quicksand. We frighten an owl. Resembling a Halloween cutout, the bird hangs eerily in front of us before darting away. Bats follow, wings flapping.

"I'd like to have a videotape of that kitchen scene to play back in court."

"You sound like Lance Haggerty." I turn the collar up on Jenna's new, oversized St. Anthony's windbreaker, recalling how strange the parochial school seemed last May. My daughter's snug ski jacket with Scout Day patches sewed to the back in a tic-tac-toe pattern brought whispered scorn. No one else owned Wallabies.

"Hear the coyotes?"

"I hate that yowl."

"In Texas they call them 'yoties."

"*Hate* it!"

"It takes a long time to grow accustomed to their yapping. Some people never do. My mother never did."

Reg's statement crystallizes into something solid, a piece of quartz to add to the many collector's items that constitute a marriage. For some time, we stand shoulder to shoulder without speaking. I see the horses grazing close together, the donkey—Don Quixote—just ahead. Cows huddle in the next pasture, a calf bawling noisily for its mother.

"Lolly, . . . what if we lose the children?"

His words dangle in the air like the bats.

"Will . . . will you go back to town?"

Does he mean alone?

"I know these past six months have been difficult for you. Remember when you said you were a better person at the ranch just like one's tennis game improves when playing with a more skilled opponent?"

"With *you*. I said when I was with you I was a better person." Besides, we were making love, so my words didn't count.

"I think you've done well here."

Liar!

"Real well."

"Except when I locked the horses into the pasture with the orange trees and Super Star almost foundered on citrus fruit."

"I'd forgotten that," Reg admits.

"Or that time I fed Don Quixote a leftover carameled apple that stuck her teeth together."

"That was pretty stupid!"

"And the night I—"

"Still, I am proud of you!" His compliment is a throwaway line. He knocks manure from his boot heel. We're not listening to each other. I'm not even saying what's on my mind, which is: "If we joined forces and moved here to raise a blended family, is the Game Plan still valid without Richie and Lynda?"

I try to picture living in a condominium on Pasadena's swanky Orange Grove Avenue, me and Jenna and Mouse. Reg?

As if he could read my mind, my husband says, crossly, "Jenna and Mouse don't want to leave, Lolly. They like it here. Hell, last week Jenna made varsity volleyball. Mouse was elected president of the fifth grade."

RB III doesn't mention that Lynda won a place on the pep squad and I spent forty-three bucks on her uniform. Has he given up already? If he goes into court defeated, we will be. Or is this man simply doing a selling job on me?

"Have you heard the latest?" I change the subject. "Mouse and Richie are both 'going around' with people."

"What's that?"

"Mouse explained 'going around' means a boy and a girl are designated as friends so they can be nice to each other without being teased."

"You're talking about my son? Richie?"

"The girl asked *him*."

Reg shakes his head.

"But Tommy Hernandez propositioned Mouse. I met Tommy's mother for the first time at the water slides the day the children were kidnaped. She invited me to lunch last week."

"Did you accept?"

"We ate at a swinging joint on the highway called Rosie's. Even the napkins were greasy."

The cowboy looks away.

"A far cry from The Bistro, I must say, but Dos Equis is Dos Equis."

Reg pulls me close, roughly, like reefing in a sail. Does he hope to offer comfort?

"Mrs. Hernandez is in charge of Catholic School Day at Magic Mountain. I'm supposed to drive ten boys from Richie's class. A week from Tuesday."

"If he's still here."

"I'll have to go anyway. She needs drivers. Mrs. Hernandez thinks the four children are mine. Everyone at St. Anthony's does."

"You'd want to move back, wouldn't you, Lolly?"

I hide my face in his chest.

Later, Reg and I sip Grand Marnier with a twist of tangerine peel. The empty hot-buttered-rum Thermos from this afternoon still litters the coffee table. I can't concentrate on tonight's book: *The Hite Report*. It is long after the children padded off to bed in their footed blanket-sleepers, pink for the three girls, who look like small, medium, and adult rabbits, blue with LA Rams insignia for Richie.

The night grows chilly, colder than in Pasadena. After our walk, I changed into a sweat suit, which I pulled on over a ski sweater and Danskin leg warmers. We have only the cookstove and the fireplace for heat. The children made fun of me when I wore a stocking cap and neck scarf indoors.

I rub my hands together, feeling contentious because I'm cold—maybe a heated argument will warm me up. "The children have got to resent being yo-yoed."

RB III pokes a log. Sparks burst forth like Fourth of July fireworks. "I believe Lynda and Richie's biggest fear is the judge will put them on the spot. Make them choose between Bev and me."

"Did you guys talk today when you went for the mail?"

"Sort of. Lynda's reluctant to discuss the subject."

"The court won't ask a child where he prefers to live? Not at their ages?"

"Scheffer says the judge won't be direct. He'll try to second-guess them."

"Does Scheffer know whose courtroom we'll be in?"

"The Honorable Carl Petersen."

"Petersen knows me!"

"How could he?"

"He and my grandfather were acquainted."

"Impossible!"

"I guess my grandfather was much older. Anyway, Gramps disliked Petersen. I don't know why. There were a few ugly exchanges between them."

"Petersen won't remember you."

"One Easter Sunday at Annandale I threw a chocolate bunny at him."

Silence.

Then I asked, "How do you second-guess?"

"Have the children talk about school."

"Richie will say he can't stand St. Anthony's. He hates wearing a uniform."

"Doesn't he like his teacher?"

"The shirts are slipover. Don't have buttons. And he despises that."

"Sister Colleen?"

"She's so sweet. And *pretty!*"

"What a waste!"

"I *used* to feel that way."

"What does that mean?"

"Those sisters have something I lack."

"What's that?"

"Peace of mind."

"The judge will see through Richie's objections."

"You have more faith in judges than I do."

"Richie wants to live here. That's obvious enough."

"I don't know. It's awfully difficult to turn your back on your own mother. Remember how he ran to Bev in the hospital lobby. When we met with Kravetz?"

"Lynda stayed by my side."

I nod.

"What . . . where do you think she wants to live?"

I shrug. "It's awfully difficult to turn your back on your own mother. But it's equally hard to give up a cheerleader position."

"That's ridiculous!"

"I can tell you were never a cheerleader."

"Sometimes you act like my ex-wife is an Auntie Mame. But Auntie Mame's outrageousness was diluted by common sense and a goal in life. Bev lacks both. She also has a quick temper and no concern for the world beyond herself." Reg downs his brandy like medicine and inquires, "What do you think Lynda and Richie will tell Petersen?"

For a moment, backed up to the fireplace, I feel as though Reg and I are talking in the warm confines of a car parked at a drive-in theater. The movie on the screen may be frightening, but we can turn away from it and hold hands. My despair (anger?) melts like butter in a hot pan. Possibly it's just the brandy settling down on all that hot buttered rum. How will I last another couple of days? There isn't enough liquor in Ventura County. "I don't imagine they'll speak out against Bev." I finger his cheek.

"True."

"Why don't we take off our clothes and discuss this in bed?"

"Bev never cooked breakfast. She'd stay up late playing solitaire or telephoning friends, then sleep until noon. I fixed the pancakes and readied the children for school. Lynda left with a crooked part until she learned to wield a comb."

"Maybe smoke a joint and play slave. First I'm yours and then—"

"I've cared for those kids for years."

"—you know what I'd *really* like to try?"

A wolf-like howl emanates from the next room. It scares the wits and passion out of me. I spill my drink and start shivering.

Reg runs into the combination playroom/bedroom Richie and Jenna share. Slowly, I follow. My daughter sleeps undisturbed in the loft section, covered by an electric blanket in her bundle bag. She claims it's easier to roll that up than make a bunk bed.

"Richie! Everything's OK. You're just having a nightmare." I bump into Reg, who's carrying his son toward the living room.

"I . . . I dreamed Mommy put me in a cage and when she slammed the door, it locked on accident. I called. But she didn't hear. Oooooowwhhee!" He burrows into his father's arms.

Holding the sleeping boy, my husband rocks in the rocker, humming "Home on the Range."

I'm mesmerized by the rocking.

"Lolly?"

"Yes?"

"Am I wrong to seek custody?" Rock. Rock.

A burnt-out log falls, sending a puff of smoke up the chimney.

"Tell me if I am," rock rock rock.

I gulp my remaining Grand Marnier.

"If it would be in their best interests," rock rock rock, "Lynda's and Richie's," rock rock rock, "then I will concede."

I don't speak.

Rock. Rock. Rock. "Should we take Bev on in the courtroom?"

I want to ask whether or not he would require me as a housekeeper if Bev won custody. Who ever heard of children holding a second marriage together?

Rock. Rock. Rock.

I'll do floors and windows and give blow jobs . . . maybe not floors and windows.

"You ready for a fight?" rock rock rock.

Eventually I nod.

He nods.

We both nod. It's like oncoming drivers signaling with high beams in the night.

"It's going to be rough, you know."

"I know." But I didn't really. The same way you don't know about childbirth beforehand.

"Hey, that slave thing sounds groovy. Give me a minute to tuck Richie in."

"What slave thing?"

Much later.

"Are you awake?"

"Yes. Are you?"

"Yes."

We grope for each other like blind people moving through familiar territory. It surpasses anything reported in the Hite book.

"Reg, how would you rate me as a housekeeper?"

"Worthless."

"Worthless?"

"Lolly," he whispers, "I can bear to lose Lynda and Richie if I have to."

"Yes?"

"But . . . but not you."

"Darling!"

"We'll move back."

Before I can answer, the alarm rings.

16

"A permissive mother?"

Sitting on the stand, I muse that it will take years for me to sift through the events of the past couple of days, like firemen searching ashes and rubble for valuables and signs of arson.

"Do you consider yourself a permissive mother?" David Weintraub cross-examines. Scheffer objected the first time Bev's attorney badgered me, but the Honorable Carl Petersen overruled. Neither lawyer asks the right questions. Ours had requested, "Describe life on the ranch with the children." I wish I hadn't gotten so carried away telling how the three girls brought the pony into Reg and my bedroom.

"The word 'permissive' has negative connotations," I hedge, my eyes darting about the courtroom. The entire cast of characters gather. Like wedding guests, they sit to the

left and to the right fenced in by a gated barricade. Reg is
flanked from behind by Paul, Sheri, Margot, Lance, Pearl,
Anneke with her kids, my parents looking respectable and
unscathed. Bev's group consists of her parents, her sister,
and Dirt Bag.

At the counsel table, my husband perches on the edge of
a chair, sending me facial twitches of love: nose-crinkling,
winks, which I *feel*, as if we were plugged into each other
by an electric cord. Beside him, Scheffer offers no clue.
Rumpled hair and face and suit, the learned gentleman
shuffles through a myriad of papers.

Weintraub circles before me—perhaps performing a rain
dance, spiffy in C & R Clothier's gray sharkskin with suede
patches. His lithe body is held erect like a fourth grader at
Cotillion. Halting abruptly, the respondent's lawyer repeats.
"Are you a permissive mother?"

"I don't believe in spanking, if that's what you want to
know."

"You have never so much as slapped one of the children,
not even in a moment of anger?"

"Never!" Pearl calls.

"I feel physical punishment teaches a child that violence
is an acceptable means of problem solving." I glance at Anneke in the third row, filled by her offspring—hair ribbons
wrapping blond heads like festively tied packages. I don't
mean to sound preachy and mentally implore my friend's
forgiveness, realizing that when pushed she swats bottoms. I
can't. Shonburg theorized that I fear life's fragility. Reg
maintains I save my aggression for him.

"Not even in a moment of anger?" Weintraub pushes,
presumably anticipating my husband's complaint about
Bev's face-smacking.

"Especially not in a moment of anger."

"You defer punishment?"

Aha! He hopes to trap me. "Of course not. That would be
mental cruelty. Discipline should occur on the spot, be a

logical consequence. A child who throws sand in the sand-
box should be removed. When he's ready to try again, he
may go back."

"Try what again? Throwing more sand?"

"Playing nicely." I sound loony, even to myself. You either believe child psychologists or you don't. If you don't,
Gesell, Ginot, and Gordon seem cracked.

I notice our four children grinning at me from behind the
last row. When did they sneak in here? I left them playing
hopscotch near the elevator. Richie's face didn't look that
clean all summer. They are still wearing their St. Anthony's
uniforms. We had expected to send them back to school the
first afternoon with Sister Kathleen, who'd driven into LA to
testify about SRA scores and classroom behavior.

*Resembling Deborah Kerr, the nun had clutched a large
neck cross when she testified on Monday. 'Twas an Irish
lullaby. "I speak for Father Sweeney and the Sisters of
Charity. It is a joy and a pleasure to know this fine family."*

*Her eyes had sought us out. "Reginald and Laurel Ben-
nett. Our fourth-grader Richard. Our fifth-grader Elizabeth.
Our sixth-grader Lynda. Our seventh-grader Jennifer. Perhaps in the future the good Lord will see fit to send us another Bennett for the new kindergarten class."*

*Hearty laughter had followed. Except, Judge Petersen
frowned. Did he figure a baby would crowd Richie and
Lynda's space? I wanted to raise my hand and tell him
about Reg's vasectomy.*

*"Their presence at St. Anthony's has enriched our lives
and our school. May God bless them."*

*Anneke and her children had crossed themselves. Margot
followed suit. She and Lance sat adjacent, directly behind
Annele and Rye. I caught Lance doing his wonderful pig
face for Karla when she wiggled around in her chair.*

Now Weintraub crowds me. "Wouldn't you spank a child
even if he or she broke your favorite pitcher?"

"Especially not if she broke my favorite pitcher. The child would feel terrible enough already."

"What would you do?" Judge Petersen asks as he leans forward on the bench.

"Nothing, assuming the child broke the pitcher accidentally. Oh, I'd offer reassurance. Say, 'Big people, small people, just about all people make mistakes.'"

My younger daughter waves at me.

Weintraub presses his face closer. I recognize his Jovan after-shave. "What if it wasn't an accident?"

"You mean like the time Mouse used a bone-handled carving knife to dissect one of her dead frogs? I simply explained that she needed to find something from the camping gear." I beam at this child, who now gives me the family greeting: booga booga, moving both hands in spirals, fingers shaking.

"What if—" Weintraub lunges toward the spectators. I assume to silence Mouse, although she's made no noise.

"Don't touch her!" I plead as the lawyer stabs a forefinger in Lynda's direction. I'm confused. What did Lynda do?

"—she broke your favorite pitcher?"

Suddenly I vividly remember the incident to which he must be alluding and blurt out, "It was a wine goblet, and I did nothing! Well, maybe I cried a little, but I promised Lynda it was OK. To just be more careful next time. She hadn't realized that it was French crystal. Louis XVI. I bought those glasses at an auction, back when there were still 'finds.'"

"Is it not a fact that you upset Lynda so much with your carrying-on that she locked herself in the bathroom?"

"She didn't know me well enough to—"

"Are you religious, Mrs. Bennett?"

I'm mentally still dealing with the shattered hundred-dollar crystal goblet. He isn't insinuating that I worship antiques? Stalling, I straighten the tweed jumper Sheri loaned me, pulling the material down to my knees—it hits *her* at mid-calf.

Sunday night, we drove into Pasadena expecting Reg and I would spend one night at my parents' home and the four children would travel back to St. Anthony's with Sister Kathleen and sleep at the convent.

"The case might drag into the second morning, but the judge won't give it any more time than that," Scheffer predicted.

Because we foolishly didn't bring along a change of clothes, I wore the same cotton skirt for two days. The third morning, Sheri loaned me a tweed jumper and brown jacket, plus a choice of blouses.

"Oh, Sheri! How can I repay you!" I hugged her impulsively. She felt sweet and soft in my arms, like a chocolate-cream candy.

"Don't call Paul any more." His girl friend sounded similar to Jenna begging me not to put wheat germ in the pancake batter.

She and Paul dropped the CARE package off at my mother's. Pearl and I answered the door together. The four of us stood in the same dank entry hall where in the early sixties I had descended as a bride. Residue from that moment and countless others stained our greetings.

"The mirror is new," Paul observed. He radiated success in a fawn-colored Cardin suit, coordinated Paisley tie, I didn't recognize the chamois-colored shirt. Perhaps it was a gift from Sheri.

"Old, really. Seventeenth-century Italian." We looked at our reflected images framed in gold leaf making a strange family portrait.

Pearl muttered, "Sheri sounds like something to drink."

"I stuck in some slacks for Reg," Paul explained. "A change of shirts. He's not that much bigger than I am."

"That isn't what I heard!" Pearl tittered.

"Thanks for letting us borrow the clothes!"

My ex-husband seemed reluctant to leave. He always did love mother's house. *"Reg's blue crew-neck sweater and corduroy jacket saw me through college."*

I remember the sweater. *"I didn't realize that wasn't yours, Paul! The night you pinned me the clasp stuck and tore a hole."*

"That was Reg's pin. I could never afford to buy one."

Today in court I feel as though I appear in costume. I want to hold up a card that reads "Mr. and Mrs. Reginald Bennett's outfits courtesy of Sheri," as they do in TV credits.

"We're mildly religious."

"Protestant?"

"Yes."

"Yet you enrolled the children in a *Catholic* school, over their natural mother's continued objections?"

"Why did you do that?" Judge Petersen inquires, obviously shocked.

"St. Anthony's offers the best education in the Valley," I reply lamely, recalling how horrified my own mother was when she found out. I see nothing wrong with a Catholic education. Often, Basic Truths, so evident to others, elude me. I drink the water in Ensenada and wear nothing under long skirts.

"Are the children forced to attend Mass?" the judge asks as his eyes narrow.

"They like to go. Jenna says it gets them out of class. Father Sweeney is wonderful! Terry-Thomas playing the parish priest. With a thick brogue he advises, 'Honor thy blessed mother and turn off the TV set by ten o'clock!' Once, after a favorite teacher died, Father promised, 'Mr. Reese is having fun with Jesus.' I thought that was so sweet."

"Your family attends Mass together regularly?" Sister Kathleen would deem this alleged act worthy. I have the feeling Weintraub intends otherwise.

"Whenever one of the four children is involved. Richie is practicing a play for All Hallows Eve. Halloween. The night before All Saints' Day. He's a goblin."

"What's the ethnic background of the majority of the *Catholic* students at St. Anthony's?"

"Objection!"

Judge Petersen says, "I'm interested in her answer."

I don't want to respond. Not because I feel ashamed of the children's new Chicano friends—His Honor can't say anothing Mother hasn't already—but why should Weintraub single them out? Has he forgotten Auschwitz?

"Isn't it a fact that your ten-year-old daughter is going steady with a *Mexican?*"

Who told?

I can't meet Mouse's bewildered expression. "He was just elected vice-president of the fifth grade!" Besides, how can Bev care? She bears no prejudice against Dirt Bag or Hiroshima or Abdul. That lady is definitely not a bigot. Is her lawyer merely bringing this out so Reg can't attack the ethnic backgrounds of his ex-wife's male friends?

"Tommy *Hernandez?*" The lawyer slaughters this sacrificial lamb.

I sputter, "Tommy—"

"I assume you and Mr. Bennett dated before your marriage. Is that correct?"

"We went out a few times."

"Where were the four children during those evenings?"

"Mine were with Pearl. Reg's with . . . I'm not sure what his sitting arrangements were for Lynda and Richie then."

"Is it not a fact that when you and Mr. Bennett spent that January weekend in Palm Springs—"

"Objection!"

I glance at my mother, motion for her to take the children away. Tough if Petersen wants to speak with them again today. Mouse said his chambers stunk of farts and he asked dumb questions. The other three volunteered nothing.

Jenna, Mouse, Lynda, and Richie trail after Mom like a chain on a semi being dragged along the highway.

Petersen says, "I assume, Mr. Weintraub, you will establish the relevance for this line of questioning. Please continue."

"Did you spend January eleven through thirteen in Palm Springs with Mr. Bennett?"

"I don't remember the dates. We stayed with a friend of mine in Bermuda Dunes during the Bob Hope Classic."

"Were his children with their mother?"

"Bev'd asked for a visitation. She was back from a trip and had some souvenirs. Richie and Lynda hadn't seen her in months—"

"So Beverly Bennett dutifully cared for her kids while you and her *then* husband went gallivanting off—"

"Objection!"

"Sustained."

"Did Mr. Bennett have a telephone conversation with his *then* wife in your presence when you were in Palm Springs?"

"Their divorce was almost final!"

"A phone conversation discussing reconciliation for the sake of the children, which you strongly advised against?"

"No! I said—"

"Objection!"

"I withdraw the question." Weintraub played cat and mouse with me several more minutes, then spit out, "Who did you say usually baby-sat for the children while you and Mr. Bennett went out on dates?"

"*Usually* we planned outings that included the children. Disneyland. Movies. . . ." Oh, shoot! I didn't want to be jumped for those R ratings; I'd better change the subject. "We made a lot of popcorn balls. Stayed at my house and made popcorn balls."

"What happened at bedtime?"

"The children went to bed."

"At your house?"

Where else? Yet I suspect yes is the wrong answer.

"At your house?"

"In the guest room." Truly Lynda preferred to sleep with Jenna in her canopied bed, Richie in Mouse's other twin. I don't know why they changed partners at the ranch—causing Dr. Kravetz to freak. Except, the shrink could argue against two curious adolescent girls being thrown together as well. I remember! Lynda objected to the playroom's bright morning light. The sun rises early over the knotty-pine bunks.

"Would Mr. Bennett leave his children overnight there? When he went home?"

I glance at the audience and bump into my father's stare. "Yes."

"Could you speak up please! I didn't hear your answer."

"Yes!"

"He abandoned his children?"

"No!"

"It sounds like it to me!"

"Reg returned at breakfast time!"

"Oh, that explains why Mr. Bennett's car was seen at your address several mornings!"

"I—"

"Did Mr. Bennett ever spend the night there? It would be logical. His children were tucked in. You had breakfast plans."

"No!" I lie as Scheffer objects.

"They didn't do nothing you wouldn't do!" Pearl defends from the audience. She testified the day before.

The maid waddled down the aisle on wedgies. She'd covered a wig with an ostrich-feather hat I recognized as belonging to my mother. When Pearl passed Margot, the soap-opera fan declared, "I didn't leave until the program was over." *Her advice to Dirt Bag, "Sit up straight, boy. This here's a courtroom."*

Instead of screaming, "Don't separate the mothers from the babies!" the black woman acted so tongue-tied on the stand that she couldn't even pronounce her own name.

"Excuse her," Judge Petersen ordered. "It is obvious she can add nothing. I'm sure Weintraub will stipulate that Pearl Slocum knew Lolly Bennett during the years 1942 to the present and believes her to be a competent mother."

It seemed a victory of sorts.

Now Weintraub repeats, "Did Mr. Bennett ever stay the night at your home in Pasadena? I caution you to remember that you are still under oath!"

I glance at Reg. How many years would I get for perjury? My husband's gaze is steadfast. He seems trusting, like when he lets me push the control wheel on his Baron, nosing the plane up and down like a mechanical ballerina. Scheffer's expression tells me nothing. He could have a full house or zip. I suppose our attorney figures Weintraub has me either way, for making love with children in the house, or fibbing.

Judge Petersen peers over the bench. "We're waiting for your answer, Mrs. Bennett."

The judge's gaze locks with mine as if finely focusing binoculars on the past; I swear that he recognizes me as Martin Bedell's daughter's kid and thinks, "That brat once pelted me with a chocolate bunny." Oh, Grandpa, what should I say? I have not felt this frightened since the elevator doors slid closed behind the gurney that wheeled Mouse into heart surgery.

"Reg camped out on the living room sofa a couple of times."

Weintraub sneers. I suddenly realize how violated rape victims must be made to feel in court. The lawyer eases his slight body toward the table. I rise, thinking my testimony is over. He snaps back toward me like a boomerang. "Please be seated. I'm not finished with you yet."

As I sink down again, Judge Petersen asks, "Did it occur to you that your openly intimate relationship with their father might be detrimental to Mr. Bennett's children? Or do you deem this sort of activity acceptable—according to your permissive philosophy?"

"Objection!"

I look over Reg's mussed blond head to Paul's dark, perfectly groomed blow-dried hair. Did they, as Bev suggested, really have interchangeable parts?

Yesterday, after Paul testified, he hesitated on his way down from the stand and shook hands with Reg, a wonderfully spontaneous kind of action on which the director rules, "Keep it in!" . . . like Brando with Eva Marie Saint's white glove in On the Waterfront.

Reg had invited Paul and Sheri to join Scheffer, the Haggertys, and us for lunch. We crowded into a taxi and sped over to Chinatown.

"Can you imagine speaking out in your ex-wife's behalf?" Sheri cooed, dark hair coiled snail-like above pixie ears. Earlier, Lance had saluted Paul with, "Say, hey, Whitman. Old home week, what?" My ex-husband introduced his girl friend as Ms. Perkowitsch. I hadn't known her last name before. She rode along welded to Paul's lap.

"Why shouldn't he?" Margot inquired.

Lance echoed his wife's statement. "Lolly was a super mother. Remember when Jenna felt sorry for the ants in the ant farm and turned them loose in her bedroom?"

"It was Mouse." Paul and I spoke simultaneously.

Reg requested an upstairs table at General Lee's. Our party hid behind folding screens, visible only to an old oriental couple who quietly dined in the far corner. Paul, figuring his day in court was finished, ordered a round of Singapore Slings.

"Where are the children?" Scheffer wondered.

"Bev's parents took them to Knott's Berry Farm for the day."

"What are Reg's chances of winning?" Sheri asked my husband's lawyer.

"I can't tell." He gnawed on a barbecued rib.

"How do you think it's going?" I inquired.

"I can't read the judge. Except, I'm sure he's anti-Catholic."

"I used to be," RB III admitted quietly.

"I thought Sister Kathleen's testimony was well rehearsed. Very moving." Margot reiterated, "They're a fine family. May God bless them!"

"Maybe if all else fails, she'll let me join the convent."

Reg passed the fried won ton. "So far, so good. Paul, you were splendid. Telling what a capable mother Lolly is. I appreciate that."

They nodded at one another. Perhaps it was a secret fraternity nod, similar to a handshake, because the nodding caused them both to smile affectionately at one another. I felt like a folding gangplank between two ships who've sailed the seas together. The golden dragon painted on the far restaurant wall lacked a jeweled eye.

"Lolly is a good mother," Paul repeated.

I'd rather he said I was a good lay.

"Maybe she should have concentrated a little more on Paul and a little less on Jenna and Mouse," Sheri giggled.

All ignored Sheri and studied their drinks. Paul sat next to me. My foot accidentally bumped his leg; I jerked away from the man who used to shave my crotch so I could wear a string bikini.

"I mean," giggle, giggle, "you can P-TA a person to death!"

Margot raised an eyebrow.

"Sheri, you were sweet to lend me clothes!" I rescued her.

My ex-husband lifted his glass to me in a toast, his way of saying thanks, I imagine.

"No one's mentioned money. Neither side." Lance mulled this over. "Is it passé?"

Scheffer untucked the napkin lodged between his neck and shirt collar. "Everything depends on Bev's testimony. Nothing else matters now. The other witnesses are a dog-and-pony show. Petersen will either fall for her story or he won't."

Hearing this, my stomach closed up as tight as a clam. I laid aside the chopsticks and downed three more Singapore Slings, paid for by Paul, who kept up with me drink for drink. We sneaked glances at each other on the sly. Scheffer noticed. It apparently gave him an idea.

My ex-husband looked billboard handsome, seemed nice. I forgot for a moment how sullen he acted if the girls' bikes blocked the driveway. Had we just met at a party, I'd have flirted with him. Except, I don't flirt any more.

For one thing, Reg exhausts me, and life at the ranch is more basic. When a mare teases a stud, she gets either mounted or killed.

I stuck the gardenias from two drinks behind my ears. Paul helped pull my chair out. We ended up sitting knee to knee in the taxi on the way back to court. I glanced in the rearview mirror once. Sheri perched on my current husband's thighs.

The five of us (sans Reg and Scheffer) collected in the front row of the courtroom like fans at a football game. Scheffer passed back a note that said, "I'm going to put your ex up there again. Clue him in!"

But I couldn't.

Paul had stepped out to the men's room. He returned just as the overweight bailiff called his name. My ex-husband looked startled.

"Paul's smashed," Margot deduced after he fumbled the first several questions.

"*Did the two of you, you and your ex-wife, share a mishap regarding childbirth?*"

"*What's this?*" *Anneke whispered from behind.*

"*He wants Paul to talk about my miscarriages.*"

"*Hospitalization?*" *Scheffer coached.*

Was that a leading question? (Couldn't you lead the other guy's witness, but not your own?) I didn't know and couldn't tell any more anyway. Petersen's rulings confused me. They didn't sound consistent and seemed to favor Weintraub. Our attorney held to the theory that the more credentials you have the harder the judge comes down on you. Being a former family-law commissioner, Scheffer was fair game. Also because he was reputed to be the "custody specialist of the stars." A framed photo of Marlon Brando in sailing clothes decorated his desk.

Weintraub probably wanted the subject of miscarriage introduced. He no doubt hoped to show me as a lunatic who ran around trying to grab off other people's children to compensate for my loss, à la Dr. Kravetz.

I realized something was wrong the third time Scheffer repeated "Hospitalization?" and Paul continued to rub his palms together as if trying to grind corn to meal.

"*Totally smashed!*" *whispered Margot.*

My ex-husband stared at the audience, looking perhaps for clues as to what to say. I gave no sign. The Singapore Slings sloshed in my empty stomach. Paul continued gazing toward me. He must have thought he could suck out information as through a straw.

"*Hospitalization?*" *Scheffer now coaxed.*

Suddenly my ex called out, automatically and at a rapid clip like a professional typist, "Lolly requested that all the machines and the IVs be hooked up in a special way so she could hold Mouse in a rocking chair instead of having her pinned to the mattress like a monkey about to be shot to the moon. Our daughter vomited. The barf ran down my wife's

*nylons into her new Bernardos. I wiped it away the best
I could with my handkerchief but—"*

Judge Petersen interrupted, *"Is he talking about one of
the Whitman children? I have no record of hospitalization."*

Scheffer shrugged.

Bev whispered to Weintraub, who had just risen, *"Mouse
—er, Elizabeth Whitman had heart surgery in 1975."*

"Who pays her medical bills?"

"Paul Whitman," Scheffer retorted after a conference
with Reg.

I stared at Paul. Was our daughter's life-saving operation
to become an issue in other people's battle for custody? This
was more than I'd bargained for. I wanted to scream obscenities at them all.

"I said Paul Whitman pays the bills!" Scheffer sounded
angry.

My ex must have heard his name and taken it as the nod
to continue. The professional typist had quit. Now it was
strictly hunt and peck. *"But the oscilloscope turned blank.
That and the smell of the vomit. I—I panicked and ran. I
don't know where I went."* Paul implored me to believe him
with a sad-eyed stare.

"It's OK," I whispered. He seemed to read my lips.

*"I— I . . . much later. I crept back. The hospital corridor
seemed silent. Deathly quiet. But as I approached Intensive
Care, I heard singing."* He'd found the key he wanted:
*"'Hush, little baby, don't say a word. Daddy's gone to buy
you a mockingbird.' Lolly. She sobbed between the words.
Her tiny voice—she can't carry a tune—sounded so . . .
brave . . . I . . . I couldn't face her. I turned and walked
away."*

Pearl, magnificent in gold lamé (I presume the float was
intended as a bathrobe), called, blowing her nose loudly,
"That's OK, Paul. You had to go find that mockingbird."

"I . . . I walked away."

Tears blurred my vision.

"I'm sorry, Lolly." Paul's voice broke.

"What a sweetheart!" Sheri exclaimed.

"That will be all, Mr. Whitman." Scheffer motioned him down.

Judge Petersen butted in, "Had you planned to bring up the miscarriages? I'd be interested in this man's version. Since he was then married to Lolly Bennett. Dr. Kravetz devoted four pages to the subject in her evaluation."

Margot suggested, "The judge has no sense of drama. Anything Paul says now will be anticlimactic. He still loves you, Lolly. What in the hell kind of a hold have you got?"

"Were there any pregnancies your ex-wife did not carry to full term?" Scheffer asked with a note of resignation.

"Three or four."

"How did Lolly react at these times?"

"She felt very sad. She—she'd cry softly at night when she thought I was asleep."

"Thank you. That will be all."

"Very sad in a normal way," Paul amended.

"Could you be more specific?" Petersen probed from the bench.

"Lolly wanted a large family; I wanted a son."

"Paul!" I gasped, hunched forward in the row of people like a dancer out of step in a chorus line. He'd never said this before. Margot forced me back against the chair, as mothers did with small children in the front of a car before the era of seat belts.

"I guess, on some level, I blamed her when Chip died."

Our shrink, Shonburg, told Paul that. I never believed it.

"Who died?" Judge Petersen referred to his notes.

"A seven-month miscarriage," Scheffer clarified. "You and your wife were understandably upset."

"I . . . blamed her."

"Did Paul and Lolly Whitman seek marriage counseling before they divorced?" Judge Petersen asked, conceivably confused.

What business was it of his?

"Yes they did," Reg informs Scheffer, who repeats it to Petersen.

"You and your wife fully recovered from this tragedy after an appropriate amount of time, didn't you, Mr. Whitman?"

"Objection!"

"Sustained. Please rephrase your question."

"Did you and your wife fully recover, Mr. Whitman?"

Paul seemed unbalanced like a teeter-totter with a fat kid on one end. Yes. Just say, "Yes," I prayed. However, I was curious to know what troubled Paul now. Pearl seemed to have an ear cocked, as did Margot. Did he suspect, as I did, that that was the beginning of the end for our marriage? We could not forgive each other the loss of our son?

Paul focused on me again. He grabbed hold of the stand. I rose slightly. We faced each other across the space like enemy soldiers who've lost their incentive to fight.

Heck, it was a very good war.

"Yes." Paul spoke evenly. "We fully recovered."

"I love you," I mouthed.

My ex-husband did not reply.

"He's all world!" Sheri chirped.

As Paul passed by Reg, my second husband stood to his full height and the two aging fraternity brothers embraced.

Currently, Judge Petersen calls the lunch recess.

The first time I crossed to the stand, I felt confident. Now my legs shake so that I can barely walk. I haven't reapplied lipstick or combed my hair, because we are late returning from Little Tokyo, where we ate with Anneke. We filled three booths at the Lotus Gardens: three adults, eleven children. I think the owner of the restaurant preferred World War II.

During the morning session, Anneke had entertained the whole crew in the courthouse cafeteria. The kids played Klomp It, Electric Battleship, and hide-and-seek under the tables, and bought twenty dollars' worth of desserts. Meanwhile, one by one, I escorted several of the Van Vetchen children to the judge's chambers.

Lunching on fortune cookies, Hendrika refused to squeal. "Petersen asked if any grown-up had told me what to say."

"And?"

"You did, Moeder!"

My girl friend and I chugalugged Japanese beer.

Karla bragged, "When he asked me if the nuns hit us, I said, 'Only with a ruler.'"

Anneke sighed. "I figured out why Paul and Sheri were so gushy about you, Lolly. They're afraid they might get stuck with custody."

"Read that last question," Judge Petersen requests of the court reporter as the trial commences.

The efficient-looking stenographer says, "'Did it occur to you that your openly intimate relationship with their father might be detrimental to Mr. Bennett's children? Or do you deem this sort of activity acceptable—according to your permissive philosophy?' Objection by Mr. Scheffer."

"Your objection has been noted for the record, Counsel. I want to hear the answer."

I don't comprehend if I'm to speak now or not. I place a hand over my mouth against the consequences of gulped chicken teriyaki. Evasively, I reply, "Mostly we took the children to Disneyland."

Weintraub spears me. "We're not talking about Disneyland."

Scheffer sends eye messages, but I can't decode them.

"What *are* we talking about?"

"Your openly intimate relationship with Mr. Bennett. In front of his children."

"You mean hugs and kisses? Holding hands? Maybe a little grab-assing?"

"Is that what went on the nights Mr. Bennett stayed overnight with his children?"

"What's grab-assing?" Petersen wonders.

Can you imagine not knowing? Grandpa did, I'm sure.

"You don't think we had sex in front of Lynda and Richie? Never! We *always* checked to make sure they slept soundly!"

Reg cringes.

Bev smirks. What about her? She's downright promiscuous. Sequentially monogamous at best. Maybe she doesn't do anything with her son and daughter at home. But they are never there!

For some goofy reason, a smile unravels across my mother's face. We exchange glances. Barbara Bedell Andrews winks slyly at me.

"You *always* checked to make sure the children slept soundly?" Weintraub dramatically flaps a typewritten sheet of paper under my nose.

"Who woke up?" I clutch the podium. "Lynda? Of course. Who else? No wonder she knows the six positions. What does that report say?"

"You had several miscarriages during your marriage to Paul Whitman?" the attorney changes course.

"Was it Lynda?"

"Six miscarriages?"

"It *was Lynda!* I'll kill her!"

"Were you deeply affected by them?"

"I–"

"Did you read the psychiatric report?"

"I–"

"Dr. Kravetz concludes that you see Lynda and Richie Bennett as surrogate children."

"I know, but–"

"No further questions."

17

"Court is nothing like..."

On Thursday morning, Reginald Wendell Bennett III mounts the witness stand: a cowboy swinging onto a horse. Reg runs fingertips through his golden hair, tossing it like a salad. He looks undressed, vulnerable, wearing a pinstripe business suit, no boots. It's the same as seeing Santa Claus in underwear.

Margot leans forward to suggest, "At that podium Reg could pass for the President giving a press conference."

Scheffer suddenly stops pacing and drops the routine questioning. "Why indeed, Mr. Bennett, should you, the father, have custody of those two minor children!"

My husband, no doubt unconsciously, loosens his tie. "Be-

cause I am prepared to provide a stable environment for
them."

The words sound as stiff as his collar.

I turn and see Margot shaking her head. The day before
yesterday, she acted her scene perfectly.

*Yes, she'd been present when Jan Van Vetchen fell into the
swimming pool. No, he had not been unattended. Yes, Reg
Bennett rescued the child. No, Richie and Lynda Bennett
weren't in any danger swimming there.*

*Then Helen McElhinney, of "Day by Day," posing as Mar-
got Haggerty, ad-libbed a truly sensational one-act play.
The Honorable Judge Petersen would have granted her custody on the spot had he owned a casting director's couch.
The drama told of the transformation of Lucky-at-Love-
Lolly from Social Butterfly into Earth Mother abetted by
Cute Kiddies and Country-Fresh-Anneke. The turning point
came when Lucky-at-Love-Lolly finally foiled the wily vil-
lain, Corrupt-but-Tempting-City-Life.*

Pearl gave a standing ovation.

*Weintraub asked one question on cross-examination:
"Did you or did you not tell Beverly Bennett on the telephone, when she asked if Richie and Lynda were at the
ranch, quote: 'How in the world should I know? There's a
kid a minute drowning in the pool'?"*

"Mr. Bennett, have you found a school for the children—out
there in the country, where you live?" My husband's attorney's strategy seems to be to pose the standard questions
Weintraub will ask, but in a hostile manner so that Reg's
ready answers sound profound. I pray that the plan doesn't
backfire.

"St. Anthony's serves three hundred of our valley's students. The grammar school, encompassing grades K through
8, is run by Irish nuns. In the sixties, when virtually no
American girls entered teaching orders, the Church looked

to Ireland to 'manpower' her convents. Lolly and I feel fortunate to have our children exposed to these highly educated, charming women. Most of them attended English
boarding schools, except for Sister Shannon. She was abandoned at three months and raised by the Sisters of Charity
in Dublin."

"Then, you like the children's teachers?" Scheffer cuts in.

"The nuns are bright, dedicated, devout, truly inspirational! Why, Mouse is ready to convert!"

My mother gasps.

Judge Petersen raises his eyebrows.

"Is the school a great distance from your ranch?" Scheffer
moves things right along.

"Seventeen miles, twenty minutes each way." Reg acts
confident of his information, having clocked the distance to
school, church, hospital, orthodontist, Cotillion, the beach,
campgrounds, and the zoo in preparation for today. "Unless,
of course, you have a heavy foot."

"What?" Father asks quietly.

"Heavy on the accelerator," I translate for him. The whispered reply, "Reg doesn't drive that sports car of his too fast
with you and the children along, does he?"

There is general laughter from the rest of the audience. I
hear Paul's deep chuckle. I know both my husband and ex-
husband mentally calculate: eleven minutes Porsche time.

Judge Petersen scowls.

"Is this a difficult drive? Unpleasant for the children?"
Scheffer continues.

"Not at all! A fast, four-lane country highway. Nothing
but wide-open spaces and a few friendly truckers. Lolly
feels that this is her special time alone with the children.
They formed a car-pool choir and sang at Mass last week:
'Peter built the church on the rock of our faith' to a disco
beat. My wife drives the morning run and Anneke Van
Vetchen picks up in the afternoon. That way, Mrs. Van
Vetchen can stay to help coach the girls' volleyball team.

Both her daughter Hendrika and Jenna made the varsity."

"How many children are in this car pool?" Judge Petersen asks as he glances at Anneke, who had left her brood behind today.

"Nine," Reg replies.

"How do they all fit into a car?" His Honor demands to know.

"They like to crowd into the Jeep. Oh, sometimes Lynda complains about mussing her hair. But she'd kick if she were in swimming!"

Anneke laughs. Judge Petersen doesn't, but Reg can't see that. My husband has, as they say in show biz, "warmed up." Why did he mention the ranch Jeep and not the roomy VW bus that I now drive?

"Have the children adjusted to St. Anthony's?" Scheffer softens a bit, perhaps no longer confident of his client.

"Mouse was just elected president of fifth grade. My step-daughter says the secret of her campaign was *not* concentrating on the popular kids. She passed out candy to the fat girls and the Mexicans."

This sounded incredibly hilarious when my ten-year-old related it at the breakfast table. It isn't funny now. Margot hisses in my ear, "Get the hook!"

Possibly aware that he's bombing, Reg blurts, "Therefore, I'd appraise St. Anthony's as a not terribly well-endowed but efficiently structured educational institution. A *modest* place. Run on love and devotion."

From the bench, Judge Petersen nags, "Would you consider Flintridge Prep, your alma mater, a 'modest place'?"

"Hardly!" Bev replies to Weintraub in a booming voice. "Reg thinks his kids should grow up knee-deep in cow shit because he wasn't allowed to."

"No further outbursts," Petersen admonishes Bev.

"Are medical facilities readily available?" Scheffer asks quickly. This is one of the weak spots in our defense.

"Forty-five minutes to a hospital. But, heck, sometimes during rush hours it takes that long to drive across LA."

"Can the Whitman child, the one with the heart problem, receive proper and adequate care? Are there specialists in the immediate area?" Judge Petersen seems curious.

Nope. Just GPs. And it used to really frighten me. But I've learned that the farther I am from a hospital, the better off Mouse is. I can't rush her into emergency with the slightest complaint. You don't need a pediatric cardiologist to investigate a stomachache. But Reg doesn't realize how my opinion has changed.

He wrings his hands. "No, I'm sorry to say there are none. But I've told Lolly I'll fly Mouse to Children's Hospital any time night or day."

"How many bedrooms are there at the ranch?" Scheffer anticipates Dr. Kravetz's complaint.

"Currently only three, but we've plans for a bigger house."

"What are the sleeping arrangements?"

"I sleep with Lolly."

Bev snickers.

"Richie sleeps with Jenna, and Mouse sleeps with Lynda."

"Your son sleeps with his stepsister?" Judge Petersen feigns innocence. We all know that he has studied the psychiatric report.

"What's wrong with that?" Anneke asks me. "I've got four kids in one room in two double beds."

"It's a question of propriety," I mutter.

"Oh, cow poop!"

"They share a large room with a loft." Reg pulls against his tie as if it were a noose about his neck.

"Is there a screen or divider of any kind for privacy?"

"The children take turns dressing in the bathroom."

"Bathroom? Singular?"

"One bathroom."

Anneke comments, "My boys pee outside."

"So, in the morning the six of you wait in line?" Judge Petersen seems fascinated.

"I—" Poor, flustered Reg. He doesn't know what goes on in the morning. The cowboy's either off to the mine by 5 A.M. or sleeping soundly.

By the time Scheffer covers the "living at the ranch" versus "life in an apartment with Bev," Reg looks like a victim of the rack. He takes the questions too seriously and tries to be overly fair and objective. "No, I don't think my ex-wife would physically abuse the children."

Finally, Judge Petersen interjects, "Can you tell me, Mr. Bennett, any reason why you believe your former wife would not provide a proper home for the children?"

This stymies Reg. Why doesn't he label Bev a red-haired cunt? The word must not be in his vocabulary. "Well, Bev's not home very much. At least she wasn't home much during our marriage."

"Were you!" Bev lashes out.

"Mrs. Bennett, I've warned you about such outbursts!"

"Lolly is. Lolly's always there."

"I don't want that flake to raise my children!"

"Order in the court!"

Too bad Reg didn't shout that he doesn't want several different men raising his.

Scheffer rushes toward Reg. "Describe the circumstances under which your wife left the family home."

"When she signed over custody to me, Bev professed to want her freedom. She said she'd 'earned' it. I told her that if she left, she could not take the children with her."

Judge Petersen cocks his head. It *does* sound like a threat.

"Bev replied that she hadn't planned to."

A few "ohs" from the spectators on Bev's side. Reg's ex-mother-in-law, Mildred Dinklebauch—her hands folded as if for prayer meeting—sports a ridiculous navy blue straw hat with a daisy that has flopped over the brim. Later, when tes-

tifying, she will swear Reg had read Mickey Spillane on
Christmas Eve instead of stringing cranberries.

"When you say, 'signed over,' are you referring to this
handwritten document which was the basis for the court's
temporary order?" Scheffer waves a sheet of notebook
paper.

Judge Petersen inserts, "That's not an issue now."

"Did you seek a divorce from your wife at this time?"

I think Scheffer expects Reg to say, "Yes," because the
lawyer's hand flies to his temple when my husband replies,
"Bev just wished a separation. I filed later so I could marry
Lolly."

"Oh, Christ!" Margot exclaims, echoing my sentiments,
Scheffer's, too, from the shocked expression on his face.

"Where did your wife go at that time?"

"She moved into a one-bedroom, *adults-only* apartment
with the grand piano that had been a wedding present to
my mother."

"Does she plan to keep the children there?"

"Lynda says—"

"Objection. That is hearsay."

"Sustained."

"Has Bev told you where the plans to live if she obtains
custody?"

"She hopes to have me buy her a small house."

Evidently another surprise to Scheffer. He quickly drops
the subject of the *adults-only* apartment, asks, "Has Beverly
Bennett made an effort to support herself?"

"I give her money."

"Does she attend school?"

"Not that I know of."

"What does she do all day?"

"Objection."

"Sustained."

"Has your ex-wife mentioned to you how she spends her
time?"

"She practices the piano."

"Does she plan a career as a concert pianist?"

"I believe she did at one time. But this is mostly for her own enjoyment. Although she recently held a piano-playing job in Las Vegas! Bev said she couldn't keep our instrument in tune at home. The children always banged the keys. And Richie used to stuff vegetables from dinner into the strings."

"To your knowledge, has your wife been dating other men?"

Reg hangs his head.

"Did she in fact desert her family in order to see a young surfer?"

"Objection!"

"Overruled. Mrs. Beverly Bennett's morals may have some bearing in this case. However, I don't care for sordid details."

"Did she!"

My husband studies his hands.

"First the young surfer? Then a Japanese student? Recently an Iranian nightclub singer who has since been deported?"

"Objection."

"I'll withdraw the question." Smart move. Reg isn't going to answer anyway.

The cross-examination proves worse.

"What in the world is wrong with you?" Scheffer berates Reg during a recess. My husband, his attorney, and I drink lukewarm coffee in a conference room.

"I can't say anything with Bev's mother sitting there," Reg explains. "Besides, I don't want to give Dirt Bag the satisfaction. He keeps grinning at me like the butcher's dog."

"Bev's life-style comes across in her deposition, doesn't it?" I ask hopefully. "Petersen saw that?"

"No. It should be brought out in the testimony."

Scheffer dumps pipe ash into his empty coffee cup. "I

know you want those kids, but let me tell you something.
Petersen's not going to hand them to you on a silver platter.
Not over Kravetz's recommendation. To the contrary. Be-
sides, statistically he favors Bev, despite the efforts of the
United Fathers Organization and the Joint Custody Law,
which went into effect January 1, 1980."

"I know. I know." Reg acts wrinkled like cotton before
perma-press.

"You're making the judge's job easy, pal."

"Maybe Kravetz is right. Maybe I do just want to punish
Bev."

Scheffer grasps Reg by both shoulders. "You go out there
and simply answer yes or no to Weintraub. Don't say anything else if you can avoid it. Get off that stand as quickly as
possible. Do you understand?"

My husband walks dejectedly ahead of us. Scheffer
confides to me, "I misjudged. I figured him for an excellent
witness. He's doing more harm than good. I should have left
you up there longer. We need to crucify that cunt."

Judge Petersen, not Weintraub, detains Reg.

"Do you discipline the children, Mr. Bennett?"

"I don't spank them."

"You never have?" Dr. Kravetz's report belies this.

"Not since I've been with Lolly. She gave me this book
Parent Effectiveness Training, by Dr. Gordon. I only wish
I'd read it before. It would have been valuable when the
children were younger. I'm afraid I used to engage in power
struggles with Lynda."

"Then, you and Beverly Bennett basically agreed on
child-rearing methods when you were together?"

Reg suddenly seems to remember Scheffer's advice. "Yes!"

"When you lived with her, you both pretty much believed
in spanking?"

"Yes!"

I practically leap over the rail, carbonated blood pulsing

through my veins. "Mr. Scheffer! May I go back up there and discuss discipline? The word's a derivative of *disciple*, for Heaven's sake. You don't go around hitting kids, you lead them!"

Petersen calls for order.

"Too late now. You should have made your points when Weintraub asked if you were a permissive mother," the attorney whispers.

Anneke squeezes my arm. "It doesn't matter, the judge's full of sour owl shit anyway."

Weintraub calls Mr. Dinklebauch as his first witness. Bev's father lists his occupation as retired chiropractor. Scheffer cross-examines like a skilled surgeon. Snip. Snip. Snip. Slice. He asks, "When were you last in close contact with your daughter, Mr. Dinklebauch?"

"It's doctor, not mister. Anyway, we had supper together last evening at a Mexican restaurant with her and her new beau, Mr. Weintraub."

"When did she leave home?"

"Bevie had a hankering to move on. She used to sit on the bridge and watch the trains heading west."

"Have you witnessed your daughter's capabilities as a mother firsthand, Mr. Dinklebauch?"

"It's *doctor!*"

Scheffer remains impassive.

"One Sunday each month, Mother and I telephone long distance. At Easter Reg put Richie on. My grandson told me he'd had roast *beast* for dinner. Said his dad cooked a roast beast. He meant roast beef. I got such a kick out of that."

"His dad baked the roast. I wonder where Bev was. That Easter Sunday."

"I think it was a Sunday."

"No more questions, Mr. Dinklebauch."

Weintraub doesn't act perturbed. Perhaps he feels, as

Scheffer does, the case will be decided on the strength of Bev's testimony alone.

After being sworn in, Bev sits demurely, playing continuously with the fringe ends of a macramé belt. She appears Valium-tranquil to me. Reg's ex has stuffed her copper-colored hair into a pillpox hat complete with a veil that half covers her eyes. This enhances the crossed effect, which instead of looking sexy now seems to be a real ophthalmological problem.

Weintraub asks questions quietly. I miss several of them, listening to Margot talking to Paul behind me. She asks my ex if he finds Bev attractive. I strain to hear his answer. Bev's attorney must have been building to a crescendo like an orchestra leader, because she suddenly cries, "None of Reg's friends ever thought I was good enough for him."

"You're not!" Anneke hisses, barely audible.

"Lolly especially. She made fun of me because I wasn't college educated. Reg and her spent hours discussing books and bridge hands. She scoffed because I used stew meat in a beef stroganoff recipe."

"Stew meat!" Mother Van Vetchen seems horrified.

"Lolly's been in love with my husband for twenty years. She stole him away. And now, to make things worse, since she can't have more children of her own, she wants mine!"

The irony of it all! I remember saying to Reg, "Have we always loved each other? Is that why both our marriages failed?"

"Sure," he replied, to shut me up.

Judge Petersen searches through the audience until he locates me. I am now sitting between my mother and father, feeling protected by their club memberships and expensive clothes. Earlier, Lance Haggerty had generously offered to take a turn watching the four children: he seemed glad to have an excuse to bug out to a matinee.

"Stole him away!"

"Shake your head no, Lolly," Paul cautions. "The judge is watching your reaction."

"Liar!" Margot stage-whispers.

"*Hoer!*" Anneke offers in Dutch.

Judge Petersen continues to appraise me.

Mother—I will never forget this—reaches over and presses my hand. She speaks conversationally: "Pretend you're at the White House." I realize how hard this must be on her and am impressed by the Andrews loyalty. Breeding *does* tell. That "Pretend you're at the White House" was the only advice she ever gave me growing up. That and "Don't go all the way."

The support of the surrounding people buoys me like bath water under Richie's yellow plastic aircraft carrier. This love seems tangible. I hope it touches Reg, slouching beside Scheffer at the long table. I swear that Judge Petersen feels it. His eyes sweep over our group. He must be musing, "Lolly Andrews Whitman Bennett couldn't be a home-wrecker. *That's forbidden by the rules at Annandale.*"

The judge glances briefly at Bev's entourage—Dirt Bag, a gal I recognize as the waitress from Two Ee's Drive In, the Dinklebauchs—then back to our side. Instinctively we—my parents, Anneke, Margot, Pearl, Paul, Sheri—square our shoulders. I'm sure we look better qualified to provide an enriched environment for Lynda and Richie. Flintridge Prep, 6; St. Louis High, o.

Weintraub evidently senses this too. He strides forward purposefully. "Did the then Lolly Whitman gain admittance to your home under the guise of friendship?"

"Yes! She even gave me a baby shower. I trusted her. We were confidantes."

"What did she confide to you?"

"She suspected that Paul had a girl friend."

"So the unhappy Mrs. Whitman turned to you and to your husband for support."

"Yes." Bev can't look me in the eye.

"That support, on your husband's part, grew into something else?"

"Yes!"

"That isn't what happened!" I look to Mother for confirmation. She purses her lips.

"Lolly was always suggesting ways for us to be together as couples. Once, I had to entertain some executives. Well, Lolly insisted that we bring these men to her house, so she could see Reg and show off her cooking."

"Did Lolly ever come right out and admit how she felt about your husband?"

"Yes. She said that she loved him."

"Loved him!"

Bev shrugs. "At Lolly's thirtieth-birthday party, at The Bistro, she said it in front of everyone."

"You did! I was there!" my ex-husband maintains.

"Reg had just handed me a bottle of *thirty*-year-old scotch and said the whiskey and I had aged well!" I retort.

"You said you loved Lance, too. And Avery Snider," Paul adds. "Not to mention the waiter who served the cake."

"*Mrs. Bennett,*" Weintraub accentuates the name—which I stole as well—"why did you leave your children?"

"I stayed as long as I could. But finally I couldn't take it any more. It hurt too much to watch her and Reg. The sly looks. The innuendos. *Playing footsie under the bridge table*. I felt helpless. Depressed. Confused. Betrayed. Mixed up. Resentful . . . I— I had to get away. Think things through. It was torture for me to be around Lolly. She was always playing Supermom."

Weintraub points at me. "Lolly Whitman forced you to leave your home."

"I was an emotional wreck. Helpless. Depressed. Confused. Betrayed. Mixed up. Resentful . . ."

Anneke quietly suggests, "If I was in that situation, I'd

throw the bastard out. I wouldn't leave my home. No woman would."

But, listening to Bev, incredible as it sounds, I could believe her story. Rather, I could believe that she could believe it. I probably was in love with Reg back then. Hot shame washes over me like volcanic lava.

". . . Resentful. Living with a husband who no longer desired me."

"Excuse me!" I jump up, stepping on my mother's foot—she doesn't flinch—and make a speedy and ungraceful exit to the ladies' room. Later, after pressing thirty wet paper towels to my forehead, with guilt still clouding my thinking, I conclude that Bev and I perceived the events differently, like two witnesses at a traffic accident. Or, she lied. At any rate, she forgot about Dirt Bag.

I think, "Court is nothing like I expected—hasn't a logical beginning, middle, and end the way legal showdowns in the movies do. It's a pot of mush that the lawyers and judge stir, once in a while turning up lumps."

I'd had a recurring pornographic nightmare—a sort of *Emmanuelle for the Defense*—because I'd permitted the children to see R movies. No one mentioned that. Instead, I'm clobbered for telling Reg I love him at a birthday party eight years before. I was stoned, no doubt.

Not mush, a boiling kettle of chicken soup. The lawyers and judge ignore the meat and potatoes and onions and carrots that constitute our life. They simply skim the grease from the surface of the custody issue.

"Bev is lying!" I yell at the tiled walls.

I try to sneak back down the aisle. When I seat myself, Margot pinches my arm. "Why did you leave? This stuff is fascinating!"

"What's Bev talking about now?"

"Your last miscarriage!"

Bev dabs her eyes with a balled tissue. "Reg insisted on buying Lolly carnations. They were her favorite flower. He

traipsed over to the hospital after work, stayed until late.
And then, when he did come home . . ." Bev blots running
mascara.

"She's been crying for ten minutes," Margot informs.
"The academy award is hers."

". . . he acted so upset."

"Probably because Bev wasn't there!" I quip.

"So worried about *her*."

"Yes?"

"Said the dead baby's name was 'Chip.'"

"Yes?"

"So upset . . . that . . . that I began to wonder if maybe
it wasn't *his* child Lolly aborted."

Mildred Dinklebauch screams.

My mother gasps.

I turn to Paul for solace. His mouth hangs open.

"Ohs" and "ahs" ripple through the audience. As Scheffer
later said, "The tide turned."

The trial for the custody of Richie and Lynda Bennett
was virtually over, thanks to Bev's perjured testimony.

I could just hear Dr. Kravetz: "So that's why you want
Richie, to make up for the illegitimate son you and Mr. Bennett lost."

Great story line, huh, Lance?

"Why did you leave?" Reg turned from the counsel table
to ask. "You should have stayed put. It didn't look good.
Your running away like that."

Bev did squirm a bit under Scheffer's cross-examination.

During the last recess, Reg's ex and I met inadvertently in
the restroom. She borrowed a Tampax from me because the
machine wasn't working. "I couldn't wait to get down from
the stand," Bev confides. "Just my luck to be wearing a
white dress! Is there a blood stain in the back?"

"Bev, how could you say I took Reg away? Didn't you dump him for Dirt Bag?"

"Hey, Lolly. Don't be pissed. Weintraub said my only hope was to give you the shaft. I warned you one night on the telephone. Don't say I didn't. Look, it was just a trial. Are you going to let a thing like that come between friends? Remember Dr. Wilson?"

"My OB?"

"Inexperienced as hell and scared to death." She watches me tuck in Sheri's blouse. "Reg hates flat-chested women. Has he told you?"

Judge Petersen announces his decision immediately following lunch recess, as promised. Not everyone in the audience has returned. Only Reg and I, Scheffer, Bev, and Weintraub listen. Earlier that morning, Scheffer's summation had been brilliant, probably too much so, like shooting a rabbit with a cannon. Weintraub's humbling D+ performance seemed to elicit the judge's sympathy. Americans tend to root for the underdog.

Now the judge floats above the high bench on the black-winged sleeves of his robe, similar to a raven with sighted prey. "I would first like to say that I resent having to make a custody decision for two intelligent adults who should be able to render their own regarding the welfare of their children."

His Honor clears his throat. As he recites the reasons for his decision, it becomes clear that Reg has lost the battle for the custody of Richie and Lynda Bennett. I blank the judge from my mind. Blank the U.S. flag. Blank the California bear flag. Blank the wood paneling. Blank the fat bailiff. Blank the efficient-looking court stenographer with silvered fingernails.

"And I object to sending Protestant children to a Catholic school where they are required to attend Mass."

The audience drifts back in as Petersen rambles on, defending his position.

". . . the primitive nature of living conditions at the ranch. The inaccessibility of medical aid and lack of group activities for the children such as scouting, which would be readily available in town."

Blank. Blank. Blank. I shoot him with my indifference. Group activities! Wasn't Petersen listening when I told about 4H? Richie dislikes the club because it's hard work raising a pig. You have to walk the animal every night. *I visualize the scene in the judge's chambers. "Richie, would you like to be a boy scout?"*

"My uncle made it to Eagle!" Why didn't my stepson say he used to ditch the meetings! That his mother refused to lead a cub den?

". . . a situation conducive to possible incest between a young boy and a pubescent stepsister."

Doubleblank. Doubleblank. Doubleblank.

". . . and I had to take into consideration the fact that Reg Bennett has a loving wife and two charming stepdaughters, whereas Beverly, if deprived of her children, would be alone. Have no one."

Only the United Nations, junior grade.

Blankety-blank. Blank.

". . . and relying heavily upon the recommendation of Dr. Kravetz in her detailed report . . ."

I push off from my seat, as from the edge of a swimming pool, float toward the aisle, into the long, silent corridor that seems an aquarium of trapped afternoon sunlight. I press my head against the fourth-floor window glass. Rain-washed Pasadena lies tucked into the mountains like a shiny Christmas-tree ornament wrapped in purple tissue paper. Then I do what I had wanted to do that awful day in Dr. Kravetz's office and have wanted to do for six months. I scream. I scream, and I kick the wall, beating it with clenched fists.

"Oh, my my my! We're angry, aren't we?" a familiar voice cajoles.

I turn suddenly, bumping into Dr. Miriam Kravetz's bulk. "I had a long rape case and just got away. Although I'm *not* here to testify. Scheffer stipulated to my report. I'm merely curious."

"Petersen's decision sucks!" I sob, letting her hold me as Pearl used to, stroking my long hair.

"There. There."

"Poor kids. Bev'll go out on them all the time."

"You're concerned?" Dr. K. wipes my tears away.

"I love them! I love Richie and Lynda!"

"You have strong feelings about your stepchildren?"

"I'm devastated."

"There. There."

"Bev lied about me!"

"That upsets you!"

"You're not here to testify?"

"No."

"You were against me, anyway."

"Was I?" Plump but nimble fingers loop strands of my hair into soft curls.

In the parking lot, Reg and I wait with Bev for Lance to return from the movie. The sun sets behind the downtown skyscrapers, lighting them like iridescent candles. Margot and Anneke have gone on to The Chronicle for a drink with Sheri and Paul. My parents have driven home with Pearl. "I hope you're going to be a good loser." Bev buckles a trench coat and hooks an umbrella over her arm. Then she lights her own cigarette.

"You wouldn't be," Reg retorts.

"No. But I'll be a good winner." My husband's ex exhales smoke rings.

Lance pulls up, spraying wet gravel. Loud rock music blares from the car radio. Lynda sits beside the actor. The three other children ride in the back seat of the Mustang convertible. Jenna's hair blows like spools of thread unraveling. Mouse's braids bounce. Richie holds on to his Dodger hat.

"We saw *The Empire Strikes Back!*" The boy darts up to us.

Bev hangs back, puffing on her Marlboro. Will she open her black umbrella and fly off with the children, Mary Poppins style?

"Is that rated R?" Reg asks wearily.

"It doesn't matter any more," I murmur.

Lance saunters over. "Say, that was an experience. Every fifteen minutes, someone needed to go potty. And the popcorn they consumed!"

"Can we ride back to the ranch with Lance?" Lynda begs. "I got his autograph."

"I'm afraid you won't be returning to the ranch." Reg swallows the words, bitter medicine.

I read disbelief, horror, shock, fear in my stepdaughter's dark eyes. Or perhaps I simply want to. Then nothing. A bleak stare. Reg and I sandwich her between us, suffocate the child with hugs and kisses. Richie worms in, whimpering. I put a free arm around him. Mouse and Jenna press against their stepbrother and -sister. My husband and I move back to include them, trap the four children in our joined arms like prisoners in the game London Bridge Is Falling Down.

I think about the black Angus we pastured late last spring. During the day, one female baby-sat the thirteen calves. The other mothers wandered off to graze in another field with the bull. Eventually, the babies stopped crying, even seemed content in their open-air nursery.

But, come evening, those four-hundred-pound heifers stampeded to the water trough, knowing that thirst would drive their mothers back for the night. Maybe, on some basis, everyone needs his own mother back for the night. I'll have to mention this to Anneke. See what she thinks.

Lance pouts. "Such a lovely family! Oh, what a dirty trick! It's just a dirty trick."

I recognize the line: Catherine's death speech to Lieutenant Henry.

Bev's high heels tap on the asphalt as she marches over. "Break it up. Enough is enough." But her voice lacks its usual verve. Reg's ex sounds like Lynda in The Miss Fit dressing room asking if she looked OK.

We watch the three of them walk away.

"She's a *witch!*" Lance cries.

At the curb, Richie half turns and tries to sprint toward us. Bev clutches him tightly by the arm. Lynda never looks around. That kid is a survivor. Maybe Mouse will grow into the cheerleader outfit. We wait until they disappear around the corner of the building.

At a dirge-like dinner that evening in my parents' formal dining room, a sniffling Pearl cries, "How could he do that?"

No one answers.

I eye the empty places at the long table where Lynda and Richie's place settings have been removed. The maid waves a basket of homemade biscuits under my nose. "How could the judge do that? Swoosh me away without letting me talk? I've got my rights. I've got my equality."

18

"Home"

On the way back to the ranch, we cruise through Pasadena's tree-lined streets, heading northwest toward the 134 freeway. Reg pulls the VW bus curbside on the wrong side of the street in front of a sloping driveway that climbs some distance to an elaborate porte cochere. The newscaster on the car radio agonizes about Iran. Our personal crisis overshadows world events.

"Isn't that Mommy's favorite house?" Mouse asks. Saturated with architectural tours in her youth, she usually acts oblivious to any building design other than McDonald's golden arches.

Jenna turns her head for a quick look and returns to the pages of *The Black Stallion and Satan.* "Yeah, Mom thinks it's all world."

The estate was refurbished for use in the movie *China-town.* Hollywood prop men added the yellow-and-white-striped awnings. The house on the corner starred in *Tora! Tora! Tora!* Since three palm trees tower over the second story, the locale was passed off for Hawaii.

Meandering gracefully behind the elegant Huntington Hotel, El Molino Avenue is one of Pasadena's grandest addresses. Mansions built as winter places by wealthy Easterners in the 1920s and '30s string along this road like pearls on a basic black dress. Wrigley and Gamble settled in the neighborhood.

Today, strollers and buggies manned by Mexican maids congest the wide sidewalk. These women chatter in a language that sounds out of place here, like hearing American slang spoken on the Paris Métro.

Prominent young families breathe life back into these huge homes, which were struck down in the sixties by exorbitant taxes. Doctors, lawyers, and stockbrokers with their wives and children fill the libraries, butlers' pantries, and ballrooms with energy and Tonka trucks. To afford the tariff, these people rent their houses to film makers. The TV show "Family" is shot at a friend of mine's. The studio has duplicated Buffy's kitchen for routine interior shots. She asks permission to change curtains.

"It's for sale," Reg announces.

Does he know I've wanted to live in this house my entire life? I stare at the grounds. A canopy of oaks, elms, and sycamores arc above the expanse of velvet lawn, unblemished by a realtor's sign. Here properties sell by word of mouth. Upwardly mobile couples change residences every few years just as the rest of the country change cars. Everyone dreams of trading up to something sensational by age forty.

Clients stand in line to purchase certain old places from brokers who scalp listings. The eager buyers wait, like vultures and relatives, for owners to die—or more usually to divorce. That's how Paul and I acquired our first Greene and Greene bungalow and the Barker house on Milan Avenue:

one death, one legal separation. You don't usually refer to an *address* in Pasadena, but to the *architect* or the *original* owner.

"What are they asking?"

"Seven hundred thou."

"You could have had it for half that a few years ago."

"Supposedly the owner is desperate and will take a low-ball offer."

"Can we afford it?" I don't have a clear picture of our financial situation. Reg squawks at the price of four pair of Nike shoes, then orders six thousand dollars' worth of lumber for barn siding.

"Sure!"

"We can?" I involuntarily clap my hands together.

Jenna and Mouse spring up, Levi's-clad jack-in-the-boxes.

"Sure. *If* we sell the ranch."

"Not the horses!"

I gaze at the Chinese elms guarding the entrance like sentries. My grandmother called this tree a saucer magnolia, because the large pink blossoms resemble a teacup on the flat green leaf. The trellised roses explode with color, as does the garden of camellias and azaleas.

Reg rolls up the sleeves on his western shirt. "You want to go inside?"

I don't need to. I know the interior by heart. My brother Randy's former girl friend Pamela Warner lived here. The wrought-iron stairway spirals down from the mezzanine like a sausage curl. Tall leaded-glass windows imprison the afternoon light in colored shapes. Rare pink marble imported from Africa leads to the terrace where Faye Dunaway breakfasted.

"I could enroll Jenna and Mouse in Westridge, a nice WASP school. I wonder where Bev'll send Richie and Lynda?"

"Groan," from Jenna.

Mouse declares, "Mommy, those Westridge girls are stuck-up."

"I thought Christa Keyes was your best buddy? You had fun with her last night, didn't you?"

"We watched *Star Wars* two times on the video tape recorder in her bedroom. Then we saw *Shampoo*."

"How terrific!"

"Mommy, I'm too *young* to be exposed to such explicit sex."

"Mouse, look around toward the back. See the sun deck? You could have that bedroom. It has a parlor and private bath with a sunken tub."

"Mom, Christa's too sophisticated for Mouse. You shouldn't let her sleep over."

"Guy, Jenna! You promised not to tell!"

"Do you want the guest suite in the other wing? That would allow you *total* privacy," I say to my teenager, thinking of Dr. Kravetz's insinuations and mentally furnishing the living room. "Tell what?"

"Christa sniffs coke," Mouse claims.

"Snorts!" Jenna corrects.

"She has her own teaspoon and everything."

"What grade is this kid in!" Reg asks.

"Sixth. She skipped."

"I guess drugs are everywhere." I conceal my horror, since Christa's mom is president of Junior League. However, my daughters are aware of Scheffer's dissertation on comparative crime rates and drug abuse, and they may be sandbagging me.

"Are you kidding! Not at St. Anthony's. Sister Kathleen would have a wet dream. She goes into orbit if anyone cusses," Jenna explains.

"I don't understand this 'wet dream' business. Lynda used that expression the other day. Do you know what it means?"

"I do," Reg replies.

"Mom!"

"Compared to Christa and her boyfriend, Tommy and I are backward," Mouse asserts. "He hasn't even mentioned *kissing!*"

"I wish you'd told that to Judge Petersen," her stepfather comments.

"I did. Sort of. I said sometimes when Tommy and I knelt together in Mass, our tennis shoes touched."

I want to know, "Is Christa really a doper?"

"Her sister's friend is."

"If we moved back to town, you girls could start taking lessons at LA Ballet again." I recall how three years ago Jenna begged not to be a line leader in Waltz of the Seasons from *Cinderella* because it meant extra rehearsals. She refused to miss her Saturday-morning jumping lesson at San Pasqual Stables. Jon Clifford floated like a leaf caught in the current when he danced—I'd love to sign up for an adult class. My body misses the disciplined exercise. Reg believes workouts in bed suffice. "We'd be within bicycling distance of the Norton Simon Museum."

"Mom! I've seen enough Degas models to last a lifetime."

"Pearl could clean for us again on her day off from Grandma's. You wouldn't have to do any more scut work."

"I hated having her as a maid!" Mouse protests. Then she whispers to me, "Did you tell Reg about you-know?"

"What?"

"That I used to wet my bed?"

I shake my head.

"Oh, I don't care." Her voice returns to normal. "He can hear. Pearl would ask me, 'Did you go *swimming* last night?' She said she needed to know whether or not to change my sheets. It was so embarrassing."

"You don't wet your bed any more."

"Not at the ranch."

"You wouldn't in town, either! You haven't had an accident in years!"

"I did when Daddy moved out."

"That's understandable."

"I *never* wet my bed at the ranch."

"Why not, Mouse?" Reg's gentle voice caresses like butterfly wings batting against a summer sky.

"At the ranch the bathroom's just a few steps away. On Milan Avenue I had to walk forever, turn, feel my way along the hall, go past one closed door, one open door; I hated that! Then turn again. It was about a mile. Plus, I never knew where the Blue Monster Man would be lurking."

"But, Mouse, Blue Monster Man remained in the attic on Milan Avenue. You told me so yourself. You needn't worry here!"

"Blue Monster Man knows the way from Milan Avenue to El Molino. It would take him about a *minute* to drive over in his golf cart."

Jenna intercedes. "If you guys move back, could Super Star and I stay at the ranch? I'll live in the bunkhouse."

"Don't you want a break from all that manure shoveling? Not to mention getting up at five-thirty to buck hay?"

"I don't mind."

"You mind making your bed!"

"That's different."

"Have you ever heard her complain?" Reg asks. "At that hour, there's still dew on the horses' backs."

"It makes their coats shimmer," Jenna adds. "Super Star nuzzles me, and her breath feels warm. You should hike up to the barn some morning, Mom."

"I'll take a rain check."

"I love feeding in the rain. The wet alfalfa smells so good."

"I want to live in town!" I whine.

Mouse says, "If we did, Richie and Lynda couldn't go to the ranch on vacations. It wouldn't be any big deal for them to come to this house." My daughter glances out the car window.

"No big deal! Tommy Hernandez would *flip* if he saw the place."

"I'd *never* invite him here!"

"Why not?"

She studies the maids walking off down the street still jabbering in Spanish. "Where we live now, Mexicans are as good as everybody else."

Jenna chews on the end of her braid. "Richie and Lynda will probably end up living with us."

Scheffer predicted the same thing.

Reg nourishes this hope himself. Last night, in my old bedroom, we held each other, lay close like two people on stretchers who've survived a traffic accident that killed other loved ones. *"We'll have them eventually,"* Reg whispered.

I promised that if the children came back, I'd stop serving oatmeal.

My teenager continues, "And they'd much rather be at the ranch."

"Did they say so?" Reg acts curious.

"Do you think Lynda could have made cheerleader at a junior high in Pasadena? In town you have to be born into it."

"You were!"

"Mom, no offense, but I'd rather grow up to be like Reg than you."

"What's wrong with me?"

"You cry all the time."

"Not any more!" I stare at my firstborn, still as much in awe of her as when I peered through the nursery window many years before.

She continues, "Bev will drop Richie and Lynda off when it suits her, like the time she went to Las Vegas. That time Mouse and I *didn't* get to see Flip Wilson. And we have to be home waiting."

"Couldn't we wait here as well?"

Their combined silence votes no. I believe the girls resist

moving back because they don't wish to return to the *old* neighborhood with a *new* father.

Reg starts the engine. "I'll call from a pay phone and make an offer."

Jenna retreats to her book, sulking. Mouse strangles Charlie the Bride Dog.

"You'll buy the house sight unseen?" My husband claims to have rediscovered his country roots on his grandfather's ranch. Why isn't he putting up a fight? I hear the heels of Reg's boots clunking across the marble floors in my dream house. It's a ghastly noise, lonely.

"Isn't that house exactly what you've always wanted, Lolly? No more going without heat—"

"Sometimes those old convection furnaces need some work!"

Neither of us speak. I bite down on my thumbnail. "How did you find out about this place?"

"Paul told me," Reg replies.

"Mom, you and Sheri could play golf together at Annandale," Jenna taunts. "She could invite you to the member/guest tournament."

I want to smack her for the first time in thirteen years. What do you think of that, David Weintraub?

Without further conversation, we ride to the pay phone on the corner of Lake and California, across from the French Hand Laundry. I used to take my tablecloths there. Reg opens his door. A sullen look blemishes his face.

I close my eyes to this opposition. My dream house! Preston will help me decorate. We'll put the stuffed owl from the ranch living room in Reg's den. Maybe buy a cute antique hat rack for his Stetson. It currently hangs from our bedpost. In the kitchen . . .

. . . I won't be able to look out the window over the sink and watch Jenna cantering around the pines, a downhill racer, her tanned body in rhythm with the quarter horse. Nor spy the Saint Bernard cooling off by walking into the creek chest-high and then floating . . . a furry hippo. Nor smell the sagebrush at night, sweeter than jasmine. Nor hear the wind whistling through the Jeep windshield as I trek across pasture, gathering wild mustard. Nor make love with Reg among the orange groves under a tent of stars with Sissy and Governor Brown, Fang, and several barn cats staring, their eyes neon marbles. Nor study the sun as it sets fire to the Santa Susana Mountains during the entire cocktail hour, which slips by without my craving a dry martini, usually.

Sister Kathleen's quote echoes in my head: *"Thomas Wolfe said you can't go home again. Perhaps what is more difficult is leaving in the first place."*

"Mommy, Christa really keeps marijuana in a cold cream jar next to her toothpaste."

"Mom, you can have my English saddle. I'd rather ride bareback."

"Thanks for telling me after I've laid out the five hundred bucks!"

"Who paid the Master Charge bill?" Reg argues.

"Then you won't get blisters on your fanny." Jenna's braid coils about her fingers like a pet snake.

I cry, "Wait!"

Reg stops midway to the phone booth. He turns slowly, playing Gary Cooper in *High Noon*. His expression reads: "Do not forsake me, O my darling."

"Let's decide about the house tomorrow," I say.

"It may be sold by morning. There are two other interested parties."

"Maybe by morning I'll be glad if it is."

"Lolly Bare, do you or do you not want to move back to town?"

"You can't, Mom," Jenna quips. "Your bridge group's found a replacement."

One week away from the nuns, and my teenybopper develops a raging case of smart mouth.

"Let's decide tomorrow morning."

"Mommy?"

We turn west off Highway 5 and slide into our valley. The pavement swallows the sun's glare, turning yellow like the famed brick road.

"Yes, Mouse?" I swing around and touch her cheek, the little blackmailer—"*I'll never wet my bed at the ranch!*"

"Could I be called Beth and drop Mouse as a nickname? So Sister Kathleen won't call me Elizabeth. I told the judge I *hated* that."

"Beth was my mother's name!" Reg seems excited. "Say, I'd like to have a daughter named Beth."

"I found her diary at the bottom of a trunk in the tractor shed. I guess I shouldn't have read it without your permission, Reg. It said, 'This book belongs to Beth Worth.'"

"My mother's maiden name!"

"Beth wrote that she was scared at night. I used to be afraid too. On Milan Avenue. Those sirens I'd hear from Fair Oaks on their way to Huntington Hospital. I—I always thought an ambulance would come take me back. You know, to Intensive Care."

Reg reaches across the seat to squeeze my hand. Mouse's words turn my innards marshmallow-soft. The ten-year-old honesty fractures me. This isn't hype. With quivering voice I ask, "Don't the coyotes frighten you now?"

"They're not going to take me back to Intensive Care!"

"But that yowl!"

"I pretend they're singing to each other."

"Singing to each other, huh, Beth." Her stepfather trades understanding for trust like it was a baseball card.

"Yeah, like mommies sing to their babies."

Reg wipes his nose on his shirt sleeve. Neither of us slept well last night at Mother's. He looks physically and emotionally exhausted. I note a tear leaking down my husband's leathery cheek in a silver line like a snail track.

"Reg?" Jenna leans forward. She touches his shoulder.

"When we get back, do you want to ride the horses down to the Jefferson piece? I think that's where they're getting into wire. I've looked, and I can't find a thing."

"Won't it be almost dark?" I intrude.

"Let's take dinner in my backpack! Have sort of a party. I mean, if you think that would be appropriate—without Richie and Lynda and all." Jenna tries to make light of this invitation. That seems a very mature thing to do.

"Why don't we use my saddlebag?" Reg offers. "It's got more room. In fact, why don't I loan it to you on a permanent basis."

"Oh!" Jenna's face registers the kind of delight and gratitude I used to hope for when I bought her Christian Dior nightgowns.

"Do you want to come along, Mom?"

"I can't imagine anything I'd rather do than go cantering off to the last beef-jerky supper across some pitch-black field."

"What do you mean, last?" Reg chides. "There'll be lots of starry nights in the next couple of months, before the rains come."

He didn't notice my sarcasm. Neither did Jenna or Mou— Beth.

Maybe I didn't sound sarcastic.

We hang a left on Willow Lane, pass the clump of trees for which the dirt road is named. In the distance the aluminum barn roof catches the sun's last rays. As though testing bath water, I submerge myself in a feeling that slowly drowns me. It's a bittersweet emotion similar to biting into a lemon drop and hitting a sour spot. I used to experience it when coming back to my parents' house after being away at college.

"We're home," I say.

"Home," Reg repeats.

While my husband and the girls go riding, I'll straighten

up the house. Our family left in such a rush going in to court almost a week ago. No one made his/her bed. Heck, maybe I will try out Jenna's saddle and tag along. I could devil some eggs real fast. When we return from the picnic dinner, I want to change Lynda's and Richie's sheets. I must keep their bunks ready.

ACKNOWLEDGMENTS

Over the years, I've indebted myself to numerous friends and relatives. They know who they are. Thank you, dear people, for indulging my need to write. And special thanks to Jim Hoopes for knowing how to spell and give back rubs; to Marga and David Raskin for their genius and yummy cheesecake; to Marian and Larry Johnson for offering inspiration; to Hennie Monteleone for being herself; to Lynn Pleshette for keeping the faith; to Randall Greene for caring; and to Shaye Areheart for her million-dollar enthusiasm.

JR
Winchester, California
October 1980